I0691590

A
Package
Deal

MIA KERICK

Dreamspinner Press

Published by
Dreamspinner Press
5032 Capital Circle SW
Suite 2, PMB# 279
Tallahassee, FL 32305-7886
USA
http://www.dreamspinnerpress.com/

This is a work of fiction. Names, characters, places, and incidents either are the product of author imagination or are used fictitiously, and any resemblance to actual persons, living or dead, business establishments, events, or locales is entirely coincidental.

A Package Deal
© 2013 Mia Kerick.

Cover Photo
© 2013 Terry J Cyr.
Cover Design
© 2013 Paul Richmond.
http://www.paulrichmondstudio.com
Cover content is for illustrative purposes only and any person depicted on the cover is a model.

All rights reserved. This book is licensed to the original purchaser only. Duplication or distribution via any means is illegal and a violation of international copyright law, subject to criminal prosecution and upon conviction, fines, and/or imprisonment. Any eBook format cannot be legally loaned or given to others. No part of this book may be reproduced or transmitted in any form or by any means, electronic or mechanical, including photocopying, recording, or by any information storage and retrieval system, without the written permission of the Publisher, except where permitted by law. To request permission and all other inquiries, contact Dreamspinner Press, 5032 Capital Circle SW, Suite 2, PMB# 279, Tallahassee, FL 32305-7886, USA, or http://www.dreamspinnerpress.com/.

ISBN: 978-1-62798-215-3
Digital ISBN: 978-1-62798-214-6

Printed in the United States of America
First Edition
November 2013

To my children, who are my reason.

CHAPTER 1

Robby

"SHE more than meets the criteria... don't you dare try to deny it, DeSalvo."

"Don't *you* go forgetting who came up with the fucking criteria in the first place." Nonetheless, Mikey took one last long look up and down the silhouette of the female in question and conceded. "But, yeah, she's smoking hot.... You gonna do her or is it gonna have to be up to me again?"

With balled-up fists, I drilled him a couple times on his shoulder, pleased with my best pal's admission that the girl I'd dragged him over to this less-than-five-star diner to check out had sailed right through the stringent requirements of his very own Michael DeSalvo Hot Chick Test. "Nah, man, I wouldn't want to put you to any extra trouble. I'll take care of it myself this time."

"Okay, but jot down lots of notes, Robby." After a wide yawn followed by an exaggerated stretch, Mikey dragged himself from his stool. "'Cause I'm gonna want all the dirty details."

Glancing several stools over at the lady in question, and hoping like hell that she hadn't heard my buddy's last comment, I gave him a shove toward the door. "Go ahead and get out of here, Mikey!"

Yes, she was indeed a vision of hotness. White-blonde curls, nearly long enough to brush the rounded top of a fine, curvaceous ass. And as far as this babe's face was concerned, her most notable features were her sea-green eyes: wide-set, but not even slightly innocent, as I didn't go for that pure-as-the-driven-snow type of girl… never had. And a strong jaw, none too eager to allow even a hint of a smile; this girl was much more comfortable sporting an unyielding, and by now, rather predictable, scowl. Thought-provoking, slightly intimidating, and at the same time incredibly easy on the eyes. To seal the deal, my best pal, Mr. Michael Joseph DeSalvo, connoisseur of the female face and form, had been hard-pressed to control his salivation in her magnificent presence. And since I had a brain in my head, I wasn't about to let this golden opportunity pass me by.

I'd bumped into this lovely young lady at this very café at least ten times since the flood in the Tardiff Building's top-floor science lab, which had occurred right after the university opened for the fall semester. They'd needed a small commercial construction firm that was available on short notice to fix the damage, and my company had been ready and willing. And yes, Dalton Builders was just about as able as a small construction firm could be; I'd spent the better part of the past five years ensuring that. Including nights, weekends, and holidays.

Anyways, if this girl's gradually more frequent half-smiles, which I assumed were in direct response to our semiweekly, increasingly cordial banter sessions, hadn't exactly become what you'd call inviting, they had at least given me the distinct impression that I was, in her opinion, tolerable. Maybe even mildly interesting. That was enough for me to work with, seeing as it had been at least six months since I'd last had a date. Past time to make my move, unless I was moving toward the priesthood. For which I had no immediate plans.

I'd never claimed to fully understand it, but I had this peculiar "little quirk" when it came to the ladies. More specifically, in order for me to possess even a hint of interest in a woman, she had to be compelling in some nonphysical way. In other words, she had to possess more assets than a pretty face and a well-shaped backside. And I could tell this girl was complicated, in a more-than-meets-the-eye way I was drawn to. Deciphering this puzzle of a lady might even keep me mentally occupied for more than the standard three or four dates I normally endured before I typically lost interest in a woman.

But I was probably putting the cart before the horse; I didn't even know her name.

"Seems that you like the coffee here as much as I do." She spoke first again tonight.

If that wasn't an invitation to chat, I didn't know what was. "It's more of a need-the-coffee kind of thing." I let my best sideways grin fly across those two unoccupied barstools separating us, knowing fully well the effect my smile had on females. "I merely appreciate its *stimulative* qualities."

Honestly, I don't know if I was trying to be suggestive with my choice of words or not, but neither my flirtatious words nor my devastating grin seemed to make even a bit of impact. The girl nodded blandly in response. "Caffeine addiction? I can totally relate."

I lifted my mug, as if to toast her. "So what brings you to this cozy café, every... let's see... most every Tuesday and Thursday night, am I right?"

Blonde hair pooled up on top of the bar as she nodded again, this time pensively. "I have an evening class at Somerville U, and I always stop here for a latte before I catch the bus to my apartment. Good coffee makes the ride seem shorter."

Those no-nonsense eyes returned my gaze, and I knew she was waiting for my explanation of my own rather frequent evening caffeine fixes. And since I always aim to please, I replied, "My company is renovating the classrooms in the Tardiff Building... and it's a rush job, so we've been holding fairly regular evening job meetings, you know?"

That nod again. But this time her chin stayed down and just her eyes lifted to mine. "*Your* company?"

Apparently I'd caught her interest; it was my turn to nod. "Yeah.... Robert Dalton Builders. I'm Robby Dalton, CEO and president... and vice president and treasurer... and, well, I guess I'm the secretary too." Feeling my cheeks burn with embarrassment at my disclosure, I held out my hand. "Management for Dalton Builders is sort of a one-man show at this point, or, well, a one-and-a-half man show since I hired my buddy. I don't know if you noticed me talking to a guy a little while ago—he helps me part-time with the estimating. But I subcontract all of the labor."

After a brief hesitation during which she kept her stony eyes leveled on mine, the girl very loosely clasped my extended hand in her small one. "Isn't that kind of a big job for such a... a tiny company?"

"No, not really; it's only five upstairs classrooms, a length of the hallway, and a ladies' room. Water damage from a leaky roof... but they found a big name contractor to do the roof part. I still have to go to all of the meetings, though, so I've been stopping here for coffee before I drive home." I'd never been more certain of the fact that I was being sized up. The way she was examining me made me feel like a lab rat. And, at the moment, a nervously rambling lab rat. Oddly, in all of my past experience with women, I had always considered them *my* lab rats.

"Well, Robby, my name is Savannah." I must say, in my humble opinion, Savannah certainly wasn't the breeziest girl I'd ever come across, but since she was still examining me with the detached interest of a scientist, I allowed myself limited hope. "It's nice to meet you."

Okay, so this girl unnerved me. "D-do you have a l-last name, Savannah?"

Very patiently, she answered, "Of course I do."

"Oh." I mean, how does a dude respond to *that*? "Uh… well, yeah."

"Meyers."

"What?"

"It's Meyers…. *Savannah Meyers.*"

Here's where I demonstrated my witty and well-polished conversational skills. "Oh… sure. Right."

But my awkwardness, which I thought would've sunk my chances at a date with a girl like her, seemed to be the factor that won her over. Savannah finally smiled at me, her expression alive with either approval or pity (hard to tell which in the heat of the moment), and she said brightly, "We should meet here for dinner tomorrow night. How's seven o'clock for you?"

I have to admit, I was thankful she'd made the first move. Despite my alleged all-American good looks, agreed upon by a general consensus of collegiate, coworking, and bar-hopping females, my confidence when dealing with the opposite sex was minimal at best. I just had such a hard time connecting with them—all except for my sister, that is. But sisters don't really count. If Savannah hadn't asked me to dinner, I'd have been destined to lurk around this cozy café for an indeterminate number of Tuesday and Thursday evenings, waiting for her return to coincide with a fleeting moment of courage on my part. So it was with great relief that I bestowed upon Savannah my most Brad Pitt-like smile. "S-sounds r-really g-good." Yes, it seemed that I had quite recently acquired a minor speech impediment.

Savannah just stood up, shook her head as if she'd had enough of me already, and turned toward the door, glancing back once to say, simply, "Oh, Robby…." And then she tossed back her unruly waist-length curls one more time and headed for the door.

CHAPTER 2

Tristan

WHERE *is she?*

The only way I was going to get through this in one piece was by rocking my body, cross-legged, arms tightly wrapped around my shoulders. And so I did it, I'll admit not without a heap of shame weighing me down. I tried to keep the motion slight, but the very second Savannah stepped through the doorway, I could tell by her baffled expression that she noticed it. She closed the door smoothly and moved with purpose to stand in front of where I swayed on the couch.

"Tristan." She placed her little hand firmly on the several days' worth of dark scruffy growth I normally wore on my face and dragged her cool fingertips down to my chin; the physical contact served to make my rocking stop.

"You're late, Savi…. I got worried about you."

She plunked herself down beside me and somehow pulled the entire long length of me into her teeny arms. Yeah, I was a rather tall man, maybe a bit on the bony side as well, but I let my body melt against her petite one like I was just a little boy. I felt her fingers slide up my back to the top of my head. She shuffled them through my dark, shaggy hair like she was feeling around for my brain. "Well, I'm here now."

We stayed like that, tangled up in each other's arms, until we were both fairly sure my rocking had stopped for good. Then she nudged me with her shoulder, a tad less than gently, so I'd release her from the near choke hold I had around her neck. "How was your day off?" Savannah's eyes met mine with what I'd call wary interest.

"Same old, same old." I grabbed the remote and turned off the television set so that now we sat in virtual darkness as well as complete silence. "Where were you?"

"I had classes this morning, and then study group. And it's Thursday—Ethical Standards Class night—you *know* that." Savannah lifted the huge mass of blonde ringlets from off of her shoulders and, with some effort, roped them into the thick elastic band she wore on her wrist. I had to restrain myself from tucking the curly strands she'd overlooked behind her ears. "And I stopped by the S-Squared for a mocha. I'm going to have a late night. Major exam in the morning... counts for a third of my grade."

"Don't worry, Savi, I'll stay up and help you study."

She smiled at me so prettily that I had to swallow deeply to soothe the lump of emotion that had risen in the back of my throat. "You're so sweet, Tristan. I can always count on you."

"And don't you forget it," I joked as I lifted up her hands, which had by now dropped to her lap, and brought them to my lips and just held them there. But the air between us crackled with the tension of unspoken words.

"How could I *ever* forget?" Sounding just a hair shy of sarcastic, she looked away quickly.

Silence enveloped us, but after more than four years together, Savannah knew me well enough to wait. I'd say what I needed to say when I was ready. And it didn't take too long before my body's rocking restarted and I was rambling. "I don't care what you're doing when you aren't with me, I've *told* you that over and over, but you've got to call me when you're going to be late—I have to know that you are safe."

Leaning over me to switch on the lamp beside the couch, she huffed softly. "You do *so* care what I'm doing when I'm not with you; you care about every single detail of what I do when I'm not with you. And Tris, that's okay, because I care about every detail of your day too." Again she lifted her dainty fingers, this time to caress the length of my cheekbones beneath the slight slant of my eyes. "And by the way, there is nothing that I do at this point in my life that does not *involve* or *revolve around* you, okay?"

I ceased my rocking, but still I wondered about her words: *at this point in my life.*

"And I'm sorry that I didn't call you—it was inconsiderate. I was talking to someone at the S-Squared." She didn't look away.

After about thirty seconds, during which my brain absorbed that information, my body very predictably resumed its rhythmic swaying. "Who were you talking to?"

It took Savannah almost a full minute to respond. "His name is Robby Dalton."

CHAPTER 3

Robby

THE next morning when I arrived at my office on the third floor of a renovated but still rustic brick mill building in Cambridge, I wore on my face the proud smile of a winner. Because yes, I'd scored with a lady (well, not *scored* in the sense that most men thought of it, but still).

And thanks to that "little quirk" I had with women, my motivational level, in terms of cruising bars and clubs and collecting phone numbers from eligible babes, wasn't as healthy for me as it was for Mikey (and the rest of the male population).

Let's face it, *scoring* for most men was as basic as: 1) registering hot chick on radar; 2) collecting said hot chick's cell phone number; 3) waiting two days and making quick call to hot chick; 4) taking hot chick to dinner; 5) scoring in sack with hot chick. Simple as connecting the numbers, right? Well, not so in my case, mostly because number 1, "registering hot chick on radar," happened to me only a couple of times per year. *At the most.* Yes, hot chicks on my radar were very few and far between. And as I mentioned before, this was due to the apparently ridiculous notion that in order for Robby Dalton to experience so much as a spark of interest, a woman had to be in some way, um, actually interesting.

So, yes, last night was momentous—I'd met a woman who'd managed to light my fire, or at a minimum get the kindling to smoke a bit—and I felt like most guys do after completing number 5. I'd scored big time.

My mind fully occupied with visions of Savannah, I pushed through the door of my office and was greeted by the sight of my chief (and only) estimator, Mikey DeSalvo, or as he liked to refer to himself when he was at one of his two part-time jobs, "Mr. Numbers," laying out the architectural drawings we were using to complete an estimate for a small library addition in Medford. Unfortunately, for the time being, he had to set up shop in my own small office. But according to Mikey, in his other occupational capacity as part-time rental agent, by late spring of next year an adjacent office space in this very building was going to open up. Late spring couldn't come soon enough; Mikey could be tough to take in large doses.

"What's wit' the shit-eating grin, Dalton?" Mikey's Boston accent was prominent. He pulled his hairy, crumb-covered hand out of a white bakery bag and popped a colorful cookie into his mouth (Mama DeSalvo owned a bakery in Revere).

Snatching the bag, I asked, "You save any for me, Mr. Numbers?" Empty… naturally.

"Course not, A-hole. Not my day to feed you, 's far as I know." He turned his attention to the blueprints spread out all over my plan table. Tapping their corners with his pencil eraser, he squinted his dark eyes and stated thoughtfully, "I think we can get this one 's long as we can find the right guy to wire it."

I kept my mouth shut and waited for the rest.

"And come to think of it, my cousin Davey-boy's a pretty decent electrician, and he just got an opening in his schedule that would coincide just perfect wit' this job here. I'd bet my fine Italian ass that he'd be interested in helping us out too."

I did my best to send Mikey a stern "I'm the boss" glare, but seeing as we'd been best pals since well before our days at St. Joseph's High and that old habits, like bad friendships, died hard, it was completely lost on him. "Your job, bud, is to find the best electrician at the cheapest price possible, *not* to keep the entire DeSalvo clan employed."

As if I hadn't even spoken, Mikey retorted with, "So, back to that fucking goofy-assed grin you're wearing… wus the deal? You get lucky last night?"

Why did I take this bullshit from Mikey? And take it, and then take it some more? Maybe it was because of the simple fact that ever since I'd met him, he'd always been one to blabber on and on incessantly—enough for the two of us, in fact, so there were never any of those dreaded awkward silences when we hung out together. Mikey DeSalvo had very simply been easy for me to be friends with; I'd never really had to put myself out there too much to satisfy him.

He'd won today's first battle easily and we both knew it. David (aka Davey-boy) DeSalvo would be the electrician whose price we carried. I called to mind my mother's advice when it came to dealing with Mikey, "Robby, you've got to choose your battles with that boy." Yes, Mom always knew best. Nonetheless, I had to smile. "I got a date with that sweet babe from last night."

He tapped his pencil on the blueprints two or three more times, harder than before. "You know, Rob, that love-at-first-sight shit just don't exist. Like, no way in hell it does. And I'm not just shoveling horseshit, my man; there's lit'rally tons of evidence on the net to prove it, an' I done the research. But I'll tell you what, and you listen good: *lust* at first sight is something I've got plenty of firsthand experience wit'." Still staring fixedly at the plans, he rubbed his palm forward over his short, wiry black hair and then back again. "And that babe you showed me last night was lust-worthy."

"Whether it's love or lust, well, let's say I'm not willing to commit myself quite yet." I ran my hand over my own cropped blondish hair, which featured a slightly longer tuft in the front, an exact replica of Mikey's.

"Well, take it from me and stick to the lust, bro. And that girl was a tiny little thing, but there wasn't no shortage of T or A, which is what counts the most."

That wasn't even close to the way I thought of Savannah, but Mikey expected full concurrence with his jaded opinion, so I nodded… and then I delivered. "And major bonus—she's a blonde, but not too dumb at all."

"Well, that's a crying shame. In my opinion girls' tits can't be too big and their brains can't be too small, ya get me?"

My voice grew harsh, even defensive, surprising us both. "Savannah's beautiful, and I wouldn't say she's even slightly dumb."

"Sava-a-annah, huh?" Mikey drew out her name with a singsong Southern drawl that sounded quite bizarre when fused with his Boston accent, and then he chuckled. *"I* think it's been way too fucking long since you got laid, my man."

"Who the hell asked you?" I meant the question exactly as it came out, but I softened its harshness by erupting into a quick bout of laughter. Then I handed Mikey the coffee I'd picked up for him at the convenience store and pulled the top off of my own to let it cool. "Anyways, I talked to her for a while—she's a good kid. I'm going to take her to dinner tonight."

Mikey reluctantly lifted his dark eyes from the drawings. "Jesus, she looked on the young side, but… you gonna be doing a teenager? There's a term for that. It starts wit' statutory and ends wit' rape."

"Christ, Mikey!" I nearly choked on my first sip of coffee. "She's a fucking college student, maybe even a grad student. That's plenty old enough!"

"Okay, then. So this bitch is cute—young, blonde, not lacking in the two most important qualities a girl can possess: T & A—she got a twin sister for me? Preferably one who puts out?"

If I was going to hold back from slugging him, I needed to refocus my mind onto business. "Anyways, you're going to need to get a price for drywall and flooring."

"Sure thing, bro. That won't be no problem." Mikey started typing notes into his iPhone. "So, tell me, where you gonna take her?"

"Um, I'm…."

He lowered his unibrow and stared me down.

"We're meeting at… at a place near the college." That response was surely not going to even come close to satisfying Mikey. "A diner." I tried to make those last words sound very small.

"That lame S-Squared place from last night?" He was predictably appalled.

"M-maybe." There was no use asking for his approval. I already knew I was not going to get it.

"You get what you pay for, buddy. And if all's you pay for is dinner at a shit-hole diner, don't expect that bitch to fuck your brains out tonight, and that's a fact." Mikey was glaring at me now, shaking his head in unmasked disappointment. "Jesus, Rob… but at least you're going out wit' a female. I was beginning to wonder about you, man." He lifted his wrist and let it fall limply in the universal gesture for an effeminate male.

"No need to worry about my *machismo*, man. I've been saving it up, that's all." Confident that Mikey was going to now want to hear a detailed listing of what items were going to be on tonight's sexual agenda, I decided to change the subject. I just wasn't that sleazy and I couldn't fake it well enough for Mikey to buy it—no sense trying to bullshit a bullshitter. "So talk to me about this little library job, Mr. Numbers. You know, if you land it, I'm going to reward you with a finder's bonus, since it was your Great Uncle Tony who put it on our radar!"

CHAPTER 4

Robby

FIDGETING with the popped-up collar of my crisp white polo shirt, I sat alone in a corner booth at the S-Squared Diner, trying to imagine how I could've possibly ended up at a less romantic spot for a first date. And I'd arrived here forty-five minutes early, as if there would be a line of hungry diners, all competing for the opportunity to enjoy a gourmet meal in the quaint ambiance of this extremely well lit, if I don't say so myself, establishment.

Okay, so maybe I was a smidgeon overeager for my dinner date with Savannah. Not because I hadn't taken a girl out for at least six months. After all, getting RD Builders off the ground consumed most of my waking hours—I'd simply had no time to wine and dine women. And also not because I actually believed that I'd be, as Mikey would phrase it, "getting some" at the end of the night. I had absolutely no intention of jumping Savannah's bones after a single dinner date.

My nerves were acting up because this girl was actually *interesting* to me; Savannah just didn't seem as one-dimensional as most girls did. Now I wasn't going to lie; finding Miss Right had never been an obsession of mine. And that was an understatement. I'd figured this much out by my senior year of high school: the effort of trying to keep at an arm's length all of the enthusiastic and hopeful future Mrs. Daltons just wasn't worth the minimal pleasure I got out of a couple of dates and a quick trip to the sack with them. I was labeled as an "obsessed jock" and that was pretty much how the story went.

More recently, particularly since college, specific titles had been bestowed upon me, including Mr. Frigid, The Ice Man, The Cold-hearted Snake, The Commitment-phobic Builder, R.E.M. (Robby the Emotional Nomad), Popsicle-Boy, The Money Hugger, and my personal favorite, Driven Mr. Dalton. There were several very distinct themes running through all of these lovely pet names. Yes, Robby Dalton was cold and Robby Dalton was ambitious. And I guess that was me.

Nevertheless, here I was, still in the fucked-up game of love, my ass planted in a shiny pleather booth, the fluorescent lighting enhancing my forehead's nervous perspiration to a less-than-subtle gleam. I guess being alone all the time sucked more than my urgent need to flee from time-consuming, predictably unsatisfying relationships with women. I shook my head to clear all of those evil nicknames out of my brain. Tonight was going to be different. It was going to be the start of something better. Because yes, I still had hope that the right one would come along.

And then there she was, that slight feminine form crowned by a heavy mass of blonde ringlets barely held off of her heart-shaped face by a colorfully woven headband. Savannah's appearance at the diner's entrance proved more jarring than I had anticipated. I can't say my gut exactly clenched with unbridled attraction; it was more that my brain froze in fascination. Something told me there was certainly much more to Savannah Meyers than met the eye.

Savannah strode evenly to our corner booth, and despite her small stature, long tanned legs emerged from her loose off-white skirt with each step. She was one of those hippie-looking girls, her draping tie-dye blouse gathered low on her hips with a loose chain belt. And although she was dressed like a trendy magazine model, her eyes were what caught my interest. Yes, they *were* a beautiful aquamarine color, but that wasn't what fascinated me. Those eyes were light in color while being dark in spirit; maybe it sounded crazy and even fanciful, but that's how I saw it. And they were shadowed eyes, hiding secrets I already knew I wanted to uncover.

This evening, my first impression of Savannah, based simply on the expression she wore, was: a complicated woman leading a complicated life. And didn't people say that first impressions are everlasting?

Jumping to my feet, I briefly wondered what she thought of me. When she reached the table, Savannah pulled me against her side in a brief hug. The girl smelled good, like some kind of wildflower, or maybe even a whole wildflower garden. She overwhelmed my senses.

"I've been thinking about you all day." That cagey gaze met mine with a force. I didn't fight my urge to stare back.

"Same here." It was all I could come up with. My cheeks burned.

"Oh, Robby...." She shook her head, then smiled wide and for the first time I got a good look at the little space that separated her two front teeth. No, nothing about Savannah Meyers was conventional, but all of the details added up to a nontraditional kind of perfection.

"Hey, Savannah, you look fantastic tonight!" So maybe that was a lame way to start things off, but again, it was all that came to mind.

She didn't thank me for the compliment. Instead, Savannah dove right into conversation. "You know, I used to work here when I was an undergrad. See the fry cook behind the breakfast bar? That's Gus, and check out that waitress over there by the door...."

After a quick peek at the portly, balding fry cook, I then looked toward the door to take in a matronly middle-aged waitress, who, incidentally, was glaring back at me with very little warmth. The woman smoothed back a few strands of unnaturally colored dark-red hair that had pulled free of a well-sprayed twist, narrowed her eyes at me, and then shifted her glance to Savannah. And as she did so, she burst into a grin of good cheer. "That's Lil, Gus's older sister. She's worked here since he bought the place like twenty-two years ago, or close to it."

"I don't think she likes me much."

"Oh, don't worry about it. Lil's not really a people person."

"I can't say I'm feeling too many warm fuzzies coming at me from her direction." I shuddered. "Don't you think that maybe she's in the wrong line of work?"

What was that sound? Oh, it was delicious, an almost bell-chiming sort of... of laughter. And it was coming from between Savannah's no-nonsense's lips. "You're funny!" she chirped with yet another bright smile. But after that moment of mirth, she quickly settled back down to business. "Gus and Lil are good people; they're always the first ones to donate to my charity drives. They love kids, like I do." One more time, Savannah allowed a brief, but fairly sunny, smile. "Oh yeah, and I hope you don't mind, but I asked my roommate to stop by later to grab a bite to eat with us."

I shook my head, no, I didn't mind at all if her roommate came by. She must really like me a lot if she wanted her roomie to come and check me out, I figured. And I was ready to ask her about how she'd said she loved kids when Savannah gave me an appraising look, as if she was a pitcher and was sizing up me, the batter. "Last night you told me you were a contractor, so tell me, what made you decide to go into that field? And then I want to hear about where you grew up."

To say I unloaded the story of my life in vivid detail would be an understatement. Sure, I gave Savannah a somewhat abbreviated version of "Robby Dalton in a Nutshell," but it was not lacking in the pertinent details. After all, she'd asked, hadn't she?

Happy childhood in upper middle-class suburbia, check. Doting parents, married to each other for thirty years, check. Football, basketball, and you guessed it, baseball star, at private Catholic high school, check. Carefree, beer-drinking college career at a Boston technical college, check. Older sister married to perfect man with 1.75 children, check. Smooth transition from college to workplace, check. I guess it must have sounded idyllic, and much of it had been.

And as I divulged my personal history, Savannah listened, pretty much on the edge of her seat, which just so happened to have been a booth. So enraptured was she by my little tell-all that I would not have been at all surprised if she'd pulled out her iPhone and started taking notes. In many ways our date was unfolding like a job interview; however, she was far more concerned with my upbringing than my work experience.

But the questions she interjected into my soliloquy were not typical of those of other girls I'd dated, which were always along the lines of "What kind of car do you drive?" or "Do you own a house or just rent an apartment?" No, Savannah's questions were odd. "Did your family sit down to eat supper together every night when you were growing up?" and "Who taught you to ride a bike?" Whenever I tried to bring the conversation back to the topic of my business plan or sports I'd played, she interrupted with something off-the-wall like "Did your parents get you and your sister a puppy when you were kids?"

And the next thing I knew, I was blurting out the tragic story of how Waldo, our family's beloved Golden Retriever, got hit by a car and died when I was in third grade. Those typically all-business eyes of hers actually filled up with tears.

Enough already, I thought when I'd finished filling her in on the habits of the Easter Bunny, the Tooth Fairy, and Santa Claus in my childhood home. "So, where did *you* grow up, Savannah?"

And that was when I met with a tiny, blonde, gap-toothed brick wall. "Oh, I went to school in Somerville, mostly." Her voice was listless.

"So you're from Somerville?"

"No, not really." Vacant eyes stared past my head.

"Oh… well, where'd you grow up then?"

"Not too far from here." Silence.

"Do you have any siblings?"

"None that I know of." More silence.

I received similarly concise responses to "Did you play town sports when you were little?", "Do you keep in touch with your high school friends?" and "Do you see your parents much?" In fact, her responses to those inquiries were precisely "No," "Not so much," and "No." It was like pulling teeth; I simply could not get Savannah to put the "life-story-telling shoe" on the other foot, so to speak. And by now, her pretty ocean eyes had darkened to a point where they were completely unreadable. She seemed to become hard… and cold.

Miss Frigid, I guess you could say. Takes one to know one.

Out of sheer desperation, I turned my questions from Savannah's past to her future. "So what do you see yourself doing in like, say, ten years?"

At that question, my date lit up like the sky over the Boston Esplanade on July 4th. "Well, I'm getting my master's degree in School Counseling, with a concentration in Family Therapy. My goal is to work as a guidance counselor in either an urban school or a very rural one…." She hesitated, and added, "I'm not sure exactly where yet."

"Wow, that's cool." I was king of the lame-ass comments tonight.

"Yeah, it is *cool*. I still have about six classes, a practicum, and an internship left to complete, but I'd like to take some time off of school soon to do some service work with teenagers. I'm looking into that right now."

"What makes you want to work with kids?" For a minute, I thought I was going to see a return of Miss Frigid because her narrow-eyed gaze shifted up and over my left shoulder rather shrewdly, but then she tilted her head as if in deep thought, somberly reconnected her eyes with mine, and answered, "It isn't easy to be a teenager, Robby. And some kids have it much harder than others. I want to make a difference for *those* kids."

BY THE time we were served our dinners, Savannah knew the concise, yet complete, story of my life, and all I knew about her was that she wanted to be a high school guidance counselor. Well, I guess I'd actually learned a few more pertinent details about her: Savannah was a liberal Democrat, she was more than willing to stand up for causes she believed in, she regularly volunteered as a way to give back to society. And she was passionate about helping disadvantaged kids. But I knew absolutely nothing about her childhood, which made me even more curious. Somehow, though, I knew the topic of her youth was closed, and I respected that. So I didn't drill her with any more questions—for now, at least.

Just as we were finishing dinner, I, along with everyone else in the diner with a pulse and functioning eyeballs, couldn't help but notice an extremely good-looking dark-haired man step rather hesitantly into the diner. He stopped beside the cash register and then scanned the tables and booths urgently, as if he was looking for someone; that was when I caught a glimpse of his eyes.

If I didn't know better, I'd say that I'd been Tasered. On the back of my neck and right over my scalp, my skin puckered and tingled in an involuntary response. And the air in my lungs got stuck there for a couple of seconds before I was able to somewhat forcibly push it back out. I also experienced another conspicuous, but thankfully only to me, physical response between my legs. It was immediate and gripping, not to mention disturbing. In all truth, I was completely overwhelmed by my own reaction to this... to this *man*. It was just I'd never seen eyes so intense, so striking. So beautiful, really. And I wanted badly to look away, but it was like I was trapped in those deep brown doe eyes, that were now fixed squarely on me.

Or rather, on Savannah. When the young man spotted Savannah, he dropped his head and dragged his fingers almost coyly through his shaggy brown hair, winked at her once, and then broke into a smile so disarming that I swear I'd lost my breath again. Savannah and I both gaped at this poster boy for angelic perfection as he breezed his way over to our table. And Savannah, clearly overjoyed by his arrival, smiled more brightly at him than she ever had at me, and then slid right over in the booth so he could sit down beside her.

I was pretty much dumbfounded at this point. First, my reaction to this *dude's* eyes and smile was something close to inexplicable. Second, my date was beaming up at him with what I took to be unconcealed love in her eyes. Yes, "dumbfounded" worked fairly well as a descriptive term for Robby Dalton at that particular moment.

"Robby, this is my roommate, Tristan Chartrand. Tristan, meet Robby Dalton."

The strangest expression I'd ever seen on a man passed over Tristan's face as he gazed down and our eyes met. One word simply couldn't describe it. I saw complete vulnerability in the shape of fear, insecurity, hopefulness, and maybe even neediness, all competing for position on his fine-boned face. Before my analysis was complete, he smiled sweetly, extended a slender hand to me, and said, "I'm so pleased to meet you, Robby. Mind if I join you guys?"

For some reason, peering into those now clouded but still stunning dark eyes felt awkwardly intimate in this public place. I mumbled something about how glad I was to make his acquaintance, and by all means he should sit down, hoping like hell that I sounded more sincere than I felt. Because I was still thunderstruck. I couldn't seem to get control of my rapidly beating heart and my skittish breathing. I was sweating; I was freezing. Okay… I was losing it.

For the life of me, I couldn't figure out what the hell was happening to my sanity. I somehow managed to mentally regurgitate and then practically choke on Mikey's "love at first sight is nothing but hogwash" speech. I took a deep yet ineffective breath for steadiness, and reflected once more on the significance of first impressions.

And if my mouth hadn't been hanging open from the initial shock of my own physical reaction to this perfect specimen of manhood, then I'm pretty certain what happened next took care of that. I mean, even before the words "my roommate" had a chance to fully sink into my muddled brain, I could actually feel the slight swinging of my jaw as it dangled limply in its socket when I witnessed what followed: Tristan wrapped both arms around Savannah and pressed his lips to hers. He even closed his fucking eyes as he did it! No tongue, but it was a mouth-kiss, nonetheless…. And Savannah, well, I couldn't help but notice that she hadn't pushed him away in angry indignation. No, she'd closed her own fucking eyes and kissed him right the hell back. And then she squeezed his fucking hand. I had no choice but to look on during this entire interaction, kind of the way you were compelled to look at a car accident on the side of the highway. You didn't want to see it, but you just had to look.

I remained pretty much tongue-tied, which was probably a good thing given the circumstances. Wasn't kissing one man while on a date with another a major dating *faux pas*? I sat staring in bewilderment at the literally breathtaking man who had just moved in on my date as well as on my mind.

But Savannah was now smiling so much more genuinely than I was used to, and Tristan also seemed so happy to meet me that he was ready to pee his pants. "I'm super glad I didn't miss you guys—I would've been very disappointed." The hypnotic stare of those deep brown eyes pulled at mine insistently.

"Lil, Lil!" Savannah flagged down the perma-frowning waitress. She proceeded to order *for* Tristan a tuna melt on rye ("very light on the butter, and we'll take it to go"), a Caesar salad ("dressing on the side, if you don't mind, Lil"), and a tall glass of water ("don't hold back on the ice"), and then she went so far as to tuck her *own* napkin into the collar of his starched white dress shirt.

Okay, so maybe the napkin part didn't happen, but you get the picture, right?

I wasn't out of this game yet. Hadn't I always been the one my teammates could count on under pressure? To stand at the foul line and score the game-winning basket, to toss the long pass into the right set of hands, to hit the walk-off home run right the hell out of the park?

Yes, I had always been The Man.... I swallowed back my shock and decided that right now I'd be *the better man*; I'd make polite conversation with this date-wrecking, brain-scrambling loser. Maybe if I kept Tristan's mouth busy with idle chat I could prevent Savannah from locking lips with him over his Caesar salad (with dressing on the side). And hopefully, in the process, he'd let something megastupid fall out of his mouth that would break me out of my unwelcome enchantment with him.

"So, Tristan, who the fuck are you and how did you manage to become my future girlfriend's frigging roommate, huh?" That is what I *wanted* to say, not what actually came out from between my trembling lips. Instead, I stuck to the safe zone for all male-on-male interrogation, or rather, *discussion*: our jobs. "So, Tristan, are you just getting off from work? You certainly pulled a late one, huh?" In a futile attempt to appear casual, I glanced down at my watch. Sure, the asshole'd worked well beyond business hours, especially for a Friday, but he wasn't nearly late enough, if you asked me.

Looking vastly relieved that I'd initiated small talk with him, he replied, "As a matter of fact, Robby, I just left work at Michael's on the Waterfront. And often times I work much later than this."

"Uh, that's a great restaurant; my sister and I took our parents there for their thirtieth anniversary. Are you in management there?"

Glancing at Savannah, who'd folded her hands beneath her chin and appeared to be observing our little dog and pony show with not an inconsiderable measure of trepidation, Tristan cleared his throat. "Oh, no…. I'm not a businessman. I'm a waiter."

A waiter? Okay, so this dude was a fucking waiter. I was now absolutely certain I had nothing in common with him except for the fact that we both wore dress shirts to work. Oh, yes… and Savannah. We had Savannah in common, didn't we?

"How… how was business tonight?" I was stalling for time, trying to put my finger on how he and Savannah fit together. And then it hit me: Tristan was Savannah's gay roommate! The man was pretty (alright, he was frigging beautiful), he was a *waiter*, he had a female roommate… and he was wearing skinny jeans. It all added up. This dude was no threat to my relationship with Savannah; he was just her queer roomie! I *almost* felt fully comforted by my newly gained realization about Tristan's sexuality, but somewhere in the dark recesses of my mind there remained a niggling but nameless concern about that very same issue.

In his quiet, controlled voice, the man replied to my question. "Not so good. I would've expected it to be a bit busier on a Friday night in September, but I did all right with tips, considering I only had four parties." He tilted his flawless face to the side, as if in deep thought, and added, "Thank you for asking, Robby."

This dude may be too pretty for his own good, but he was certainly no asshole. I actually felt a measure of guilt at my mental accusation from a few minutes earlier. I mean, how many guys did I know that were this fucking sweet?

Ah, let's see…. Zero.

"So… uh, where's your apartment?" A fair enough question. Extremely civil.

Tristan leaned across the table toward me, a serene smile on those perfectly sculpted lips, evidently pleased with my continued interest. "Savi and I live about seven blocks east, right here in Somerville Square. It's not a fancy place, but we like it."

Savi? How quaint. For some reason, I had begun to feel irritated again. So I hastily turned to the conversational topic that I always kept in my back pocket, ready and waiting for desperate moments: sports. "How 'bout those Red Sox, man? They're having one hell of a season!" I directed that question to the back of the booth midway between their heads. That way, either of them could answer. And it was well past time that Savannah rejoined the conversation anyways, wasn't it?

After a boyish shake of his shaggy hair, and possibly a slight pinkening of his cheeks, Tristan answered. "I don't really follow the Red Sox too closely.... I mean, I *try* to watch the games, but there are so many rules.... I just get lost."

Nope. Tristan Chartrand, the pretty waiter, and Robby Dalton, the athletic builder, had absolutely *nothing* in common. It was clearly time to call it a night. "Well, I have an early job meeting tomorrow morning, so... can I give you guys a lift home?"

At that moment, Tristan was chomping on his final mouthful of Caesar salad (is there a market for lettuce-eating male models to work in salad-dressing commercials?), so Savannah had no choice but to chime in. "Oh, no. We're fine. We're used to taking the bus."

So much for a goodnight kiss, I surmised. Robby Dalton was not going to be "getting some" in any sense of the words, tonight. I reached into my jeans to pull out my wallet, but before I had a chance to lay down some cash, Tristan had swept up the check and was hurrying like a man on a mission toward the cash register. Glancing back, he shouted with a grin, "I've got this one, Robby!"

My head was spinning. *What the fuck is going on here?* I asked myself. I knew this wasn't an expensive dinner date or anything, but wasn't *I* the guy who should be forking out the cash for Savannah's six-dollar dinner?

And since wonders never cease, apparently now it was Savannah's turn to lean in over the table to get a little bit closer to me. "I was about to thank you for dinner, but... well, Tristan seems to be taking care of that." She gazed at me across the table, her ocean eyes shining, her narrow lips parted. I had to admit that she was every bit as pretty as her roommate. "I had a great time getting to know you."

Yes, tonight had ended on a rather strange note, but what the hell? With my next question, my caution and the wind became closely acquainted. "Um… maybe I could get your number and I could call you sometime?"

Savannah glanced over her shoulder to where Mr. Perfecto stood at the cash register, head tossed back in laughter at something Gus the fry cook had said to him. When she faced me again, I must confess, she appeared almost taken aback, like she hadn't expected my interest in contacting her. "That sounds great, Robby."

I pulled out my cell phone and plugged in the numbers she'd quickly scribbled on a napkin. As I did so, Savannah slipped out of her booth and moved across the table to sit next to me. Again I noticed that fresh scent of wildflowers. I turned to her and before I knew it, she had placed her tiny hands on either side of my scruffy face, and right there under the watchful eyes of matronly Lil, burly Gus, and the devastatingly gorgeous stare of Tristan Chartrand, she pressed her lips chastely to mine, as if it had been a *real* dinner date at a *real* restaurant, not macaroni and cheese at a diner.

And then she was gone. The soft hands, the floral scent, the lingering warmth…. I glanced over to where she had joined Tristan at the cash register and watched as the two of them made their way to the door. And strange, just after Tristan hooked his arm affectionately through hers and pulled her tiny body against his lanky one, he raised his hand to wave to me. Not in the "Nah, nah, nah, nah, nah—I've got the girl" way, but in the "I really enjoyed meeting you" way. His doe eyes shone at me with unrestrained warmth, drawing forth further physical and emotional discomfort.

Stranger still, before the two passed through the door onto the street, Savannah looked over at me and chirped, "*We* can't wait to see you again!"

Looking back…. Savannah

TRISTAN hadn't screamed or cried out. Not even once. In fact, he hadn't uttered so much as a single sound during the entire ordeal, which had lasted no more than fifteen minutes. I did, however, recall very clearly the noises his attackers had made, ranging from guttural grunts to sighs of satisfaction. Sounds that had been forever burned in my mind. Sounds that no child should ever have to endure.

Strange how fifteen minutes can change the entire direction of your life.

Until that night, I'd been in a daze, but I'd never been truly afraid. Tristan had always taken care of things for me. From the moment I'd left my mother's house, he'd been there. He'd found me—scared and crying by the subway stop—and he'd more or less scooped me up and swept me off. Not exactly to safety—the streets could never be considered safe. But Tristan had never let me discover the ugliness of my own desperation. I'd never had to figure things out for myself.

But I couldn't go back. Not after that night. Not even for him.

CHAPTER 5

Tristan

"NOT her too!" I shot right up in our bed, still screaming. "Just me! Don't you all go fucking with her! *Just me*!" There was no hiding it from your bedmate when you basically screamed bloody murder in the middle of the night into the pitch blackness of a tiny bedroom.

And she didn't startle even slightly at my outburst. But I had to face it: this was pretty much par for the course with us. Not a nightly routine, or weekly, or lately, even monthly, thank God. But I'd had my share of sleep-disturbing nightmares, and since Savannah had slept right beside me every night for the past four years, her sleep had often been interrupted as well.

"Now stop that, Tristan." Yawning, she pulled me back down and snuggled right up to me so that her breasts pressed against my back. "You don't need to go through that again, now, do you?" Her breathy crooning soothed me; it always did. Her nearness kept most of my fears away. "Once was enough, hmm?"

"Savannah… honey, you're okay… you're right here…." I reached back to touch the toasty skin of her side, just needing to be sure.

"Of course I'm here—where else would I be?" I felt her lips on the back of my neck, kissing me in between words. "Want to tell me about it?"

"We were… w-we were back at that party… they were gonna hurt you… b-but I know it's all over. It's all over now."

"Yeah, Tris, it's all over and nobody hurt me, thanks to you." I got a big wet shoulder-kiss for emphasis.

"I could've fought them."

"You could've fought, but you couldn't have won. You were just sixteen and a rack of bones—you'd missed more than a few meals, if you think back on it. They were grown men." I squirmed at the painful memory. A few more tiny kisses were deposited onto that sensitive place between my shoulder and my neck.

Maybe she was right. Maybe I did do the best I could have under those impossible circumstances.

"And there were four of them...." Her words trailed away into silence. Then Savannah's probing fingers slipped into my hair and I knew what was coming, and I knew it was going to feel so good. The little circles that she drew on my scalp soothed me like nothing else. They brought me back to the present, to our bedroom, to the person who'd saved me.

I accepted the silence between us and momentarily embraced it because it was just so peaceful. But before a full minute had passed us by, I broke it. "They changed me that night, Savi. They *ruined* me.... It's like I.... I c-can't be with a guy, and you, of all people, know I'm not what you'd call straight—I'm not *any* kind of man anymore!" This particular conversation had become as routine as my bad dreams.

"Nobody changed you—and you *are* a man, Tristan. You just aren't ready for the physical part of love, that's all. Things haven't... it just hasn't been exactly *right* for you yet."

I seriously considered what she'd just said and what I wanted to tell her next. I liked to think a lot about what I was going to say before I let any words out of my mouth, especially when it was this important. "Robby's really nice." Buried in my hair, her fingers froze; I knew her ears had perked up. "And you have a chance to be *normal* with him."

Savannah sat up, leaned across me toward the nightstand, and switched on the lamp. When I looked up at her she was staring at me, speechless.

"All I'm saying is, I think you could be happy with him. He seems crazy about you."

Her expression remained unchanged; I'd classify it as *shocked and horrified.*

"I think I'm gonna back off… let you two see what happens with each other, okay?" I exhaled sharply, having said my piece.

"No, it's not okay." She'd managed to speak, but she was still gawking at me, her expression now a cross between angry and bewildered. "And who ever said I wanted *normal*?"

I sat up and gaped back at her, racking my brain for an argument that she'd consider, or even listen to.

"I'm not gonna see him again." Savannah was shaking a bit now so I reached out with both hands to steady her fragile shoulders. "Not unless it's the three of us."

Shaking my head, I replied, "He's not gonna go for it, Savi; no normal guy would. He's gonna ditch you, can't you see that?"

"Why are you so stuck on 'normal'? Nothing about either of our lives has ever been anything remotely close to 'normal.'" She did this air-quote thing with her fingers. Savannah could be so stubborn sometimes. Her chin was already set in this certain position that I'd seen on plenty of other occasions in the past, occasions when she was bound and determined to get her own way. "Anyways, I thought we had a deal."

A lengthy and exasperated breath puffed out of my lungs. Savannah was living in some kind of a dream world if she thought she could make her crazy plan work. But the only way that she'd agree to go on dates with other men had been if I went along with it—if I went along with *them*. She knew fully well that I wasn't… how to phrase this delicately… I wasn't able to participate in *any* relationship—not with her, certainly, or anyone else—in an *intimate* way. And she'd never push me like that. I comforted myself with the assurance that all I really had to do was pretend to be of one mind with her in this bizarre little plot she'd concocted. I'd just hang out with Robby and Savannah, staying on the outer edges of their relationship until they became a couple.

I could do that for a while, couldn't I? In any case, I *was going* to do that for Savannah.

"Promise me you'll try, Tristan."

What choice did I really have? She deserved more in life than a platonic future with me, her asexual best friend. So I nodded.

"Swear it." Savannah was one tough customer. "Or at least say it out loud."

I smiled. "I'll try, but I won't ruin your life. If I think it isn't working, and Robby's getting freaked out, I'm backing off."

She looked at me and laughed heartily, but strangely there wasn't a trace of a true smile on her lips or in her eyes. And for the life of me, I couldn't figure out what was even slightly funny about this situation. "The third piece of our unusual puzzle is out there, Tristan. I think I've already found him."

CHAPTER 6

Robby

I COULD barely even see Mikey's rather oversized nose above the huge pile of Maria's Mouthwatering Mega-Mountain of Macho Nachos. And yes, that embarrassingly descriptive name was actually listed on the menu next to a snapshot that really didn't do the monster justice. Okay, maybe I was exaggerating a little bit about how high the pile was, but still, there was enough cheese, fried beef, and sour cream on that plate to bring on heart attacks in half a dozen men.

"All I can say is it was fucking strange. They acted like a married couple, but at the same time there she was, openly out on a date with me." I tried to find a tortilla chip that wasn't completely smothered in the offensive ingredients, but I didn't have any luck, so I took a sip of my Coke instead. "It just wasn't normal."

Mikey didn't seem to share my revulsion in regards to the fatty ingredients. Licking the grease from his fingertips, he offered up his version of sound advice. "You shoulda told her that if she wanted a threesome so bad, you want it to be wit' you and two girls." After that insightful suggestion, he fearlessly dove headfirst back into the potentially heart-stopping plate of appetizers.

Trying to use Mikey as a sounding board had been a miserable idea. I tossed him my napkin, thinking that what he really needed to use to mop himself off was a full-size beach towel, and then I rolled my eyes. "Can you get your mind out of the gutter, man? I like this girl and I want to see her again." I left out the whole part about how my first glance at

Savannah's stunning boyfriend, Tristan, had given me a woody—the likes of which I'd heard of but had never experienced firsthand before. And how when I was lying in bed last night, I didn't know which of the two to fantasize about.

"Then go out wit' her again, for Christ's sake, Rob. Give it to her good at the end of the night and she'll know which one of you two is the real man, huh?" Over what now looked like the slaughtered remains of some extremely unfortunate animal, Mikey sent me this get-your-head-out-of-your-ass glare, and delivered his final piece of questionable commentary. "An' prob'ly the dude's a big fag and you're reading way too much into their relationship. Now, I've had enough of this chick-flick shit; I'm losing my goddamn appetite."

"Well, I wouldn't want this gourmet food to go to waste." I spoke rather sarcastically, but have to admit I wasn't too worried about poor Mikey starving to death. As long as the food was free, which it usually was when we dined together (for him, at least), Mikey's belly was an endless black hole.

"So shut the fuck up and let me know when you bang her—and I'm gonna want details. Sights, sounds, smells, tastes, touches... you're gonna hafta engage all of my five senses, you hear?"

Mr. Sensitivity. *Jesus*, I wondered to myself, *when did I start calling Mikey the same names that women usually called me?* Nonetheless, when I opened the contacts on my phone to press S for Savannah, the image of haunting brown doe eyes lurked disconcertingly close to the front of my mind.

"YOU'RE staring at me." Our eyes met over our healthy stir-fry dinners, in stark opposition to my lunch with Mikey. I'd met Savannah at a Japanese steak house in Harvard Square after a late afternoon potential job walk-through near my office. The chef had prepared our meals right at our table, his dramatic chopping and stirring blending with occasional bursts of fire and the sound of our mingled laughter. This dinner date was certainly several steep steps up from macaroni at the diner.

"Robby.... I'm not going to apologize for staring. You're a very intriguing man."

Intriguing? I had a reoccurrence of the Robby-the-lab-rat feeling that I'd first experienced on the night she'd asked me out. I glanced down at my plate. "I'm glad you think so."

When I looked back up at Savannah, she was licking her lips, but not at all suggestively. "Well, I can't eat another bite. That was delicious."

The light from the many well-placed candles and the spontaneous bursts of flame coming from different corners of the room highlighted Savannah's face. The mood was certainly set for romance, so I reached across the table and drew her dainty hand into mine. She squeezed my fingers harder than I expected, and I looked up quickly, catching her point-blank stare. For some reason, Savannah's absolute directness, her complete lack of flirtation, allowed me to relax a little. Yes, The Ice Man, as I'd been referred to more than once, melted a bit around the edges.

Now, to attack the area of Savannah's reticence. "You haven't told me anything about when you were a kid." I could only watch as the candor of her gaze repositioned itself into the wariness with which I was far more familiar. "Why's that?"

"Not my favorite subject, I guess." She lifted the tiny crockery cup of tea to her lips, but didn't drink it; she just held it there. "My childhood was nothing like yours."

She spoke with such a note of finality that I knew her intention was to have slammed shut the subject with that one cryptic statement, but I stuck my foot in the door. I continued to look at her expectantly.

Savannah placed the cup back on the table, and then withdrew her other hand from mine. "I'm going to keep it brief, if you don't mind. No house with a white picket fence, no Waldo the Golden Retriever, no happily married parents, no private Catholic school." So she really *had* been listening intently to my life story. "Just my drunk of a mother, her lowlife boyfriend, and me. A crappy apartment. Food stamps. Get the picture?"

Wow. I was not expecting to hear that. In fact, I didn't know anyone else, not personally at least, with life circumstances like hers.

"That is, until Tristan came along." She lifted her blue-green gaze nearly to the ceiling, and this wistful smile shaped her narrow lips.

Bingo! She'd given me exactly the opportunity I'd been waiting for. "So, how did you meet Tristan, anyways?"

If I'd thought her eyes had grown shadowed before, then right now I'd have to call them fully eclipsed. Nonetheless, she graced me with a rather vague answer. "We met on the street."

Once again, she'd managed to yank the rug out from beneath my feet. "On the street?" I asked. From what little she'd already told me, I highly doubted that they had been two precocious ten-year-olds playing hopscotch on Brookline Avenue when they'd been formally introduced by their hovering nannies. The circumstances must have been more sinister. I didn't have to voice my query, though; my face betrayed my confusion.

"Both of us took off from home when we were teenagers."

That was blunt. "Y-you g-guys were *r-runaways*?" As could have been expected, I displayed behavior that was the polar opposite of calm, cool, and collected.

She nodded but offered nothing more in the way of explanation. *Typical.*

I was forced to examine the curly top of her blonde head as she picked up her chopsticks and thoughtfully drew lines through the rice that remained on her plate. "Why did you run away?"

If I had to bet my life right then, I'd have bet that Savannah wasn't going to answer my last question. And I'd be dead. Because after at least a full minute, during which she'd expertly used her chopsticks to move the rice from one side of her plate to the other and back again, she didn't look up, but she did start talking. "My mother's boyfriend was a creep. He couldn't keep his hands to himself."

"Are you saying that he made passes at you?"

My most recent inquiry served to make Savannah smile at me in an annoyingly patronizing manner, as if she believed I'd been born only yesterday. "That'd be a polite way of putting it." She thought for a minute, and then the direct side of Savannah reemerged. Looking at me squarely, she replied. "If I'd stayed, my mother and I would have shared a lover. How's that for me having 'a close family unit'?"

I was stunned. What kind of a mother would allow that sort of thing to go on under her roof? "Did she kick him out?" I asked hopefully.

Sour laughter preceded her answer. "She didn't care if I was part of the deal or not, as long as her boyfriend stuck around. Anyways, I left before he could get what he was after, if you know what I mean."

That was a pretty messed-up situation, to say the least. "How old were you when this was going on?"

"Oh, about thirteen or so, and fourteen when I'd had enough of fighting him off and split." I had no idea how she managed to do it, but Savannah kept her expression completely blank as she informed me of her youthful plight. She may as well have been listing the ingredients of banana crème pie. "And things were much worse at Tristan's house…."

Suddenly, I didn't want to hear any more. I didn't want to imagine those soft, trusting brown eyes of his red-rimmed with tears or swollen with pain. For some inexplicable reason, the concept of Tristan suffering was simply intolerable to me. I had to make this conversation stop. "Well, that sure sucks for him." I used a note of finality in my voice that I hoped would push Savannah on to the next topic of conversation.

I failed quite miserably; she looked at me as if I'd kicked her puppy. "Yeah, it really did *suck for him*." More accurately, she was glaring at me as if I was an asshole who'd stuck his foot deep in his mouth. Which was exactly who I was and what I'd done.

Was it too late to redeem myself? "Sorry, that sounded cold. And Tristan seems like such a great guy—he didn't deserve to be treated poorly."

She wasn't buying what I was trying to sell her.

"I mean nobody deserves that, especially not a kid."

Savannah might as well have looked through me; it was as if she was in a trance of some sort. Her voice dropped to a tone so low I could barely hear her. "His uncle succeeded where my mother's boyfriend failed."

The blood froze in my veins. I was shocked. I was pissed. I was repulsed. Why in fucking tarnation did Savannah feel the need to share that little tidbit of information with me? I had no need for the grisly details of Tristan Chartrand's tragic childhood. My mind was already fucked-up enough when it came to that dude, the last thing I needed was to add pity and compassion to the mix.

We sat there, our arms folded politely on the table. Savannah was stone-faced and I'm sure I appeared completely distraught. Yes, Robby Dalton, The Cold-hearted Snake, all shriveled up in the grass in complete emotional devastation. And I had absolutely no idea what to say next, so for the longest time I said nothing. Finally, when it had become sufficiently clear that Savannah was not going to be the first to speak, I sputtered, "I don't blame him for leaving…. Uh, I'd have jumped ship too, if that shit was happening to me."

Savannah nodded like maybe I'd passed (as in, barely squeaked by) some sort of test. She reached out for my hand again, this time holding it loosely. "Thanks for dinner, Robby. Let's get out of here."

IT SEEMED like there were a lot of stairs leading up to Savannah's third-floor apartment. And a lot of silence between the two of us. *A lot.* We hadn't spoken very much since I'd stuck my foot in it back at the restaurant. Conversation in my Jeep had been pretty much restricted to the directions to her place.

"Tristan should be home by now." Savannah knocked on the door. "Hey! Open up, it's me!"

And me—the guy who wined and dined your girlfriend tonight, I thought, but wisely chose to stifle the words.

The door swung open wide and suddenly all I could see was a fucking gorgeous smile. It was too perfect for words… and then there were those expressive eyes of his. But I couldn't dwell on them too much right then; they brought to mind the pain I now knew he'd experienced as a child. However, I couldn't help but notice that at the moment, those soulful eyes actually seemed to be sparkling with genuine enthusiasm at seeing me again.

No sooner had I stepped through the door than I felt Tristan's palm slap down gently on my shoulder in greeting. I shivered. "I was hoping you guys would come back here after dinner!" I could tell he meant each word. "Can I get you a beer, Robby?"

"Uh, sure… if you're gonna have one." It seemed like I'd just asked him to join Savannah and me, didn't it? And it also seemed like the two of them caught each other's eyes and smiled.

"Can you get me a Diet Sprite?" Just as Tristan removed his hand from my shoulder so he could head off to the kitchen, Savannah started tugging insistently at my arm. "Come on. Let's go sit down."

A couple of minutes later, seated alone on the oversized tan couch as Savannah had gone to visit the bathroom and Tristan was still in the kitchen, I peered around as inconspicuously as I could manage, trying to take in the details of their apartment.

It was interesting. And if I had to describe it in a few short words, I'd say the place had a "We are the World" theme going on. It had been tastefully decorated with what looked to be African pottery and Navajo baskets, artfully placed on well-used but sturdy wooden trunks. Middle Eastern-looking rugs and South American wall hangings covered almost every square inch of wall space. This was not Savannah's college crash pad, nor was it Tristan's bachelor pad. This apartment had been thoughtfully and lovingly decorated. It was a home.

Just then Tristan emerged from the kitchen balancing three frosted mugs. "I wasn't sure if you liked your beer in the bottle or not, and then I remembered I'd stuck some mugs in the freezer, so…." He handed me a mug, placed the one filled with soda on the coffee table in front of the couch, and took his own to the puffy fake suede chair that was placed diagonally to where I sat. I took a couple of deep breaths to calm my already raging hormones, which seemed to act up almost involuntarily when in this dude's presence, and forced myself to take a long look at him.

Tristan Chartrand was no doubt one of the most beautiful human beings I had ever set eyes on. Yes, that sounded dramatic, but it was really just me being honest. His features were perfectly even; his tan skin was smooth and flawless; his hair was shaggy and casual, like he'd just stepped in from a windy day. And he had this pixie-like quality, a little spark of spirit in his eyes, all buried beneath his shyness. It was nothing short of adorable. Tonight, in his snug Goo Goo Dolls concert T-shirt and these oversized gray sweats tied loosely at his hips, he looked very young and innocent. I made a feeble attempt to remind myself that I wasn't into the pure-as-the-driven-snow type. *Right.*

Lifting his sock-covered feet onto the coffee table, Tristan asked, "Did you and Savannah have a nice dinner?"

"Uh huh. It was great." I had no choice but to continue staring across the coffee table at Tristan's picture-perfect face. *And body.* Wouldn't want to miss out on that important detail, now, would I? Don't get me wrong, Tristan wasn't buff or anything, but from what I could see below that scrap of a T-shirt, the dude had himself a decent set of abs. "Fashionably slim" would describe him pretty well, not at all gangly. And the guy had a respectable amount of definition in his pecs and biceps too. He'd obviously spent a bit of time on a weight bench.

"Where'd you take her?"

What the fuck am I doing? I was acting like I was in some European art museum scrutinizing Michelangelo's sculpture of David.

"Um, Robby, where did you guys eat dinner?"

Suddenly realizing that Tristan had asked me a question, I dragged my gaze up from the strip of his belly at which I found myself staring, and met his eyes. "Uh… oh, we had Japanese."

"I don't think Savi's ever had Japanese before."

Well, I guess you'd know, wouldn't you? Again, I didn't say it out loud. I just shrugged.

Savannah returned to the living room, now dressed in an oversized Red Sox baseball jersey, which had "PEDROIA" printed across the back in bold letters, along with tight black leggings, her hair pulled up in a messy bun. "And Tris, they cooked our dinner right in front of us—at our table!" When she was around her roommate, it was as if she was about fifteen years old. "And it was so good! I brought you back our leftovers. They're in a box in the fridge. But it's too bad you couldn't have come with us."

Yes, it's a crying shame, I thought drily.

Tristan smiled at Savannah like they shared some kind of big secret. "Somebody has to work in this relationship." He wasn't being cruel; he was just teasing her (and evidently financially supporting her).

Savannah laughed and then asked, "Speaking of work, how did it go tonight?"

As the pair exchanged their "how was your day, dear?" small talk, I took the opportunity to further check out my surroundings. Speckling the multicultural décor like spots on a dog, were framed photographs of Tristan and Savannah. Always smiling, always touching. At the beach, at Savannah's college graduation, in front of what looked like a bar in Quincy Market… looking like the world's happiest couple. Making me wonder what the fuck I was doing with my ass planted on their comfy couch. That was when I noticed that there were only two doorways in the very short hallway off of the living room. The one at the end of the hallway stood wide open: clearly a bathroom. And there was only one other door. The bedroom.

Only one goddamn bedroom?

So caught up in their domestic chitchat, the loving couple didn't even notice that I leaned as far back as I could on the couch so I could sneak a peek through the slightly open bedroom door. And that's how I managed to see it—one fucking queen-size bed!

There was only *one* fucking bed in that *one* fucking bedroom!

What the fuck was going on here?

That was when I noticed a persistent brushing against my shin. It nudged and pushed more and more forcefully until I finally broke out of my daze and glanced down. A huge black cat pressed its forehead into my dangling palm.

"His name is Runaway. We found him in a box behind the S-Squared Diner when he was just a kitten." Savannah leaned over and picked up the monstrosity of a cat, and soon she was nuzzling him as Tristan fondly looked on.

How fucking sweet—the happy couple had a baby!

Now, seeing as I'd just become aware of the cozy love nest shared by the girl I was dating and the guy I was apparently lusting after, I didn't have too much left to say to them.

"Don't you like cats, Robby? Oh, no... you're not allergic, are you?" Tristan held his breath, waiting for my answer.

"No, no, cats are fine. I'm fine with cats." That's about all I was *fine with* in this apartment, though. I stood up.

Tristan, Savannah, and Runaway all leaped to their feet (and paws) as well.

"Where are you going?" Tristan looked alarmed.

"I thought maybe we could all watch a movie together." Savannah did her best to catch my eye, but I was having none of it. "I rented *You, Me and Dupree*—Owen Wilson's in it." I needed to go home, to be alone, to think this fucked-up shit over.

"I, uh, have to go, um, to my sister's for breakfast, like, real early... the breakfast is."

Those brown eyes fell softly on me; I could almost feel their weight. But still I focused my eyes on the door.

"It's early, Robby. Stay a while." Tristan and those fucking gorgeous eyes moved between the door and me. But I shoved past him and didn't glance back to see the hurt on his face.

"I *said* I had to go." And I was out the door.

CHAPTER 7

Robby

WORK was dragging. And Mikey was driving me fucking crazy, whining about how "frigging starving" he was. Christ, his mother owned an Italian bakery. That spelled free food too, didn't it?

"You oughtta take me out to dinner, seeing as I charmed that old hag of a veterinarian into spilling the name of the contractor who they were *gonna* hire to do the addition."

"You did a good job by getting that information, Mikey, but Dr. Peverly isn't exactly an old hag." I'd long thought that comments like this one about Dr. Peverly came from Mikey's misguided attempts at being funny. It crossed my mind that I'd been giving him way too much credit.

"Well, she sure ain't no cougar. I wouldn't do her unless I was drunk or high. Now, 'bout my dinner…."

I didn't tell him to shut the fuck up and take what he'd said back about the good doctor. No, instead I just bent my ass right on over, figuratively speaking, and made myself an easy target. DeSalvo was about to con me into buying him yet another meal. I stopped for a second to wonder if it still counted as a con if I was fully aware that it was happening to me. That was when the brilliant idea hit me. "All right, Mikey, dinner's on me, but I'm choosing the restaurant."

"You ain't gonna take me to the Burrito Shack again, are you? I swear last time I got food poisoning."

Shaking my head, I replied, "No burritos tonight. How does Michael's on the Waterfront sound?"

"Shit! You got yourself a dinner date, Dalton." He was already rubbing his belly in anticipation. "Your treat, right?"

"It'll be on the company."

Mikey was definitely not one to decline a free meal. "Well, what are you fucking waiting for? I'll drive, that way we'll get there in half the time. You can call on the way over so they have a table ready and waiting for King Michael DeAmazin'."

I managed to laugh, but it came out sounding more forced than usual. *Whatever.* Tonight I was going to take a look at Tristan Chartrand when he wasn't all wrapped up in his security blanket, who just so happened to be named Savannah Meyers. What kind of guy was he when sweet, loving *Savi* wasn't around?

Tristan Chartrand was probably an asshole just like the rest of us.

I anticipated tonight's dinner with much more than a simple yearning for fine seafood.

I'D TAKEN a few girls to Michael's on the Waterfront over the past several years in my rather apathetic quest to get laid. Ironically, I was here tonight to check out a dude. But I managed to push that less than comfortable thought from my mind with great haste as I entered the vast and elegant establishment, which was located directly on the Boston Harbor.

Loosening my tie, I wandered around the regally decorated lobby, easily locating the bar, where Mikey had already started sucking down the liquid portion of his free meal while I'd parked the Jeep. "Finish your drink, man. I'll go see about our table."

As I made my way to the hostess desk, I pulled off my suit jacket and pushed up my shirtsleeves.

You're merely treating a good employee to a well-deserved dinner, I told myself breezily. But the undeniable truth of the matter was evident in my darting eyes, my rapid breathing, and my sweaty palms. I was behaving like some schoolboy with a terrible crush, ever on the lookout, more than well aware that his beloved roamed the same hallways. Yes, I was on alert for any sign of Tristan Chartrand.

I leaned against the high mahogany desk where a pert red-haired hostess stood studying an oversized seating chart. "Hello, ma'am. I called about thirty minutes ago and requested a table for two under the name DeSalvo."

"Oh, yes, sir. Ahhh, here it is." Pointing to a spot on the chart, she batted her baby blues rather invitingly up at me.

But I wasn't biting. "One more thing, I have this friend who works here and I wanted to know if we could be seated in his section, if it wouldn't be too much trouble. But I'd rather you not tell him I'm here. That would ruin the surprise."

She nodded. "Yes, I see. Who is your friend?"

I leaned in toward her a bit more, lowered my voice, and cupped my hand over my mouth. "Uh, he's a waiter. His name is Tristan Chartrand."

"I'm sorry, sir," the hostess said with a tilt of her head and a flirtatious tug at her pearl necklace. "You're going to have to speak up."

"His name is Tristan. Tristan Chartrand." I felt like I was yelling, but I was barely speaking at an ordinary volume. "Can you just seat us in his section? Please."

"Tristan? Oh, God, he's such a sweetie! I think there's room in his section." With a bob of her red curls, she picked up two heavy menus and said, "Follow me."

As I walked in the hostess's wake toward our table, I found myself glancing this way and that, checking to see if Mikey was…. Oh, okay, if I was going to cut the shit, I'd confess that I was scanning the restaurant for a certain tall, dark-haired man with sensitive, chocolate-colored eyes.

From the small corner table at which I was seated, I spotted Tristan's perfect profile silhouetted against a spectacular view of the Boston Harbor, which was visible through one of the restaurant's enormous picture windows. He was lowering a heavy tray of piping hot food onto a waiting stand, wearing the most (annoyingly) engaging smile I'd ever seen on a waiter.

It pained me to admit that Tristan looked fantastic. He was dressed in the typical waiter attire, but to it he'd added his own urban flare. His white oxford was tailored perfectly to fit his sleek frame, his tie was solid black and narrow and was tucked into his shirt between his third and fourth buttons, and he wore jet-black skinny jeans that clung to him in all the right ways. If I don't say so myself.

Was the guy Euro? Emo? Homo? For a moment I speculated about his Metrosexual style.

After serving meals to the party of four by the window, asking them if there was anything further they required, and wishing them an enjoyable meal, Tristan looked up, and somehow directly into my wide-eyed gaze.

If I'd thought his smile was stunning when he'd opened the door to his apartment that night last week, well, all I can say is it couldn't compare to the grin that spread over his lips right now. And before I knew it, he'd practically run over to my corner table. "Oh my God, Robby—you're here!" He grabbed my hand right off of the menu on the table and shook it vigorously. "It's so great you came here, man!"

So it had been established: Tristan was happy to see me.

I stuttered out my prepared excuse. "I-I'm here for b-business—to, uh, to m-meet with an employee."

Tristan swiped the menus off of the table and grabbed my arm. "Well, you certainly won't be sitting way over here. Come on!" He led me to a table for four directly in front of one of the huge picture windows. "This is much better."

After seating me carefully, like I was made of fine china, he picked up the two extra place settings from the table.

"You really don't need to go to this trouble for me."

"This is no trouble whatsoever, Robby. I'm just so glad you chose Michael's for your meeting tonight! Now listen, I want you to just relax, take in the view, and sip on your water; I'll be right back with crackers and cheese. Oh, and let me put in an order at the bar for you while you wait for your associate."

"Oh, well, sure. Grab me a Heineken, I guess."

Just then, Mikey swaggered over to our new and improved table. "Nice spot, D-man. And by the way, I think that perky little hostess over there wants my meat 'tween her thighs." He used both hands to create a disturbingly vivid visual image of exactly how he'd get that job done. I'm pretty sure I blushed in response.

Tristan's eyes widened measurably at Mikey's vulgar display, but he politely inquired as to what he could get my asshole coworker (my words) to drink and headed off to the bar.

As soon as Tristan was out of earshot, I admitted the truth to Mikey. "Our waiter—he's the *other man*."

"Come again, Rob-ster?"

"The waiter who just took your drink order. He's Savannah's roommate."

Momentarily, an expression of genuine injury crossed Mikey's face, which actually surprised me. "So, you're saying we're not here to celebrate my 'job well done' and we're actually here to check out some fucking queer dude?"

I looked around us coyly to be sure no one had overheard Mikey's latest verbal blunder. "Keep your voice down, DeSalvo. And remember, it's still a free meal—and a damned good one at that."

Mikey yanked his napkin out from underneath his silverware and dropped it onto his lap without taking his eyes from mine. "This is frigging bullshit."

"Hey, man—"

"Just shut the fuck up, Rob. I shoulda remembered there's no such thing 's a free lunch. Or dinner. But I s'pose I'll get over the pain once I taste the surf 'n' turf." He was definitely still pissed off, but at least he seemed willing to work with me on this.

For the rest of the evening, Tristan treated us like royalty. Now, I was there to do a job, to evaluate Prince Charming when Cinderella wasn't in the vicinity, so although I was enjoying myself thoroughly (the food was magnificent and the service impeccable), I took mental notes on Tristan's behavior. Over the course of our *very extensive* meal (Mikey was paying me back for the insult to his pride by ordering just about everything on the menu) Tristan showed his true colors. And it appeared that his inner shades were as glowing as his outer ones.

Tristan was consistently prompt, patient, courteous, efficient, and generous. His warmth and friendliness knew no boundaries. And he showed these qualities not only to Mikey and me, but to all of his other customers, each and every member of the restaurant staff, and even to a random little old lady who dropped her cane on her way to the ladies' room.

Three baskets of rolls and butter (I actually thought Tristan was going to butter my roll for me). Humongous salads, extra dressing, even additional croutons (I'd merely mentioned to Tristan that I liked the croutons, and he'd gone and returned with a soup bowl full of them).

Enormous dinner portions (so huge I found myself avoiding the envious stares of other diners).

Mikey and I were treated like kings, which didn't stop my partner in crime from behaving like a complete asshole. When I introduced him to Tristan, Mikey refused to raise his eyes from his seafood chowder long enough to say hello. But he did manage to inform Tristan that his last drink was "way too frigging weak", and could he please tell "that fucking barkeep to stop being such a cheap prick wit' the booze."

"I am so sorry, Mr. DeSalvo. I'll make your next drink myself," Tristan responded with patience. I barely resisted the urge to insist that Mikey shut the fuck up.

And when Tristan came back with Mikey's made-with-love-and-extra-tequila drink, he said so sweetly it made my teeth ache, "Now, let me get you gentlemen some dessert. I would highly recommend the cannolis—they're amazing."

Despite the fact that the eating machine sitting across from me was still salivating at the prospect of more free food, I politely refused. I'd finished observing Tristan. My question had been answered: the man was a virtual saint, whether or not Savannah was present. Plus, we were both stuffed to the gills. "No, thank you. We're fine. You can just bring me the che—"

"We'll take our dessert to go. Pack 'em up in a big box and don't forget to put in some tiramisu."

Mikey, Mikey, Mikey. I shook my head in frustration.

"That sounds like an excellent plan, Mr. DeSalvo. I'll send the busboy over with your dessert when it's all packed up. And Robby, there won't be a check. You gentlemen are *my* guests tonight."

Uh-huh. *Saint Tristan of Somerville.* "No way—just bring me the check, man."

"This is my treat. Please, Robby, I want to do this."

"I didn't come here to suck a free dinner out of you!"

"Of course you didn't." Momentarily, Tristan appeared offended. His brown doe-eyes clouded over, and then briefly dipped to stare at the floor. But he recovered quickly. "You came here for a business meeting. And I want to show you how grateful I am that you chose Michael's for your meal."

Christ, Mikey and I had chowed down like two fucking pigs before the slaughter and it was all going to be at Tristan's expense.

"Thanks a shitload, uh, Tristan. That's your name, right?" Mikey was in top form tonight. "And, on second thought, can you stick a few slices of sweet pie in the box too? I'm having me a craving."

I shot my dining partner an annoyed glare. Actually, it was more of a look to kill. Mikey smiled back at me innocently.

"Of course, sir. It'd be my pleasure."

Both of us watched as Tristan headed off to the kitchen. And I didn't waste a minute before I leaned over the table and asked my dinner guest in a scheming whisper, "So what do you think? Is he gay or not?" I waited for his answer with bated breath, knowing that this should not matter so much to me. It wasn't as if I'd fallen in love with Savannah and my entire future hung on her pretty roommate being gay. Nonetheless, for some reason I wanted so badly for Mikey to bellow, "That boy's as gay as a frigging spring parade!"

Sucking on his fingertips one by one, Mikey appeared to be seriously considering my question. Finally he replied, his tone nonchalant, "I sure's shit don't have a clue if that dude's a faggot or straight as you and me, but I gotta say, he'd make somebody a frigging perfect old-school Italian wife. He lives to serve."

And no, Tristan didn't bring me a fucking check, but on the outside of the box from the bakery, he'd drawn a smiley face and scribbled, *Give Savannah a call! T.*

CHAPTER 8

Robby

AS IT turned out, Savannah called me.

I wasn't sure if getting together with her again was such a good idea, for a multitude of reasons. Nonetheless, here I was, bottle of wine in hand, standing at Savannah's apartment door waiting eagerly for her to answer my knock, although my slumped shoulders represented my battle-worn brain. Violently conflicting thoughts had been doing battle there since she called last night, inviting me to dinner at her place. I was just so fucking torn, and not in the "I'm just not that into her, so what should I do now?" way I was accustomed to. No, I'd finally met a girl who was perfect for me; she was smart, committed to her own worthy causes, not at all needy. Well, not at all needy *for me*—I wasn't certain precisely how much Savannah needed Tristan. And how much *I* wanted Tristan. Therein lay the problem.

As expected, she looked ravishingly beautiful. Savannah was one of those girls who seemed effortlessly flawless. Tonight was apparently "denim night." A loose cowboy-styled denim shirt, unbuttoned to reveal a lacy bra-thing, torn denim jeans rolled up at the ankle and snug where it counted, hair pulled up tight into a high bun, and tons of homemade-looking beaded jewelry adorning her wrists, neck, and bare ankles. I was happy with my jeans and white T-shirt choice for tonight. It was going to be a casual dinner.

"Robby." She always said my name in this certain way I couldn't exactly put my finger on. It was kind of like she was partly saying hello or good-bye, depending upon the circumstances, partly giving me a little pat of approval and partly just barely tolerating me.

I leaned in and gave Savannah a quick kiss in an attempt to assure myself that it was strictly the "hot chick" I was here to visit. But I couldn't help glancing around to see if we had an audience.

"He's not here," she said mildly as if in answer to a question. "Tris has to work tonight."

A potent feeling rushed into my awareness, but again I had trouble either identifying or admitting it. "Oh, oh, okay." If I *had* to name the feeling, though, I'd call it disappointment.

She led me into their spotless kitchen, which, in opposition to their living room, was quite stark. There was no decoration here whatsoever, not even curtains on the window. "Tristan likes to keep his kitchen bare."

His kitchen? Again, she offered no explanation.

"Does Tristan like to cook or something?" Even when Tristan wasn't here, it still felt as if he was.

She smiled. "He sure does. And he's good at it."

I was suddenly reminded of Mikey's words about Tristan before we left the restaurant: *he'd make someone a frigging perfect wife*. How true.

The table was set very simply with rustic white crockery plates and heavy flatware. The cloth napkins were charcoal gray, folded neatly into rectangles. A long loaf of what looked like home-baked bread rested in a narrow basket. Savannah went to the refrigerator and pulled out a large matching crockery bowl. "It's Thai Chopped Chicken Salad."

She proceeded to serve us each a plateful. It looked delicious. "Did you make this, Savannah?"

In response to that question, Savannah released a spurt of laughter. "You'll be glad I didn't when you taste it."

I took a big bite. It tasted like heaven on a fork. "Tristan made this?"

She nodded. "He loves to do all of the homemaking stuff for us— you know, cooking, cleaning, laundry, decorating. Probably because he never had a real home before this one."

I fought like hell to squelch the compassion I felt swelling in my heart for Tristan, the boy. All alone on the streets. But I didn't say anything; I didn't think I could have.

"I was only out on the street for six weeks all together." Now her attention appeared totally focused on the salad.

"Six weeks? Why only six weeks?"

Beads of moisture had collected on the narrow strip of skin above her upper lip. Savannah took a few more bites and then she put her fork down. So I did the same. But she kept her eyes on the plate while my eyes were stuck on her. "Something, um, something *happened* to us—to *him*—out there, and I decided that state care was a better option, uh, for me, than living on the street. I went into foster care for the next four years, until I graduated from high school."

I didn't know why, but I had to ask. "What happened to Tristan, you know, when you went into foster care?"

Savannah's attention shifted toward the bare kitchen window that overlooked the city street. She spoke quietly. "He stayed out there."

Without hesitation, Savannah picked up her fork again and I followed suit. For the next few minutes, we ate in silence.

My subsequent query was much more calculated, I must confess. I needed to know how Savannah and Tristan fit together; the answer to this would hopefully provide me with a clue as to the nature of their current relationship. "Did you stay in touch with Tristan during high school?"

Shaking her head in regret, Savannah answered, "No. I lost touch with him for a long time. And I'm talking about years, Robby." Then a spark of enthusiasm lit her eyes. "But when I started my undergraduate degree at SU, I managed to track him down. Or more honestly, I bumped into him. He was working at the diner. You know, at the S-Squared. Once we'd hooked up again, we moved in here. And I'd gotten a job at the diner, too, so I worked there until I started grad school. The rest of the story is pretty much what you see." She gestured to her surroundings.

Very gradually, the picture was coming together. But, exactly what did "hooked up" mean?

WE WERE sitting on the couch in the living room drinking wine when Tristan came home. He trotted right over to us with eager eyes and a wide smile. Savannah reached up as he bent down, and they embraced briefly. And then—*what the fuck?*—Tristan bent right down and hugged me as well. Chills rose up my spine and, disappointingly, it wasn't at all unpleasant.

"Hi, Robby!" God, he was so fucking cute. "Did you like the salad? I wanted to make some hot and sour soup too, but Savannah said that enough was enough."

Before I could answer, I heard Savannah suggest, "Grab a glass and another bottle of chardonnay, and come join us."

I threw in awkwardly, "Oh, and, yeah, the salad was awesome. You sure *can* cook!"

I was sent the most devastating smile I'd seen so far, and that was definitely saying something. "Really, Robby? I'm so glad you liked it." He strode off to the kitchen mumbling something about the fact that he was originally planning to make a grilled chicken Caesar salad using some croutons he'd brought home from the restaurant, but he'd decided maybe that was too boring.

"You don't mind that I asked him to join us, do you?" I got one of those pointed glances from Savannah.

Quickly, I shook my head. "No, of course not. It's fine." But I was already planning my exit strategy. I'd felt the surge of my overly interested hormones the very second Tristan had come through the door. I knew I had to get out of here before… before I stopped feeling so satisfied with the evening I'd just shared with Savannah. Before I was reminded that when I was with her, *something* was missing. Before I admitted that when I so much as laid eyes on Tristan, that *something* wasn't missing anymore.

That unexpected realization was nothing short of earth-shattering to me. I stood up and moved swiftly toward the door. "I think it's time I called it a night."

Shit. In my rush to get to the door, I nearly slammed into Tristan, who was returning from the kitchen, wine and wine glass in hand. "I thought you were going to stay a while." His eyes reflected a disappointment so bitter it hurt me to witness it.

"Come on, Robby. Stay for an hour or so—we can play cards," Savannah piped up from her corner of the couch. Her voice showed markedly less passion than Tristan's, yet I could tell she hoped I'd stay.

"I guess I can stay for a while."

Savannah purred with the smug satisfaction of a feline; if Tristan had a tail, it'd be wagging a hundred miles per hour.

And I really was much more of a dog person.

WE DIDN'T play Bridge, Rummy, or Black Jack. And we most definitely didn't play Strip Poker. No, the three of us played every single kids' card game that I'd ever heard of. We faced each other in War, Crazy Eights, Go Fish, and Slap Jack. Spoons and I Doubt It were absolute battlegrounds. At first, I felt rather detached from the excitement of it all, and I sat back and watched my date and her roommate compete like a couple of determined elementary school kids for what I would have considered meaningless wins. I figured their enthusiasm was probably some kind of unconscious attempt to recapture a bit of their stolen childhoods. But before too long, I caught the fever and did whatever I could to make victory my own. Soon all three of us approached each and every game with equally high intensity. After each game concluded, we sucked down wine, discussed our strategies, and laughed together.

It was the most fun I'd had in way too long.

It was the most fun I'd had in way too long?

That in itself was incredibly fucked-up.

After several hours of play, a comfortable sense of camaraderie emanating among us, I felt my face split into a wide grin. "No offense to Savannah, but you, Tristan, are a master of children's card games."

Tristan beamed at me from across the room, his cheeks turning red like I'd admitted he was the master of the universe. And, yes, it warmed my heart.

Savannah got up and lithely strolled across the room to stand in front of Tristan's chair. "No offense taken." I think the reply was directed to me, but she was staring directly into Tristan's eyes, and she was nodding. "You should challenge Tris to a Chutes and Ladders marathon. He's a force to be reckoned with in that game." Even as she spoke, she gazed into her roommate's eyes. Tristan stared back. The affection between them was palpable, but it was more than that. They were communicating without words. I found myself wanting in on their clandestine messaging system.

And that spelled "Time for Robby to Leave."

I stood up and stretched. "I had a great time, you guys, but you know what they say about all good things."

My words almost broke their spell but didn't quite get the job done. Without removing her eyes from Tristan's, Savannah said, "I'll walk you to the door, Robby."

Tristan nodded at her slightly and headed to the bedroom without saying good-bye to me at all. *Strange.*

Savannah followed me down the hall, and then sort of crowded me up against the door. And since I was the red-blooded man here, I decided it was my turn to make a move. I bent down and pressed my lips against hers, knowing fully well that my head and heart were consumed with affection for a blurred image of two people.

"I had fun tonight—it was really great." I had so much more to say, because being with Tristan and Savannah was so much more than fun.

But who should I say it to?

"I like you, Robby. I really do." Savannah kissed me again, not so much with desire as with a powerful sense of need that I could practically taste. When she withdrew her lips from mine, she whispered, "We really like you, Robby. Do you like us?"

CHAPTER 9

Robby

I MUST have heard her wrong. Because it had sounded a fuck of a lot like she'd said, "We really like you, Robby. Do you like us?"

That was "we" and "us," not "I" and "me."

I sat at the desk in my office attempting to crunch numbers for the vet clinic addition, but nothing was adding up. On top of that, Mikey had been driving me absolutely crazy all morning with questions about how far I'd gotten in the sack with Savannah, seeing as I'd taken her on the three necessary dates prerequisite, in his opinion, to even a nice girl "putting out." Yes, Mikey's words.

Finally, I'd sent Mikey to the scrap yard with aluminum, copper, and steel from a recent demolition, just to get him out of my hair. I couldn't really think when he was here babbling away about "hot babes," and "huge tits," and "getting laid." And if I'd introduced the concept of our little "threesome" to Mikey, neither of us would get any work done all day.

A ménage à trois? I mean, was that what Tristan and Savannah were after? I didn't even know how those things worked. Technically, I'd seen a porn flick or two that had featured a ménage à trois as the main event, but that was just sex. Not a real relationship. And the movies I'd watched were always strictly two women with one man. Once, I'd even been invited to participate in one of these girl-dominated threesomes in college, which I'd quickly refused. I'd never been a guy who'd thought with my little head, and my big head had told me, "Bad idea."

I simply had no life experience to help me categorize what was happening here. My big head knew Savannah was the right choice for my very conservative family's traditional lifestyle. My little head was far more invested in my relationship with Tristan. I was clueless as to what their interest was in me. Was Savannah's interest independent of Tristan? Did Tristan's extreme friendliness suggest that he had feelings for me? What if he did have feelings for me? And what if I had feelings for him?

Suddenly, I grabbed my cell phone. I was going to give it one more try with Savannah. This situation was far less complicated than I was making it out to be. I was a decent-looking heterosexual man who was dating a beautiful, sexy blonde bombshell who just so happened to have an overly friendly male roommate with a pathetically sad life story. And that was it. There was nothing more to it.

I'd take Savannah to a movie. There was absolutely nothing whatsoever complicated about going to a movie.

I PARALLEL-parked my Jeep on the street directly beneath Savannah's apartment. Looking up into her curtainless kitchen window, I saw *two* shadowy figures standing close together. *Naturally.*

It's now or never, I guess.

I headed purposefully toward the stairway that I was confident led to my future girlfriend. Yes, I was going to give it one last shot with Savannah. Tonight she'd be my girlfriend or she'd be nothing to me.

Savannah opened the door on the very first knock. With her, there was no knocking and waiting incessantly, like there'd been with other girls. When the door opened, all I could think was, *smolderingly beautiful.* She'd let her hair fall in cascades of yellow-white curls that tumbled freely down her back. Draped in a deep-red velvet dress, she resembled a queen of bygone years. More importantly, tonight Savannah held a queen's power over both of our destinies and as soon as her self-assured eyes met mine, I became aware of the fact that she probably knew it.

"Geez, Savannah, you look beautiful tonight!" I couldn't help staring at her, but her reaction to my compliment was the same as always. Nonexistent.

"Robby." With a slight shake of her head, she said my name *that* way and led me inside.

"You did hear me correctly when I said I was taking you to the movies and not to the opera, right? I mean, you're dressed to kill!"

That chiming bell sound, her laughter. "Go say hello to Tristan, he's in the kitchen. I'm gonna get my shoes."

I did as Savannah asked, assuring myself as I went that I had nothing to fear. Tristan was not in control of my mind or my body. Control of Robby Dalton's physical and emotional (and sexual) behavior was exclusively mine. And I was going to get the girl tonight. It was the only rational thing to do, the only choice I had that fit into my lifestyle.

I went into the kitchen and there he was. I steeled myself in anticipation of his enchanting eyes and wistful smile, but it wasn't necessary. Because Tristan was different tonight. No bright eyes, no wide smile. He sat at the kitchen table staring at his hand, which was wrapped around a beer bottle.

"Hey, man, what's up?" I tried to catch his eye, but he seemed almost mesmerized by the sight of his hand on the beer. "You working tonight?"

The right word to describe Tristan was withdrawn. He shrugged a bit and then shook his shaggy head. "Nah, worked lunch today."

"Going out tonight, then? Have a hot date?"

Tristan looked squarely at me, and a spurt of bitter laughter shot from his lips. "Not quite."

And then there was awkward silence.

With a pair of strappy black wedge sandals dangling from her two little fingers, Savannah entered the kitchen. She looked at her roommate and then at me. "Tristan's not himself tonight," she said bluntly.

Well, any moron could see that, but I didn't ask either of them what was bothering him. And I admit that I felt a pang in my heart at my cruel evasion.

Moving behind him, Savannah draped her arms around Tristan's chest. "Come with us to the movie, Tris." She looked directly over the back of his head and into my eyes; this was a challenge. "Robby and I would love your company."

I looked back at her, my face carefully devoid of expression, and still I said nothing.

Tristan shook off Savannah's arms, stood up, and went over to the sink. He placed the bottle down on the counter and then turned around to face us with what I'd call a smirk on his lips. "No, you guys go ahead and have fun." He was obviously making an effort to appear more upbeat, clearly for our sakes. "I'm bushed anyways. I think I'll turn in early." He turned to the refrigerator and pulled out another beer. "Now, get outta here, you two. You'll miss the previews."

I swore I could actually see Savannah's brain in action. She was thinking on her feet, rearranging our night, setting things up exactly how she wanted them. "Robby, tell Tristan that we want him to come with us tonight."

What the hell am I supposed to say to that?

And so I didn't say anything until those melancholy brown eyes gazed over at me, effectively melting away all of my best intentions. "Come with us, Tristan."

Tristan's eyes stayed glued to mine, but he still appeared as despondent as before I'd spoken. And for some fucked-up reason, his pain was my pain. My heart lurched.

All I could do at that point was speak the plain truth. "Tristan, I want you to come with us. We'll have a great time, us three."

For a few moments, the kitchen was silent.

Trying like hell to act casual, to hide his need to be included, he asked me slowly, "Are you sure, Robby? 'Cause it wouldn't kill me to stay home."

And even as I spoke the truth yet again, I felt my heart sink. Because I knew that it was over with Savannah and me. Or, more honestly, with Savannah and Tristan and me. "Yes, I'm sure. I want you to come with us tonight." I just couldn't categorize what I was feeling and what's more, I didn't want to. Because sometimes the truth provided far more information than you really desired.

Savannah Meyers didn't want a partnership with me. She wanted me to become a part of a twisted little trio. And maybe I wanted that very same thing a little bit too much for my own sanity. I just couldn't deal with this crazy situation any longer. After tonight's movie, I wouldn't see them anymore. They could find another man to be their third.

And I could find another way to become complete.

THE three of us sat in a row with Savannah in the middle, all of our eyes fixed on the big screen. And Christ, I was thankful that I'd chosen an action/adventure movie. I couldn't have handled a romantic flick tonight.

About a half hour into the movie, Savannah shifted in her seat so she could lean against my shoulder, and it felt so nice to have her soft, sweet-smelling curls falling over my shoulders. I leaned my head onto hers, catching Tristan's warmth-filled eyes as I did so, and to be honest, that was when I stopped watching the movie. Because that was when my mind started spinning out of control. And there was no apparent rhyme or reason to my self-inquisition.

Have I made the right decision to call it off with Savannah?

Is Tristan hurt that Savannah is cuddled up with me right now?

Am I falling in love?

Who am I falling in love with?

Should I give myself a bit more time to figure things out?

The questions swirled around in my brain. As Tristan and Savannah happily watched the movie, I suffered with my staggering confusion over what to do. By the time the movie was nearly over, I was mentally exhausted, but I had *almost* convinced myself that I was straight, Savannah was my girlfriend, Tristan was gay, and Savannah and Tristan were simply friends without benefits. And that I was okay with all that. The operative word being *almost*.

Then when I looked down at Savannah, who was snuggled against me, I saw it. In her lap she held Tristan's hand, their fingers entwined. And I knew right then that I couldn't do this any longer. Because at that very moment, as I was cuddled up with the "girl of my dreams," I experienced a sharp pang of jealousy that she was the one holding onto Tristan's hand.

Looking back.... Savannah

ONLY the last man had spoken to me as he'd walked out the door. Nudging my rear with his work boot as he buckled his pants, he'd said, "You owe that kid big time."

And the split second that I'd been certain those men were gone, I'd scrambled up off of the floor, desperate to get to Tristan's side. I'd stopped dead in my tracks when I'd heard his frantic voice.

"Don't look at me, Savannah!" His voice had sounded harsh, but I could still tell that he was more or less pleading with me. "I don't want you to see me right now!"

I'd dropped my butt back to the floor without a second thought. "I won't, Tristan.... I won't look at you."

It had been silent for a moment, aside from the sound of Tristan's agitated breathing, and then he'd whispered one more time, "Please don't look up here."

So I'd waited, hearing only the rustling of the party guests' coats beneath Tristan as he'd pulled his jeans up. At least that's what I'd figured he was doing up there on the bed. A moment later, he'd risen stiffly from where it had happened, moved to my side, and had run his hands up and down my body from my head to my ankles, as if he was assuring himself that I hadn't been hurt. But he'd refused to make eye contact with me.

"We gotta get outta here." Rigidly, Tristan had leaned down to lift our backpacks off the floor and then he'd grabbed a couple of the strangers' warmest coats from off of the bed. He'd held one out to me. "Put this on." He'd slipped one on as well.

Then we ran down the stairs and scurried back out onto the street, quickly finding safety beside a dumpster. As soon as we'd been hidden from the street, I'd roughly grasped his sweaty face and held it in my hands, trying to see his eyes. "Are you all right, Tris? Those guys... they... they...."

He'd cut me off midsentence, his voice sharp, his words enunciated, but his eyes downcast. "I'm fine."

"They were gonna do that to me... but you... you begged 'em to—"

"Are you fucking deaf, Savannah? I said I was fine." At first he'd sounded furious, but then his speech had softened. "It wasn't... it wasn't the first time for me, Savi. I know how to take it."

And I remember that his words had made me physically ill. Literally. "I can't do this anymore" had been all I could say, over and over again.

Without a moment's hesitation, Tris had wiped off my face with his coat sleeve, lifted me gently from the ground, and led me purposefully down the street holding my hand. I still hadn't managed to catch a glimpse of his eyes.

"I know where to take you where they'll help you." He'd started walking faster; I'd been stumbling along, barely able to keep up now. "The Teen Outreach Center, it's not far from here. They'll know what to do."

He'd been correct. It hadn't taken us long to walk the few blocks to the Center.

"Come in with me, Tristan. They can help both of us." At that point, I'd been crying and begging. "Then you can be safe too."

That had been when I'd seen Tristan's eyes for what I hadn't realized would be the last time for almost four years. They'd been puffy—I hadn't been sure if those men had punched him or if his eyes had swelled up from his having cried. But when those earnest brown eyes had finally found mine, they'd revealed just exactly what the world had done to him. In his fifteen brief years of life, Tristan had been so deeply wounded by everyone he'd encountered that he did not believe there was a place on earth where he could be safe.

There I'd stood, witnessing his pain and still knowing I was leaving him.

He'd reached up and touched the side of my face, his eyes filled with understanding. "I can't do that." Then he'd turned, swayed a bit when the frigid nighttime wind had smacked into his face, and staggered off into the night.

Before I'd stepped into my safe haven, I'd spoken three words; I'm still not certain if I'd said them aloud or just in my head. "I'll find you."

CHAPTER 10

Robby

PEOPLE say that if something doesn't kill you, it just makes you stronger.

I wholeheartedly disagreed with that sentiment. The past several weeks of not calling Savannah and not returning her calls were simply killing me. And as of a couple days ago, Savannah had stopped leaving voice mails altogether. It seemed that I'd survived our "break up," if you could call it that, but I didn't feel as if I was any stronger for it. I just felt emptier. I truly missed them. Both of them.

I'd never called to offer her the standard "it's not you, it's me" line. Or the expected "this just isn't working out with us" speech. I'd never been that adept a liar. But, shit, those wouldn't have been lines at all, would they? It really *wasn't* working out because I was more in love with Savannah's male roommate than with Savannah. And I had a strong feeling she wouldn't mind sharing him with me at all. No, that situation would not fit very well into my football-playing, white-collared, not-practicing-but-still-Catholic, all-American, upper-middle-class life.

Mikey and I sat staring out the window of my Jeep, having just attended a breaking-ground sort of ceremony to open up the spiffy new classrooms in the Tardiff Building at Somerville U. He certainly didn't know what to make of my recent mini-depression, but I'm pretty sure he hadn't bought it when I'd told him that *I'd* been the one to dump Savannah. Mikey's opinion was that no matter what had gone down between "you and that bitch" (yes, his words), all I needed to do was to get it on with one of the girls on the street corner, and that would "fix me up just fine." He couldn't have been further off base.

Needless to say, Mikey was an unsatisfactory substitute for Tristan and Savannah.

"Do you realize that you haven't fed me in going on two weeks now? I'm fucking insulted. Not to mention starving."

I supposed my mind hadn't been focused on food very much recently.

"Look, there's that tacky diner we met at when you wanted me to give the Mike DeSalvo Stamp of Approval to that fag hag, remember? The S-Squared." He got out of the car and headed directly across the street.

I jumped out of my Jeep. "What the fuck do you think you're doing, DeSalvo?" My mind scrambled to recall if it was a Tuesday or Thursday, Savannah's nights at the diner. I wasn't ready to see her; I'd never be ready to see her. "Get your ass back over here!"

"I'm getting something to eat, man. You may be ready to keel over from starvation and a broken heart, but I got shit to do and I need food. Do the burgers here suck?"

"No, they're actually pretty good—but I'm not going in that place!" So there I stood beside my Jeep exchanging shouted questions and answers with my insubordinate employee, all because I had no balls. And of course, that's the very moment when Savannah came out of the diner.

Over her coffee cup, Savannah sent me a half-lidded glance, an expression on her face that one would reserve for strictly the lowliest life forms. "Coward." One word, that's all she said. But she made sure to say it loudly enough to carry all the way to the place where I stood.

As Mikey disappeared into the diner, his hunger taking precedence over my anguish, I found myself rushing across the street to get to her side. "What did you say?"

"You heard me." Savannah's eyes were as dark as I'd ever seen them.

"Yes, I guess I did." I thought I might crap my pants. "I deserved that."

"Whatever." She turned in the direction of her bus stop, but I grabbed her arm to stop her.

"Robby—what do you want?" Never looking more annoyed, she shook my hand off of her arm and pulled her draping wool poncho more tightly around her shoulders. "Is there something you forgot to say to us?"

I nodded. "Well, yeah, there are a few things I want to say." I didn't know exactly where this sudden clarity was coming from. All I knew was that I missed them, and fucking badly. "Will you meet me for coffee tomorrow?"

"Why?" Savannah was not making this easy.

"I want to apologize for—"

Savannah again started to walk away. "We don't need your apology. So if that's all you want, consider yourself forgiven and we can all move on with our lives."

She was walking slowly, so I could see her face in the dull glow of the streetlight. She still looked more or less pissed off. "I want to talk."

"Yeah? Well, Tristan and I wanted to talk last week, and the week before that, but there was no Robby to be found." Savannah stopped dead in her tracks and turned to me. "You hurt him." (The "you son-of-a-bitch" part was implied in her glare.)

"I'm sorry." I was a grown man, I reminded myself; grown men do not cry in public. "I'm so sorry."

"Tristan doesn't deal well with disappearing acts." I opened my mouth to say I was sorry again, but Savannah interrupted my attempt. "Where?"

"Where? Where what?" She'd lost me.

"Where do you want to meet for coffee?" (Again, the "you dumb-ass" part was suggested by the tone of her voice.)

"You name the time and place." I'd go anywhere she wanted me to at any time she wanted me to be there.

Savannah told me to be at a small coffee shop near her apartment at ten the next morning. She gave me absolutely no clue as to what was going on in her mind.

"And, Savannah, could you come alone?"

"Robby." She shook her head. If I'd fallen to the ground in respiratory distress right there and then, I would have received no mouth-to-mouth resuscitation from Savannah Meyers. "I wouldn't bring him if you paid me." She again started down the street. This time I let her go.

There was really nothing more I could say at that point.

I GOT to the generic hole-in-the wall coffee shop at nine. A full hour before our meeting time.

Eager much, Robby?

It was a Friday, so the work crowd had already cleared out, leaving plenty of space to sit. I picked a table by the window and claimed an extra chair for Savannah with my coat. Now all I had to do was wait. And I felt like a kid on Christmas Eve. But instead of wondering what Santa was going to bring me, I wondered if Santa was going to show up at all.

She showed up. Ten minutes early too.

Savannah looked amazing and what's more, I could tell she hadn't tried, or perhaps even wanted to. Jeans and a T-shirt and a high ponytail: that was all it took for Savannah to be the prettiest girl in the city. She whisked through the doorway, walked over to my table without looking at me, and sat down.

Before Savannah even took off her jacket and scarf, she was already staring out the window as if it was beneath her dignity to acknowledge my lowly presence. She said in a matter-of-fact tone, "We're a package deal, Tristan and I."

Zero bullshit. "I sort of figured that much out."

"The hard way, huh?" She smiled, but her eyes were still far away.

"I guess."

Savannah unwrapped her bright-pink scarf from her neck and unbuttoned her jacket but didn't remove it. "There can be no us," she pointed at me, and then gestured toward herself, and one more time back to me again, "without him." She looked at me expectantly.

I nodded. "Okay."

A waitress came over to our table and we ordered cups of coffee, which neither of us had much interest in. But the coffee was the price of the table. We were promptly served.

At that point I noticed Savannah examining me skeptically. In that Robby-the-lab-rat way, but more with more suspicion. "You said 'okay.' What does *okay* mean to you?"

"It means I understand what you're saying. It means…." I couldn't continue because I really had no idea what I'd meant. I just knew I wanted to be part of their little family. I'd been strangely happy there.

"Robby, have you ever had feelings for a man before?"

My stomach clenched. I hadn't anticipated this particular line of questioning; I guess I hadn't wanted to. "I-I don't think so."

"But you feel something for Tristan, beyond friendship?"

"Yes, I feel for him." I nodded again, and then added defensively, "I feel something for you too." My face was burning. I couldn't believe I was saying these words aloud to another person—to a woman who'd passed Mikey's Hot-Chick Test. "But it's different with Tristan. I can't explain it."

Savannah grabbed my hands, suddenly impassioned. "I knew you were the one for us!"

I had no clue what she was talking about, but I was so afraid to say the wrong thing that I simply nodded like one of those bobble-head Chihuahuas on the dashboard of an old woman's car. I didn't know exactly why, but I couldn't lose this chance to get them back in my life.

"It's okay, Robby. Whatever you feel for him is, well, it's just right. And whatever you feel for me, well, that's fine too."

"I don't understand. I just don't get it, Savannah." I pushed my coffee off to the side and grasped her hands with even more vigor than she'd grabbed mine. "I don't know how I should feel."

Before I knew what was going on, Savannah had gotten up, dragged her chair around the table, and pushed it next to mine. "Listen, Robby." She leaned right into my space so that we were shoulder-to-shoulder, "I want you to just go with your feelings, okay? There is no right or wrong way to feel for Tristan and me." She took a calming breath. "But I need you to know this: I will not exclude him from *any* aspect of our relationship, and *he'll* want to do the same for me. And *you've* got to understand this next part, but remember, Tristan doesn't need to know about what I'm gonna tell you yet, and that's more important than anything else."

When Savannah touched my chin, I looked into her eyes. "Wh-what is it?"

"I want you to know that it's okay with me if, well, if…. All right, I'm just going to say this directly, no more mincing words: it's okay with me if you two get close, even if it's in ways that you and I won't."

Savannah Meyers could yank the rug out from beneath my feet and send me sprawling like no one else. I couldn't believe I was sitting here listening to this beautiful woman tell me it was okay for me to be gay with her, with her, well, I supposed the time had come to ask. "What *is* Tristan to you? Is he your lover?"

This time when she shook her head at me, it was not with her usual exasperation. "I can't tell you all of Tristan's personal business; it isn't mine to share. But I *can* tell you that Tris and I aren't lovers and we never have been."

"But I know that you share a bed—I *saw* it!"

"Tristan and I are physically close but not sexually involved. There's a big difference, Robby."

I was officially overwhelmed and had a strong urge to run for the hills. I just needed to be alone to think things over. Starting with whether or not I was gay.

"He needs closeness. He needs to feel safe. And I need you to help me make him feel that way. I'm not enough for him anymore and he's not…." She didn't finish her thought. Instead she sent me another hopeful glance. But I couldn't speak; my head was spinning. "We can do it together. Tris and I, we both need you so much."

"W-what are you a-asking me to do?" Robby the Stutterer seemed to have made a return appearance. And he needed to know what the fuck he was signing up for.

That was when she started to cry. Suddenly, the girl sitting beside me was a completely different Savannah, because the Savannah I knew certainly wasn't the type to break down in public, or in private, for that matter. This girl was scared and confused and vulnerable. She seemed so young and, somehow, so tired. And despite the fact that I was struggling deeply with my own confusion, I knew the most important thing to do right then was to comfort her. So I dropped an arm around her shoulders in an effort to ease her worries, as well as to shelter her from the prying eyes of the waitress and the other customers.

Immediately, Savannah batted my arm away. Apparently, she didn't give a shit what anyone else thought and had no need for meaningless comfort. She looked at me square in the eye in that no-nonsense way I was more accustomed to and had grown to respect. "I need you to help me love him."

I suddenly felt sick. All sorts of X-rated images of Savannah and Tristan and me splayed out inside my head. Images I wasn't at all comfortable with. "I-I don't know if I can do that." This was too much to wrap my brain around.

Savannah took my face in her hands, her grip almost too tight. "You can. Just start by being his friend, Robby, and when you discover his beautiful spirit, and believe me, *you will*, nothing will be more important to you than loving him."

"But you? How do *you* fit into this picture? Tell me, Savannah. *How?*"

"Robby, love doesn't have to mean sex; it can be just love."

I had absolutely no idea what she'd intended with *that* cryptic statement, and I was actually too mind-boggled to ask her to explain. And since she was apparently refusing to voluntarily spell it out for me, I found myself completely out of my comfort zone. Not that sex had ever been a make-it-or-break-it issue for me, but it was *sex*, and we were talking about three people here. Gently but firmly I pulled Savannah's hands from my face. "I n-need to think about all of this. I, uh, I have to figure out a few things. I'll c-call you."

Ripping a small square off the edge of her napkin, Savannah scribbled down a phone number and slid it across the table to me. "After you've thought it over, I want you to call Tristan. But only make the call if you have room in your heart for both of us."

I slapped down a crumpled pile of cash on the table, looked blankly at Savannah, and left the coffee shop without a backward glance. Once I was on the city street, I guzzled in as much cool air as I could fit in my lungs, and then I tried to mentally chop up this situation into bite-sized morsels, ones that my brain could easily chew on.

Before this morning's coffee date I was a heterosexual guy (okay, possibly bi-curious when it came to one man) making an attempt to get back on the good side of the girl he'd screwed up with. If I signed up to be part of this fucked-up gay/straight/bi love triangle, maybe that hole in my heart, the empty ache that no woman alone had ever been able to satisfy, would finally be filled. But then what would that make me? Was there even a word for it?

Attired in a business suit and Italian loafers, briefcase in hand, I started to run.

CHAPTER 11

Tristan

"UH, TRISTAN?"

"Yes, this is Tristan."

"Oh, okay. This is Robby here."

I switched my cell phone to my right hand and said nothing. I wasn't trying to give him a hard time or anything. It's just I hadn't expected to hear from him. Not even one little bit. So at this point, just managing to take my next breath was a challenge.

"Um, it's Robby Dalton."

"Yes, I heard you. I'm just wondering why you're calling me."

More silence. Well, except for the sound of dishes clattering (folding napkins didn't make any noise). But that was coming from my end.

"Robby, how did you get my number?"

"I, uh, I got it from Savannah. Uh, is this an okay time to talk?"

"Hang on a minute." I turned to Sandy, my closest friend who worked with me at Michael's. "I've got to take this call. Can you make sure my section is ready for lunch?"

Once she nodded, I took off for the back door of the restaurant where the loading dock was located. Outside, a couple of cooks were standing around smoking, but for the most part, I was alone.

"Robby? I'm back."

"Oh, okay. Great."

I leaned right up against the side of the building so that the other guys couldn't see me so well. "I... or, *Savannah* didn't expect to hear from you. It's been like three weeks."

"Yeah, well, I'm really sorry about that. I had some thinking to do, I guess."

"Thinking?"

"Uh-huh. About, well, I thought about what's important to me."

This was sort of an awkward moment. I didn't want to be too hard on Robby, but I was angry. No, that wasn't really it. I was hurt that he'd taken off on us. Very hurt, in fact. But as far as Robby knew, he hadn't been dating *me*, he'd been dating Savannah, so I knew I had no right to be upset. I just hoped I didn't sound too flippant. "So what did you come up with? Tell me what's important, Robby." *And why you felt the need to call and tell me this.*

He didn't hesitate. "You and Savannah—that's what's important."

I couldn't think of anything to say to that, mostly because my heart was bouncing all around inside my chest with emotions that were changing too fast to name.

"Tristan, I want another chance. With both of you."

"What? Why?" I was using monosyllabic words. That was usually a bad sign for me in terms of the direction of a conversation.

This time Robby hesitated. "I missed you guys. I missed you guys a lot. I was thinking that maybe we could work something out, you know, all three of us."

A light breeze could have knocked me over. "You *what*?"

"Tristan, will you try it?"

"You and me *and* Savannah?"

"Yeah, that's what I was hoping for. What do you say?" He sounded sort of impatient. "I know it might sound crazy, but can't we just *try* to be together?"

My knees started shaking so hard I knew that if I didn't sit down I was going to fall down. And even through my jeans the cement felt cold on my backside, but still, I just had to sit. "There are things about me, things that you don't know." My voice rose a couple of octaves when I admitted that.

"Well, of course there are. There are things about *me* that you'll find out too. That's part of being in a relationship, Tris."

That was the first time Robby had ever called me Tris. And I liked the way it sounded when he said it, which made this even more difficult. "I can't really be in a relationship, you know. There's so much shit in my past, *so much*, and Robby, I can't really talk about this right now...." I wasn't *ever* going to talk about it, either.

"You don't have to talk about anything right now. Just give me a chance. And believe me, I won't push you in any way that you aren't, in any way that you aren't comfortable. Know what I mean?"

Yes, I knew exactly what he meant. And because of that, my heart was beating way too fast, and I was hot and nauseated. In fact, I was pretty sure I wasn't going to make it back to work without vomiting beside the loading dock.

"Tris, this is all new for me too, in more ways than one."

I managed to make this kind of strangled sound. "Urgh."

"It'll be okay, you'll see." Robby was quiet for a moment, and then he said much more softly, "I mean, let's just take the sex part completely off the table. Us three can just work on getting to know each other, you know. And then we can see what happens, I guess."

"I, uh...." I couldn't believe he was willing to try this with us. *Am I as willing?*

"Tristan, just say you'll give it a shot."

"Will Savannah try too? Because I can't try anything without Savannah."

"I'll call her next, but I think she'll be open to it."

Oh, Savannah will be perfectly fine with it, I thought. This was exactly what she had wanted all along: a relationship for the three of us. And I'd promised her I'd try, if she could get Robby to go along with it. Who would've ever figured that he'd actually agree? Certainly not me. What's more, none of us had a clue how a love relationship would work with three people in it. But I'd do about anything so Savannah could have a man who functioned properly in the bedroom, in more ways than just changing the sheets. Maybe she and Robby would totally hit it off, and then they'd get married, have kids, be a real family, and then I could just fade away into the background.

"Okay, Robby, I'll give it a try."

CHAPTER 12

Robby

SO WHAT had been up until now merely a hypothetical plan was going to turn into reality today. *Yes, Robby,* I'd had to remind myself numerous times on the drive over to Tristan and Savannah's apartment, *this is actually happening. You are going on your first date with Tristan.*

In all honesty, I'd struggled quite a bit with what I should wear on my first official date with a man, seeing as I was also a man. And I couldn't realistically call Mikey for advice.

"Hey, dude. I'm taking this gorgeous guy out on a date to a football game and probably to dinner after. I really want to make a good impression, so should I dress in business casual or go with relaxed weekend attire?"

I'm pretty sure Mikey would toss his cookies, those colorful Italian ones from his mother's bakery, at the very thought.

And as much as I was into playing team sports, I was more or less a loner in life. I was close only to Mikey, if you could call it that, and when I went out in a group, it was usually on the fringes of Mikey's hometown cousin-filled crowd from Revere. I guess I was a one-on-one type of guy, which made it seem even weirder that I was trying to enter a love relationship with two people.

On second thought, *weird* might be too mild a word.

In any case, I ended up going with my standard weekend uniform: T-shirt, sweatshirt, jeans, and sneakers. I *was* taking him to a football game, after all.

When I got to their apartment, only one spot was left on the street. Struggling to wedge my Jeep into it, I realized I hadn't had so much trouble parallel parking since I was sixteen. In any case, I chalked that up to a case of general first-date jitters rather than to first-date-with-a dude jitters. As soon as I stopped the engine, Tristan came running out of the front door of his apartment building. I breathed a sigh of relief; I wouldn't have to face Savannah this morning.

Tristan trotted right up to my Jeep, thankfully sporting similar attire, but looking much more like a model for a fall Ralph Lauren Denim and Supply advertising campaign than I did. He jumped in. "Hey, Robby!" His flawless face was flushed in exactly the right way. I would have expected no less of the perfect man. "I could barely sleep last night 'cause I've been so excited about this ever since you called yesterday!" He looked over at me, a blush rising on those high cheekbones.

"Me too." Catching a glimpse of his innocent eyes, I felt my pulse rise. *You can do this, Robby*, I assured myself as I pulled out of the parking spot. "Are you into college football?"

I could immediately tell that Tristan was embarrassed by the way he dipped his head down, lifted off his ball cap, and ran his hand through his hair. "Well, I watch as many games as I can 'cause sometimes they're on at the bar at work. I like all of the Boston and New England teams but I really don't know too much about sports."

"Well, thankfully, today we don't have to get out there and play." I found myself wanting to make him feel comfortable. "All we have to do is grab a beer, find our seats, and watch, right?"

I glanced over and Tristan nodded at me. "I guess you're right. You know, I always wished that I had a chance to play sports when I was a kid." He offered no explanation and I didn't ask for one. "You must've played tons of sports growing up, huh?"

When I told him about the many sports I'd played, I wasn't trying to brag in the "I dominate" way so much as I wanted to impress him, like any other guy on a date would want to do. And very satisfyingly, Tristan listened with every bit as much interest as Savannah had when I'd told her about my childhood. "Sports were a huge part of my life. Not that I'd had a choice. You see, Tris, if I didn't play a sport for a season, my father would pile on the after-school chores. Dad was more into my sports than I was."

"Did he go to all of your games?" His voice sounded wistful.

"Hell yes. In fact, up until high school, he coached most of my teams. And the expectation was that I wouldn't screw up. So I didn't." When I looked over toward Tristan to make a right turn, what I saw touched me deeply, in that lump-in-my-throat kind of way I was getting used to when it came to him. It was almost as if a little boy had taken Tristan's place in the passenger seat. He gazed at me, wide-eyed with respect and admiration bordering on reverence, and practically salivated in his eagerness to hear my next glorious high school sports memory. And then it hit me: while I was blocking and passing and dribbling my way through my school years, Tristan had been busy being molested by his perverted uncle.

Well, no one said that life was fair, but that really sucked. I had to breathe deeply a few times to stop myself from reaching over and squeezing his thigh.

"Did you guys ever pull any locker room pranks like on television shows?"

"We did all of that stuff." Tris made a small sound, a "go on, I'm listening" sound, but instead of telling him about how we stole all of the point guard's clothes when he was in the shower that one time my junior year, I decided to go in a different direction. "Maybe sometime you and I could go outside, like to the park or something, and I could show you how to throw a nice spiral. You know, with a football." Every guy deserves a chance to learn stuff like that.

"Oh my God, Robby, I'd love that!" More than satisfied with our conversation, Tristan leaned back in his seat and closed his eyes, an expression of bliss on his face. An expression I was already pretty sure I was going to want to see again and again.

I SORT of felt like a replacement for Tristan's absentee father at the football game, but I actually didn't mind at all. The truth was I rather liked it. Usually my father and Mikey were the ones blabbing on and on to me about who "screwed up big-time" on the sports field and how it "shoulda gone down if they coulda got their tiny jock-brains outta their asses," and since I was the "jock" with the tiny brain, I'd always sat there passively, with no choice but to agree with their very loud and very critical commentary. But today, I was the one who got to point out the different positions in the lineups, explain the rules and penalties, and offer criticism on the plays and the calls. And Tristan wasn't a passive listener when it came to football; he asked questions about every aspect of the game. I felt smart and proud of my own knowledge of football, as well as happy that Tristan was learning so much.

To my relief, no one in the crowd had seemed to notice that we were on a date. In fact, nobody even looked twice at the two guys wearing ball caps, sweatshirts, and jeans, sucking down brews in their prime seats at the fifty-yard line. Nobody even seemed to notice us that is, except for this one crowd of more than slightly tipsy college girls.

"Hey, is that Brad Pitt and Ashton Kutcher over there?" A particularly well-imbibed girl pointed us out to her friends. I suppose if you were drunk enough, and if Brad and Ashton were each a decade or more younger, that was not beyond the realm of a vivid imagination. "Can we have your autographs?"

Suddenly we were surrounded by a disorderly crowd of nineteen-year-old girls, all of whom were clamoring for front position in the pack. One girl actually produced a sharpie marker and a large bare breast. "Sign it!" she ordered, pretty much poking the marker into Tristan's chest.

Tristan, however, seemed completely unaware of their interest. "Robby," he said, trying to peer over the sharpie-holding girl's head, not even acknowledging the existence of her exposed flesh, "I thought that it was only the third down, but that guy looks like he's getting ready to kick." If Mikey had been presented so directly with a woman's naked breast, I'm pretty certain I wouldn't have seen or heard from him for the rest of the afternoon because he'd be in her dormitory room introducing himself to her other breast as well. For some reason, I couldn't help but make the Tristan/Mikey comparison.

Tristan was literally enthralled with the game. After clearing the girls out from the area surrounding our seats, I heard myself saying, "I bet I could score us some Patriot's tickets, Tris. If you like this, you'll go nuts over the Pats!" That sure sounded like another "outing"—I'd decided I liked that word better than "date"—with Tris. And I wasn't even slightly dissatisfied with that prospect. Today's BC football game "outing" hadn't gone half-bad so far.

After the game, we wandered aimlessly through the extensive tailgate parties that the parking lots near Alumni Stadium were famous for. Tristan seemed to just enjoy taking in the rowdy adrenaline-fueled atmosphere. But it wasn't long before I was feeling hungry, and although Tristan hadn't said anything, I assumed the same was true for him.

"If you're up for a little walk, we can grab a burger in Cleveland Circle before we head home."

"Yeah, I could definitely go for a burger." He glanced at me shyly, as if he was thinking exactly what I was thinking—going out to dinner felt a heck of a lot more like a date than sitting on metal benches in a football stadium drinking beer.

And that's when the awkwardness set in. Walking side-by-side around the Chestnut Hill Reservoir on a beautiful, breezy fall afternoon was possibly just a little bit more romantic than either one of us had anticipated. But sure as shit, Tristan trudged along beside me, making an attempt to do whatever the hell it was we were trying to do together, so at least I was pretty sure I wasn't in this alone.

"This is really strange for me." I figured that the truth was the best way to go. "I mean, not the walking to get a burger part, but the walking to take a guy out for a burger part." Tristan looked down at the well-worn dirt pathway, and I could tell he was uncomfortable with what I'd just said. And it was time to make him more uncomfortable, because *someone* had to say it. "And I don't know how two men can share one woman, anyways."

Still staring down at the path in front of him, Tristan took a few more steps and then he stopped. "We're not just sharing Savannah; I mean, we're supposed to be sharing ourselves as well." He kicked at a little rock on the ground near his foot.

Shit! I hadn't expected him to be so straightforward. Was I ready for this discussion? Were *we* ready? "I guess. But what it comes down to is two men, one woman."

"True enough."

"I can see that you love her; when you look at her, it's in your eyes. Why are you letting this happen?"

He smiled at me sadly, and for the first time since we started walking, his somber brown eyes met mine. "Robby, I'm not *letting* this happen. I'm *making* this happen."

My chin dropped. I was startled. "You mean you *want* to share Savannah?"

"What I want is not of much concern to me anymore. What matters is what I am going to do. And I'm going to share Savannah, and I'm going to share myself. I'm going to share us both *with you*."

I immediately stumbled and Tristan grabbed my bicep to steady me. My arm tingled where he'd touched it; my desire for him was *that* fierce. I actually had to concentrate on putting one foot in front of the other, or else I was pretty sure I'd find myself flat on my face on the cool ground. But there was something I desperately needed to know if I was going to be able to continue in this relationship, or whatever the fuck it was. "Tristan, are you doing this just for Savannah's benefit? Or are you into it too? What I mean to ask is, are *you* into *me* at all?" I shook my head, in awe that I'd found the fortitude to ask that question.

He looked at me, totally dismayed, as if I'd stomped on his pet gerbil.

"I need to know, Tris, do you have any... *any* kind of feelings for me? Because I, uh, I've never thought of myself as gay but I, uh, you...."

I had to wait almost a full minute for his answer, which nearly killed me. Then he stopped, placed his hand lightly on my forearm, and said in a quiet voice, "Don't worry, Robby. You're not alone in your feelings." Tristan picked up the pace of our walk, almost like if he could walk fast enough, he could escape what he was about to say. But after a deep breath, he continued. "I feel more for you than I ever imagined I could feel for a man, than I ever *wanted* to feel for a man. It's just that I need time. Give me some time. *Please*." By the time he said that last part, Tristan was at least three paces ahead of me, but I still managed to make out his words.

WE MANAGED to survive dinner without having another heart-to-heart, which suited both of us very well. When we finally got back to Tristan's apartment, we were greeted quite affably by Savannah. If this was any other evening, and Savannah was any other woman, that warm glow in her eyes would have suggested that my night's fun was far from over. But this was Savannah, who was, indeed, the current woman in my life, but I had just spent a surprisingly satisfying day with her roommate, or, I supposed you could call him, *our* boyfriend. I had absolutely no idea how to read her, or this situation, for that matter.

Before Tristan spoke, I noticed a brief hesitation, as if he was working and reworking his thought in his brain before he trusted it to come out of his mouth. Come to think of it, this was not the first time I'd noticed a slight hesitation before he spoke. But at the moment, I was just barely surviving the ride, so I tucked that little observation into a pocket in the back of my brain to analyze later when I was alone. "Savi, I understand football now."

That was the sentiment he'd struggled to force from his mouth? That he now understood the ins and outs of the game of football? *Is he for real?*

"Oh, Tristan." I stood there watching in complete shock as Savannah embraced him like he was a soldier returning from war. "That's wonderful! I'm so happy for you!"

And Tristan, well, he appeared quite overwhelmed with emotion at that point. Politely, he excused himself, offering me only a shy sideways glance, and retreated to the bedroom.

Once the bedroom door closed, Savannah turned her attention back to me. Before I knew it, it was my turn in her arms. She held me tight, both hands squeezing my shoulders. "Thank you, Robby. Thank you so much."

I found myself at a loss for words, but when I was with Savannah and Tristan, that wasn't exactly an unusual occurrence. "W-why? Why are you thanking me?"

Savannah let go of me, stepped back, and then looked up into my eyes with such appreciation, as if I was her own personal superhero. "You gave him something I never could. Robby, you gave Tristan back a piece of his childhood, a little part of himself." And suddenly I was in her arms again, and she was crying and murmuring words of gratefulness.

As soon as she loosened her hold on me, I made my move toward the door. Leaving now, after having had such a great day with Tristan, and with Savannah so pleased, seemed like the right thing to do. Who was I to tempt fate? "Would you tell Tris that I had a great time today?"

"Of course." She looked back down the hall as if she expected Tristan to come up behind her and say good-bye for himself, but the only one there was that enormous black cat. When she turned back to me, her eyes were a little puffy and her lips were trembling as she said, "It's the three of us now."

Chapter 13

Robby

MIKEY swept into the office, thankfully relieving me of my jumbled thoughts regarding my jumbled love life. "Hey, Mikey. Were we the low bidder on the library addition?"

"Yes, boss-man. That baby is ours! We just hafta draw up the paperwork and get everybody's John Hancocks on it." He smirked, pleased with himself. I had always admired Mikey's youthful enthusiasm, even when I didn't agree with what he was enthusiastic about.

"And thanks to your Great Uncle Tony, you're going to be getting a hefty bonus." I could smirk too, and I proved it.

"How 'bout we hit the Nines Club tonight and celebrate? We haven't gotten wasted together in way too long, huh?" He came around my desk and slapped me hard on the back. "And then we can pick up some babes and have some horizontal celebration, what do ya think?"

I hesitated. "I'm seeing someone, Mikey."

"Holy shit!" Mikey grabbed at his heart dramatically. "Tell me you didn't fall for that fag hag?"

"Christ, Mikey. I never said I'd fallen for anybody, and I also never said that Tristan was gay." I was quick to set Mikey straight on both accounts. However, I felt like I was lying to him and, strangely, to myself, which probably meant something.

"But ya aren't up for some no-strings-attached sex, so that means ya must have it bad for this chick, Sava-a-annah, right?" He looked at me with pity. "No more screwing around for you?"

I shook my head. Mikey had no idea how far off the mark he was. Well, except for the screwing around part. I didn't see much screwing around at all in my near future.

"I guess that leaves more girls for me to screw." He shrugged and then nodded to himself like it made sense.

I cringed at Mikey's crudeness, something I had accepted as a benign part of his personality until recently. Since I'd gotten to know Savannah and Tristan, I was somehow losing my tolerance for his overly loose tongue; it was just so disrespectful. "I thought I'd take Savannah to dinner tonight, but I'm sure you'll have enough fun at the club for both of us."

"Bring her," he said, looking squarely into my eyes as if it was a challenge. "Bring her to the Nines tonight."

"Well, I don't know, she may have class in the morning and—"

"I ain't gonna take no for an answer, my man." After wedging himself between my desk and the chair I was sitting on, Mikey dropped his ass on my desk with a hard plop. "You bring smoking Savannah and I promise to try and behave myself. Deal?"

All I needed was for Mikey to get a load of us on our very first public date as a threesome and all hell would break loose. I'd never get a moment's peace and quiet again. And knowing Mikey the way I knew him, he'd go straight to my father with the big news. Then my entire life would come crashing down around me.

"I'll mention it to her, okay? If she wants to go, we'll stop over."

Mikey stood up and stepped right into my face, close enough so that I could smell the vanilla hazelnut creamer in his coffee breath. "Be there at nine sharp, and you'd better show up, asshole. We ain't gonna let no bitch come between us, right?" He glared at me in warning, and then headed out the door, saying, "Time for Mr. Numbers to put on his realtor's hat."

It looked like I was going to have to call Savannah and Tristan to see if they liked to dance.

I ARRIVED at precisely nine o'clock, ever obedient to my good buddy, Mikey, accompanied by Savannah, who looked hotter than a girl had a right to. Tristan was planning to come over and meet us after work. Tonight should prove to be interesting. I fought an urge to chew on my fingernails.

Instead, I took Savannah's hand and led her through the darkness to the lounge area near the bar where I knew Mikey and his crowd would be hanging out. The very second Mikey caught a glimpse of Savannah all dressed up like a Barbie doll, he was practically on top of her. And since Savannah was an unpredictable blend of sassy and sweet, all I could do was cross my fingers and hope for the best.

The Nines Club was really nothing but an enormous renovated warehouse space, not too far from Michael's on the Waterfront, divided into six separate rooms, each presenting different musical themes ranging from alternative rock to the Blues. There was a huge square bar in the center of the building, with low couches and chairs surrounding it, that served as a sort of common area, but in my experience it was simply the best place in the house for the guys to scope out the girls. Savannah somehow managed to blend perfectly into the dark, sultry atmosphere, while simultaneously standing out with her eclectic and eye-catching style. Tonight, the focal point of her outfit was her tall black equestrian-looking boots, which she wore with lacy black leggings, a snug-fitting white tank, and what looked like a riding jacket hanging loosely off of her bare shoulders.

"All's your gal needs 's a crop, huh, Robby?" Mikey, as expected, spoke loud enough for Savannah to "accidentally" overhear, which wasn't an easy task to accomplish since the walls themselves were vibrating from the earsplitting volume of the music. "I take it one of you is in for a bumpy ride tonight." He looked back and forth from me to Savannah and made some clip-clopping horse noises with his tongue and then a cracking of a whip sound, which made me want to fade right into the sticky floorboards.

I knew people tended to judge you by the company you kept, and Mikey had been pretty much the one constant friend in my life since before high school. I also knew it was well past time to ask myself what that fact said about Robby Dalton. That disturbing concept started me off in a tailspin of worry about the conclusions Savannah would very likely draw about me when she got the complete picture of her "boyfriend's" BFF, Michael Joseph DeSalvo. But what could I do about it now?

Since it was a Thursday night, Ladies Drink Free Night at the Nines, I was hopeful that there would be a high enough female population traipsing around the club to distract Mikey's attention from my official "hot chick" of a girlfriend and me—oh, and Tristan, of course. Placing my hand tentatively on her waist, I directed Savannah toward Mikey's gang, who were sprawled out all around the left side of the bar. Mikey followed close behind us. He pushed on her shoulder a bit to turn her in his direction. "Name's Savannah, huh?" He clearly wasn't finished with us yet.

"I was about to officially introduce you. Mikey DeSalvo, meet Savannah Meyers. And Savannah, this is Mikey, an old friend." Who I probably should have left in my dust somewhere along my path from high school to this very moment, but apparently I'd been too lazy to put myself out there and make new friends. I thought it best to keep that convoluted thought to myself.

Mikey was dressed in his usual all-black—snug dress pants and a clingy, silk T-shirt, his stereotypical heavy Italian chest hair poking up from its V-neck. Not being into the club scene like he was, I'd just stayed in the white oxford shirt and Dockers I'd worn to work. Mikey reached out and grabbed my shirt by the right side of its collar and yanked on it a few times. "This here preppy look was the best you could come up wit' for a night on the town, Rob? You need to loosen up; get yaself some style."

In response, Savannah raised her hand and placed it delicately on my left shoulder. She directed her stormy ocean eyes at Mikey's jet black ones, but leaned in and spoke to me, loud enough for him to "accidentally" overhear. "You are *by far* the best-looking man here, Robby." I could practically taste the venom in her voice; the compliment was actually a poison dart, aimed squarely at Mikey's heart. Like many of the other women we had encountered through the years, Savannah had apparently acquired an instant dislike for my dear old friend.

Not one to be trumped, Mikey chuckled, his fingers still wrapped around my collar, "If you think *he's* a man, you should take a ride on the Italian Stallion." Then he let go of my shirt so he could gesture grandly toward his own crotch with both hands.

The withering glare Savannah sent in Mikey's direction would have made a lesser man weep. So what did Mikey choose to do to encourage his best pal's new girlfriend to warm up to him? The man stuck an arm out, sunk his fingers right into her golden mane, lifted a few strands to press against his lips, and then, between his teeth: "Bite me, Savannah."

I didn't know which one of them to gape at first, but I felt Savannah shudder against me. She said rather curtly, "I'm going to the bar. I'll get you a beer, Robby."

As we watched her walk away, Mikey said, "That went well, don't ya think?"

I MANAGED to keep the two of them apart for the next hour. After apologizing profusely for Mikey's bad behavior, I asked Savannah to dance, and we actually started to have fun. I honestly could have watched her dance forever. The way she swayed her shoulders and rolled her hips had me rather habitually thinking about dragging her outside to the parking lot for a short make-out session in my Jeep. But then I saw an image of Tristan's beautiful brown eyes in my head and all I wanted to do with Savannah was dance. It was nice, it was fun, and it was enough.

A little after ten, I suggested to Savannah that we stop dancing and order Tristan a drink so it would be ready and waiting for him when he arrived.

"He'd like that." She bestowed upon me an expression so pleased that it bordered on pure delight. I felt my face heat. Getting my date's *other* date a beer was really no big deal, just common courtesy. It was the least I could do.

While we waited for Tristan's beer—I was informed that he preferred an American light beer by the woman who certainly knew him best—I noticed that Savannah's eyes were no longer planted squarely on mine, as they had been for the past hour while we'd danced. Now they shifted back and forth from me to the club's entrance. Savannah was obviously anticipating Tristan's arrival with great eagerness. And she wasn't alone—I also was having trouble concentrating, knowing that his arrival was imminent. I tried not to analyze that too much.

"You're watching the door for him, Savannah."

She nodded. "I miss him. But there are three of us now. So I plan to watch plenty of doors in the future for you too." Savannah smiled wide and then stood on her tiptoes to give me a quick kiss. And naturally, that was when Tristan came up behind us.

A soft hand brushed against my forearm. I jerked around to be faced with Tristan, and immediately felt guilty for having been caught in the act. But when I looked at his face, I saw it was serene. "Hey, Robby, Savi. Sorry I'm a little bit late."

Savannah moved fluidly from my arms to Tristan's and embraced him deliberately, as I'd come to expect. I waited for a wave of jealousy to surge forth, unsure as to whether it would rear its ugly head at Tristan or

Savannah, but it didn't come. Instead, I just felt happy that Tristan was here with us now. *Strange.*

"No, Tris, you're not late at all, and you certainly weren't forgotten." I handed him his beer and said, "We were waiting for you."

Although it was very dark in the bar, I could tell he was blushing. I already recognized the way he handled embarrassment: he dipped his head down and to the side, and then ran his fingers through his hair a time or two.

"I had to take a few minutes to wash up and change before I left work, or I'd still smell like baked stuffed haddock." He dropped his head and did the hair thing again.

Leaning against his side, I said right into his ear, "Well, I wouldn't have minded that at all. I love seafood." *Oh God, am I flirting with him?*

Tristan did the head dip and hair rub again; I guess three times was a charm because at that point, I wanted badly to run my own hand through his hair. So I did the next best thing I could come up with; I placed my hands on Tristan and Savannah's lower backs and guided them to some couches in a corner where we could catch up.

Savannah and I sat on a sleek, velvety black couch and Tristan sat diagonally across from us in a shiny leather chair, just like how we'd sat in their living room. He looked sleek and classy in a fitted gray V-neck sweater and dark narrow jeans.

"So, Tris, you were up from bed and out the door early this morning." Savannah's comment did not make me feel as uncomfortable as it should have.

"Yeah, I've been trying to get to the gym early in the morning before I start thinking of all the other things I should be doing with my time."

"Where do you work out?" This was my type of conversation; talking about gyms was like speaking in my native language.

"One of those fitness chains opened a gym right down the street from our place that only charges like eleven dollars a month. I go there as much as I can," he said dully.

"You don't sound too thrilled with it."

Savannah piped up. "Tris gets bored just staring at the gym walls when he works out. He'd rather play some kind of game, or be outside and actually get somewhere when he exercises."

I had the perfect solution. I looked across the coffee table at those stunning tilted eyes, their sensuality only enhanced by the darkness. "Then I'm gonna take you to my gym as a guest this weekend. We can play basketball, and there are racquetball courts, and even a couple of tennis courts. There's a pool too. And plenty of weight machines and free weights. I won't let you get bored. Don't worry about that, buddy!"

Savannah and Tristan both stared at me, their mouths forming matching O shapes.

Shit! I shouldn't have assumed he'd want to stay in shape in the same ways I did. "Only if you want to, I mean, if you like your own gym, then...."

"No, no, that'd be the greatest thing. The greatest thing ever." He leaned over the coffee table, as if to get nearer to me. "But I'm not a great basketball player, not at all. I know as much about basketball as I knew about football before you taught me." He did that head drop/hair rub thing again.

This guy had missed out on more growing up than I'd realized. "Well, then, you're going to learn the game of basketball by playing it, not just by watching it. We'll have fun."

Again, Savannah chimed in, helpful as always when it came to getting Tristan and me together, "And Tristan's tall, doesn't that help in basketball?"

"It sure does. Pretty soon, he'll be dunking the ball—it'll be impressive!"

All right, both of my dates were looking at me as if I were God. All I'd offered to do was play basketball with Tristan. I guess little things meant a lot to some people; I just wasn't accustomed to associating with those types. I smiled, genuinely pleased that something so small could make them both so happy. And it was something I enjoyed as well. Win-win-win, all around.

"I've come to claim my dance wit' Robby's little sex kitten here." Mikey offered a hand to Savannah. "Wanna get my paws on all those soft pussycat curves. What do ya say? Meow once for yes, baby."

Savannah refused to even acknowledge his presence. She stood up and said, "Please excuse me, Robby, Tristan. I have a sudden need to visit the ladies' room." She walked away without a backward glance.

Mikey looked at me, as if for an explanation, and like the dedicated defender-of-the-innocent that I was, I just shrugged.

But Tristan cleared his throat and spoke up. "Savannah doesn't like to be treated as if she's a sex object. Because she's a *person*." Then he also shrugged without malice. "Just saying."

Dragging his eyes up and down Tristan's body with revulsion, as if he was nothing but a disgusting piece of slime that had just washed up with the seaweed on Revere Beach, Mikey replied, "You, pretty boy, can tell your snobby bitch girlfriend that I wouldn't dance wit' her if she was the last frigging broad on earth! Jesus, this is what I get for trying to be a nice guy."

Tristan's eyes narrowed just slightly at Mikey's words, but he didn't challenge him. And for some reason, I felt compelled to smooth things over with my oldest friend. "Come on, Mikey, I'll buy you a beer."

"Fuck the frigging beer—get me a couple shots of tequila. And get a few for yourself too. You're gonna need 'em if you have to go home wit' that bitch!"

Apologetically, I glanced at Tristan, who sent me a passive stare in return, and then I followed Mikey to the bar. Somehow I sensed that I'd let my partners, and even more than that, myself, down.

"Fuck, Robby, where'd you find them two?" He was completely pissed. "A snobby fucking bitch who thinks she's all that, and her faggot roommate who probably has some sexual-transmitted fucking disease. You found yourself a couple of real winners, you know that, Dalton?"

It seemed that shrugging was the name of the game for the next fifteen minutes or so. I listened calmly and shrugged intermittently, as Mikey ranted that out of all the millions of people on earth I had to pick those two "fucking losers" to cozy up to, when what I really wanted to do was to go back to the table in the corner where my friends were. Rather, where my *other* friends were. Thankfully, it didn't take long before Mikey became distracted by a redheaded "piece of ass" who'd made it clear that she was selling if he was buying.

"This ain't over, Dalton. We're gonna discuss this whole thing tomorrow morning. And bring me coffee—an extra-large one. You know how I like it, right, buddy?" He slung his arm around the woman's shoulders. "Come on, honey. Show me what you got out there on the dance floor!" They headed for the disco room.

By the time I returned to our table, Tristan and Savannah had gone into the classic rock room to dance. I knew that because one of them had scribbled a message on a cocktail napkin and had left it on the chair where my blazer was hanging. I was certainly not accustomed to this type of consideration.

I watched from the shadows as the two of them danced. They moved in unison like they belonged together. I wasn't exactly sure how I felt about that, but I realized that moments like this, moments of feeling like the odd man out, were bound to occur when three people shared. *Shared each other*.

As soon as they saw me standing there, they both signaled with wild enthusiasm that I should join them on the dance floor. After taking a glance around me to make sure that neither Mikey nor his cousin/buddies were within eyeshot, I made my way across the crowded floor. And although it may seem rather bizarre, the three of us danced together to rock 'n' roll classics, sipped on our beers, leaned in to make an occasional joke, and it felt like all was right in my world.

But I knew I'd pay for it tomorrow.

BOTH of my dates dozed a bit on the drive home. Savannah had crashed with her head in my lap, blonde curls covering me from waist to knees. In the backseat, Tristan kept on closing his eyes and then completely startling for some reason when he found he'd drifted off. I decided to help him out, since he clearly felt the need to stay awake.

"Okay, Tristan, summarize the game of football for me, top to bottom. And I'm looking for major detail here." As instructed, Tristan repeated (and I'm talking word-for-word) what I'd taught him at the game last weekend. When he was finished reciting, he looked at me as if checking for my approval. I immediately recalled all of the times when I'd made decent plays on one field or another and had looked to my father for a smile of reassurance, and he had turned his head away.

I smiled widely at Tristan in the rearview mirror. "You're an excellent student; I don't think you forgot a single thing I told you." He beamed back at me. "The only area you stumbled a bit was on defensive positions—but just a little. Okay, it's time for your final exam." I heard Tristan exhale a nervous puff of breath. "Name the defensive position that is farthest from the line, usually in the middle of the field."

Tristan tilted his head in deep thought. "Um, a safety?"

"So far, so good. Now tell me about a fair catch."

"Um, it's when a, uh, a kick receiver waves his arms around over his head before he catches a kick, and nobody can tackle him. Then they play it from the twenty-yard line, right?"

"Not bad. But I'd like to sense a little more confidence in you, okay? Last question, and this one is gonna be tough. How many points can you score in a two-point conversion?"

He hesitated, probably unsure as to whether or not it was a trick question. "Um, two points?"

I laughed and lifted my hand off of the wheel and tilted it back toward him so he could slap it. "You know the game inside out! Are you sure you didn't play football as a kid?"

I immediately wished I hadn't asked him that. In a split second, Tristan's lips transformed from a giddy grin to a pencil thin line. "I'm sure, Robby. There was no football for me… when I was young." We stayed quiet after that, but Tris had no trouble staying awake.

When we arrived at their apartment, I pulled into an open spot and turned to look at Tristan, at least as much as I could with Savannah on my lap.

"You want to come in for a while, Robby? I can make us some coffee." Tristan's expression revealed the blend of emotions he felt: hopefulness mixed with abundant fear.

He clearly wasn't ready to take the next step, and since I wasn't exactly sure what the next step was, I was fairly certain I wasn't ready either. "Nah, I can't. I've got an early meeting tomorrow."

I watched as his facial muscles relaxed. "Okay, maybe next time."

"So, do you want to come to the gym with me Saturday morning? At about, maybe seven?"

"Oh, yeah! Robby, that'd be super. But remember, I'm no Larry Bird."

"Don't worry, Tristan. Neither am I. We'll play for fun and exercise."

Savannah started to wake up and immediately Tristan jumped out of the backseat and came to pull her from my lap. "Come on, honey, let's get you to bed." Gently, he assisted her as she rose unsteadily to stand on the sidewalk.

This part of the night, I had to admit, was kind of weird.

"Good night, you guys," I said softly.

Hands full of a wobbly but still rather adorable Savannah, Tristan looked back at me and offered a tolerant smile.

And I asked myself yet again how a definite feeling of genuine warmth could be growing in my heart for two separate people at the very same time. And how could I not even be slightly sorry that it was?

CHAPTER 14

Robby

"ALL'S I know is, you're fucking warped!"

Mikey was in rare form. He'd been basically shouting at me since I'd stepped into the office on Friday morning. My first response to his tantrum had been, "I don't remember asking for your opinion, Mikey." But that had set off an even more violent demonstration of his volatile temper, probably because I had, indeed, asked that he share his personal views on Savannah and Tristan as recently as several days prior. He'd actually thrown the paperweight that my three-year-old niece had painted for me at one of those ceramics places at a local strip mall, and had smiled as it had shattered on the floor. If you asked me, *that* was warped.

And since he was Mikey DeSalvo, he got overly personal in a very ugly way. "I caught a glimpse of the *three* of you dancing last night. What a fucking heartwarming sight *that* was. So, D-man, you and that fag gonna divide your time in the bedroom wit' the bitch fifty-fifty, or are you three gonna have yourselves a big orgy like out on the dance floor?"

At first, I just bent down to pick up the broken pieces of my paperweight, trying my best to pretend he wasn't in the tiny office with me, ranting and raving like I'd beat up his nana. And then I tried to reason with him. "You've got it all wrong, man. Tristan and Savannah are just friends." I sounded whiny and pathetic. How could I convince Mikey of something I wasn't convinced of?

"Tell me another one, Rob. I saw the way them two looked at each other and I didn't see no *friendship* in their eyes. By the way, are you gonna service that dude in the bedroom too? Is that part of the deal?"

"Shut the fuck up, DeSalvo." I'd had about enough.

"The truth frigging hurts, don't it? And from what I hear, butt-sex hurts even worse! Good fucking luck wit' that shit!"

That was it! I jumped to my feet, grabbed Mikey by his good-for-nothing neck, and being half a head taller and broader by a wide measure, without much effort I easily had him pinned up against the wall. "I *said* to shut the fuck up!"

Breaking out of my grasp, Mikey straightened his collar coolly and cleared his throat. "Just think about it." He sent me one of his more meaningful glares and then stalked out of the office, probably to go be a realtor or to eat Italian cookies or to fuck a redheaded chick or something. I didn't really care what he left to do, as long as he got the hell out of my office.

And maybe I would think about it; maybe I wouldn't. Maybe the three of us were destined to be friends, maybe we were destined to be lovers, or maybe some combination of those things. Maybe it was nobody's business but the three of us.

Maybe I'd figure it out tomorrow.

CHAPTER 15

Robby

I'D DONE some work in the Saugus home of Danny Rose, the owner of Rose's Gym. Nothing major, just refurbishing his deck, fixing a couple of holes in his drywall where he'd sunk his fists in the heat of the moment, that kind of stuff. But ever since then, I hadn't been asked to pay for my membership. Dan and I had an unspoken bartering system going, and it worked well for both of us.

It also had other perks. The indoor basketball court didn't open to the rest of the members until nine in the morning, so when the gym opened up at five for early morning workouts, the court was mine and mine alone. I figured that Tristan would prefer to learn the game unobserved by a crowd of critical ex-jocks.

Tristan was definitely nervous from the moment he got into the Jeep, and I really didn't blame him. He was soon going to have to demonstrate his lack of ability in an area in which most men took great pride: their athleticism. Neither one of us said too much until we got to the gym.

"Hey, Jake. This is my buddy, Tristan. He's gonna be my guest today."

Jake at the desk didn't take his eyes off of his newspaper. "Right, Robby."

Tristan seemed quite relieved. "So getting me in was no big deal, was it?"

"Not at all—this isn't that type of club, Tris. Come on." Since we were both already dressed in sweats and T-shirts, we didn't need to stop by the locker room. We each just dropped our gym bags on the side of the basketball court.

The next two hours flew by. Other than being slightly awkward in some of his first attempts at layups and three-point shots, I had to say Tristan was a fairly adept natural athlete. Before we'd even completed an hour of drills, he'd started asking me if we could play a little one-on-one, and I figured he'd gained enough of the basics to be ready.

And it was awesome. Tristan was competitive, but in a good-natured, nonassholish way, reminding me of when he'd been playing board games that night with Savannah and me. And when I corrected him on his ball handling, he listened carefully and made the necessary adjustments. As my father would have said (about pretty much anybody but me), "the boy's very coachable."

By the end of our game, I found myself experiencing feelings of admiration for the guy. Tristan had had absolutely no idea what he was doing when he'd started today, but he'd still put himself out there and he'd given it his best shot, no pun intended. I decided maybe I should take a lesson from him about life in general.

All sweaty and smiling and bubbly, Tristan grabbed his bag and bounced over to stand in right in front of me. In his excitement, Tristan's long dark eyelashes fluttered against his cheeks a few times before he looked at me and said, "That was really fun, Robby. *Really fun*, so thanks."

And right then I knew I wanted to see what he looked like the very second he opened his eyes in the morning. And I wanted to be the first one he saw when he woke up and greeted a new day.

What the fuck? I'd never had thoughts like that in my entire life—not about a man or a woman. But I couldn't deny them, and I realized I didn't want to.

"No thanks required, man. We both put our hearts to work, and that was the whole point, right?"

He nodded. "What are we gonna do next?" A boy on his first trip to Fenway Park: that was how excited Tristan was.

"How about we do a few laps in the pool?" And yet again, he lowered his head and shoved his fingers into his sweaty hair, and I knew immediately that Tristan had never learned how to swim. "Or maybe we should hit the hot tub. It'd feel great after two hours of basketball, you think?"

"Okay, Robby." His face brightened, but he still appeared somewhat anxious. "I brought my swim trunks and a towel." Yes, he was definitely uptight about something.

As soon as we hit the locker room, I knew exactly what his problem was. He looked around with wide eyes at the other guys, who were stripping down so easily, and by the way his knuckles had whitened on his gym bag, I could tell he wasn't comfortable taking his clothes off in front of them.

"Tris, you may want to hit the toilets before we get into the hot tub, 'cause I'm going to be heavily pushing the water bottles on you. You can change while you're in there." I don't know if what I'd said made much sense or not, but Tristan jumped at the chance to change into his trunks in privacy. And just to make him feel comfortable, I did the same.

TRISTAN was breathtakingly beautiful. He was sitting across from me in the hot tub with his hair damp and falling softly over his half-lidded eyes. His olive-toned, lean body was covered by the water just enough to suit what I assumed was his strong sense of modesty. Speaking of which, I hadn't missed the fact that the guy had actually kept his towel wrapped around his chest until he slid into the water. But now he allowed his slim shoulders to slump down, loosening with relaxation. And that was when I had another one of those earth-shattering insights I'd been experiencing more and more lately. Out of what seemed like the blue, I knew with certainty that I wanted to run my fingers over the entire length of Tristan's body. I wanted to find out if his skin was actually as soft as it looked right now, all splattered with tiny droplets of water. Holy shit, I *wanted* him.

I shut my eyes as I inhaled sharply at my startling realization, knowing that this very moment signified the end of my own personal denial. No longer would I struggle with myself as to whether or not I had sexual interest in another man, or in *this* particular man. Because there was no denying that part of my interest in Tristan was sexual, but it was so much more than that. So much deeper than that.

My admission of my feelings for Tristan left me feeling relieved and eased and somehow strangely thrilled. And more alive than I ever had before. Ever.

We sat together silently in the bubbling hot water. And I wondered with some trepidation about the nature of his interest in me.

CHAPTER 16

Tristan

WHEN I got home, Savannah was curled up with the cat on the couch. She never went to bed without me on the nights that I worked late. She'd fallen asleep once again watching one of those home makeover shows that we both loved.

I went to the television, snapped it off, and headed to the kitchen to grab a beer to help me unwind. When I came back to the living room, Savannah was sitting up, now more awake than asleep.

"Tris, it's so late, and you must be exhausted." She patted the place beside her on the couch and I stepped over and sat down.

"Actually, it's really early." I looked at my watch: nearly 3:00 a.m. "I missed the last subway. Had to take a cab home."

"Was it a wedding?"

"Yeah, and it was huge. I'd say three hundred and fifty people." Michael's housed several enormous function rooms where I often served dinners at weddings and other events. "The money was great, though."

Savannah squatted on the couch, completely dislodging a disgruntled Runaway, who gave me a look to kill before he launched off the couch, and then she moved behind me as best she could. I felt her palms on my neck, kneading away my weariness. "Robby came by tonight."

"Yeah?" I turned to look at her. "I wish I got to see him. How was he?"

"He was great—he brought me a mocha latte. He brought you something too."

"He did?"

"Look on the coffee table." Her hands stilled.

I looked at the table and actually didn't know how I could have missed it when I first came in. I guess I really *was* tired. Spread out on the table was a Red Sox jersey. I lifted it up. Number 34. Even *I* knew that it was David Ortiz's number. Underneath the jersey was a Fenway Park postcard. I turned it over and quickly placed it back down on the table as if it had burned my fingertips. There was a note on it from Robby.

Tris-

The time to learn about baseball has arrived. And we're going to do it in style. Can you get next Sunday off work? I got three tickets to the play-offs and do you know whose names are on those tickets? Yours, mine, and Savannah's—that's who!

Robby

I WAS totally disconcerted by what he'd done. I just dropped down to my knees on the floor and put my head in my hands. Why had Robby gotten me a gift? And tickets too? *What does he want from me?*

When my mind cleared enough, I lifted my head. Savannah was staring at me.

"I didn't let him fuck me, so that jersey isn't *payment* for anything." I knew my words were vulgar, reminiscent of my thirteen-year-old self who sometimes reemerged when I felt threatened. But this unexpected gift-giving just hit too close to home—my Uncle Ben had thought he could swap a new CD from Walmart for privileges with my preteen ass, and he'd let me know that I'd be acting ungrateful if I tried to refuse him. So right then I just wasn't able to control my language like I usually could. "And it's not like fucking either one of us is just over the horizon for the guy. He's bright enough to have figured *that* out. I just don't get why he'd do this."

Now when Savannah looked at me, her disappointment was obvious. "Maybe it's not all about sex to him."

Wishing like hell that were true but knowing otherwise, I picked up the jersey and hugged it to my chest. And then I shook my head. "So you actually think that Mr. Normal—Robby Dalton—the straight athlete and businessman, the poster boy for blond-haired, blue-eyed, all-American good looks—is into a cozy little threesome *relationship* with *us*?" I'd pulled myself together enough to clean up my language, but not my attitude. "Tell me another one, Savannah."

Savannah didn't answer me and I wasn't sure why. Probably, she wanted me to keep on rambling so she could better understand what was going on in my head. Of course, I obliged. "Nobody but you cares about me and no man has ever, *ever* wanted a thing to do with me for any other reason than getting themselves something, most typically for getting themselves *laid*. And I just don't buy it that Robby Dalton could have any sincere interest in somebody like me. *You*, yeah, I get that. You are perfect, and perfect for *him*. But not my nasty ass." Once I'd gotten back together with Savannah after she found me in Gus's cellar, I'd made a huge effort to clean up my act—foul language included. But every once in a while, in the heat of the moment, I slipped back to being the Tristan who had survived for so many years on the street. So I stared back at Savi, waiting for her to speak so I could shoot her words down, but she just continued to study my face with serious eyes. She knew me too well. She knew that if she waited, I'd eventually blurt out everything that was on my mind.

"Can't you see it, Savi? He's just doing this so you'll give in and be his girlfriend! And that's exactly what you'd do if you, if you used your brain!" I crawled over to the couch. "Just be his! It's okay. I'll be okay."

Savannah shook her head. "He cares about *you*."

I was stunned; Savannah never lied to me. Sure, sometimes she omitted telling me portions of the truth, but she never looked right into my eyes and lied. I grabbed her hand, needing her to steady me.

"Tristan, I saw it in his eyes tonight. When he brought over the jersey and the tickets, I saw it. Robby is falling in love with you."

"You *saw* it?" My heart was pounding. Hope, dread, elation, terror.

She nodded. "And it's okay. It's what I want for you."

"What *you* want? For *me*?" Monosyllabic words—not good.

Another nod. Then she pulled me up by my elbows so I was sitting beside her on the couch. "Tris, I love you; you're my family. You'll *always* be my family and I'll *always* be yours. Now it's time to let Robby in."

This was *so* not what I'd expected to happen when I came home from a fourteen-hour shift. *I can't deal with this and I'm going to bed.* I tried to get up but she wouldn't let go of my wrist.

"No, Tris. We're not done here."

"Well, what do you want me to say?" I tried to sound sarcastic but then the truth slipped out again. "I'm scared, Savi." *Shit, when had I started rocking back and forth?*

"Scared of what?"

"Scared to lose you, scared to feel for him. I-I'm just...."

And that's when Savannah pulled me against her chest in the way that always comforted me so well, as if *she* was the one who was six feet tall and *I* was the tiny one. "You will never lose me. But it's time to open your heart to a different kind of love." She paused and then asked the million-dollar question. "Do you think you could fall in love with him?"

It felt so comforting for me to sway my body that I didn't stop. But somehow Savannah managed to hang on. She gripped my shoulders with all of her strength and rocked right along with me, and that's when I let it spill. "Maybe I already have fallen a little bit, but it's so hard for me. Savi, it's just so hard to trust."

"I understand that. But I really do think you can trust Robby." She kissed my cheek as if I'd somehow pleased her with my honesty. "He's a good man."

"But how do the *three* of us fit together? *How*?" Maybe *this* was really the million-dollar question.

And that's when she took my face in her hands firmly, in that I-mean-business manner I was so used to with Savi. She made me look right at her, and I saw that her eyes were filled with hope, not hurt or fear, and definitely not jealousy. "I don't know exactly how it will work. But if you love me, you'll allow yourself to feel for him. Let your heart be in charge of your brain. Please, Tris—it's what I want."

Barely a minute later, as if we could read each other's mind, we both stood up in a single motion and headed to our bedroom.

Looking back.... Savannah

LEAVING *Tristan had been devastating for two reasons: first, for what it had done to me, and second, for what I was certain it had done to him.*

It was true that I'd only been fourteen when I'd met him, and we'd only known each other for a month and a half, but it had been the most volatile, life-altering time in my short life. And when you are fourteen and lonely and afraid and needy, well, six weeks is all it takes for you to fall in love.

It hadn't been a kind of love I'd ever experienced before, because I'd never known anybody who had put my needs before their own. And Tris had been nothing short of devoted. He'd come up with food for me to eat, relative warmth for me at night, and he'd given me more emotional comfort than I'd ever known. What's more, he hadn't expected me to have sex with him in return for any of that.

No matter where we'd found ourselves in the dark of night, Tristan had simply held me, no funny business at all; he'd smoothed my greasy curls and placed tiny kisses on my dirty skin until I'd fallen asleep. And he'd done that every night for six weeks.

He had also taken the rape that was meant for me.

And in return, I'd left him, vulnerable and alone.

But I'd meant what I'd said, as only a fourteen-year-old could, when I'd told him I was going to find him. For the first four years, though, all I could do was dream about the boy I loved... where he was, what he was doing, whether he loved me too. I'd fantasized that he'd grown tall and strong, that he'd found all of the men who'd hurt and used him over the years and had taught them all the biggest lessons of their lives. And I'd dreamed he was somewhere warm and safe and happy, and all he needed to be complete was me.

As one of several foster daughters of Mrs. Sarah T. Watson of Somerville, I hadn't had as much freedom as I wanted to spend hours upon hours scouring the streets of Boston in search of a runaway teenage boy. What I did have was high school classes, plenty of chores, a steady babysitting job. I'd even had a few friends.

But I'd never forgotten Tristan.

As soon as I'd turned eighteen, my dreams of Tristan Chartrand had changed into an obsession with finding him. He'd been the only person who had ever made me feel precious. I just couldn't let that feeling, or the man who'd given it to me, go. I'd searched all of the hangouts around Boston that Tristan had taken me to when I was with him, but had been disappointed time and again to find that he no longer frequented them. I'd asked about him at the Outreach Center, and they'd said that they'd actually seen him in Somerville every now and again over the past several years. But since he'd become a legal adult, he was no longer their concern.

Finally, in the spring of my senior year of high school, I'd given up the search and resigned myself to the fact that Tristan had moved on, maybe to a warmer climate, if he was still homeless. I'd also accepted that I needed to get a more lucrative job to support myself through my next four years at Somerville University. And that's when I applied for a job as a waitress at the S-Squared Diner.

CHAPTER 17

Robby

TO PUT it politely, Mikey and I hadn't exactly been seeing eye-to-eye lately. And because of that fact, I now found myself exhausted, starving, and freezing, not to mention, stranded, in a remote South Boston neighborhood. At ten at night.

Tonight Bill Cheney, the only job superintendent on the company payroll, Mikey, and I had presented a sales proposal for the renovation of an Evangelical Baptist church's parish hall. The "coworker chemistry" between Mikey and me just, well, it just hadn't been there tonight. I mean, even with Mikey's able assistance, I had absolutely choked.

RD Builders just couldn't sell its plan. We'd stuttered in the face of simple questions. Our claims of previous successes in similar jobs had come off as nothing more than hollow bragging. Our PowerPoint presentation kept resetting itself back to the beginning about thirty seconds in. Come to think of it, calling it a failure would be way too kind.

Before he'd departed, Bill had made a particularly valid observation. "Maybe you guys woulda had better luck selling your pitch to your client if you woulda actually looked at each other. Like you'd come here together and worked for the same company."

Mikey had shrugged and somehow managed to make his eyes appear as round and innocent as a child's. But I'd known Mikey as a child and he'd never been that innocent.

But yes, Bill had been right. Since the morning I'd shoved Mikey's back against the wall of my office, neither one of us had acknowledged the other's existence on planet earth. And that kind of unresolved anger made it tough to sell a client on the steadfast and consistent attributes of your company's personnel.

"Jesus, Mikey. Couldn't you have put your childish anger aside and considered the interests of this company?" I'd stood there in the flickering glow of a streetlight, my arms folded tightly in an effort to contain my rage, and attempted to shift the entire blame for our night's flop onto Mikey.

In response, Mikey had sweetly suggested that I go cry on the shoulders of "that bitch and her fag" (yes, Savannah and Tristan) and while I was at it, find my own frigging ride home. In the heat of the moment, I had less than rationally threatened him with his job, saying something like, "If you can't focus on building buildings, I'll find someone who can." No, nothing about tonight had been sufficiently warm and fuzzy to induce an Evangelical preacher and his committee of six middle-aged housewives into signing on the dotted line.

And so here I stood. Unfortunately, very few cabs frequented this area, and I had no clue where the nearest bus station was. I was stuck.

Thankfully, I still had my cell phone, and I pulled it out and pressed T. "Tris?"

"Yeah. It's me. What's up, Robby?"

"It looks like I'm not gonna make it over to your place tonight." I tried to make my voice sound slightly less pissed off at the world than I actually felt.

"Why not?" He was clearly disappointed.

I asked myself whether I should unburden myself on my unsuspecting partner. But, hell, that's what relationships were for, so I dished it out. "Not a good day. I just finished a disaster of a job interview and, well, at the moment I'm stranded in South Boston."

"Where's your Jeep?"

"Back at the office. Mikey drove me over here, but let's just say I wasn't welcome for the return trip."

Silence. *The Tristan hesitation.*

"I don't think I'd be decent company tonight anyways."

"Have you eaten dinner yet?"

"Dinner?" Sometimes he totally lost me.

"Yeah, have you had dinner yet tonight?"

"Uh, no. Not yet. But I think I have Cheerios at my apartment."

"Robby, grab a cab and get over to our place. I'm leaving work now and I'll meet you there with dinner from the restaurant."

I had to smile because I could hear the grin in his voice. He wanted to do this for me.

"What do you say?"

Dinner from Michael's with Tristan and Savannah sounded a hell of a lot better than dry Cheerios alone in my cold apartment. "All right. I'll be there, buddy. But don't hold your breath. I haven't seen a single cab go by in the past fifteen minutes. Maybe I'll try to call for one."

IT TOOK me well over an hour to get to my partners' apartment. And at that point I felt like complete and total crap. Tonight had pushed me over the edge.

When Tristan opened the door, the first thing I noticed was his beautiful brown eyes. Only after I took a few seconds to appreciate them, did I notice the delectable smell of seafood emanating from inside. I dropped my coat and briefcase by the door and followed Tristan down the hall. "This smells unbelievable." I yanked at my tie to loosen it.

Standing beside the kitchen table, laying out food cartons and occasionally tugging up those baggy gray sweatpants that kept slipping down his narrow hips, Tristan appeared quite pleased with himself. "It was one of tonight's special's—Seafood Linguine." He gestured toward a chair. "Sit down; I'll grab us a couple beers."

Before my ass hit that chair, I was drooling. Tristan had thought of everything: beer, rolls, butter, salad, and plenty of those delicious croutons. "Where's Savannah? Isn't she going to eat?"

Dishing out the most enticing food I'd encountered since I'd been invited to dinner at Mikey's mother's house last summer, Tristan replied, "She went to bed right after I got home. She had a kind of bad day too."

"What happened?"

"This girl she's friends with, Lani, from a group home in Malden, got into some major trouble at school today. She took it really hard."

"Does she need our help to deal with it?" That was what people in a relationship were supposed to do for each other, right? Plus, I hated the thought of Savannah being upset. She was such a strong person; her only weaknesses seemed to be in the people she cared about.

"She'll be okay. I've seen her deal with worse."

"You have?" This was the first time Tristan had presented me with an opening to ask questions about his and Savannah's bond. I didn't overlook it. "Like what?"

Conveniently, he used chewing as an excuse to avoid my question, pointing to his mouth and shrugging, as if he was helpless to answer.

But I was persistent. "Tell me about when you met her."

A shadow crossed Tristan's face, and he lifted his beer and took a long swig in an attempt to distract either himself or me. Then the shadow lifted and his expression was sweet again. "She was amazing. The best thing that ever happened to me, in fact. Savannah was—"

For the first time, I reached out to touch the skin on Tristan's wrist, and it was every bit as soft as it looked. When he didn't freak out at my light touch, I covered his hand with mine and interrupted him. "Not just her, Tris. I want to know about you too."

Our hands fell apart and then we both took a few more bites of dinner as he pieced his thoughts together in his mind. "Well, I'd been living on the street, you know, for maybe a year and a half or so before I met Savannah. For some of that time I'd been down in Atlanta 'cause it was warmer there, but I'd been back in Boston for about six months before I met her."

I nodded and waited. Patience seemed to be the way to get the most out of Tristan.

"Savi was really young, just fourteen. She left home to get away from her mother's pervy boyfriend." Avoiding my eyes, he buttered a roll. "Let me know when you want another beer, okay?"

I nodded but stayed focused. "Why did *you* leave home?" I knew it was blunt, but I also knew that I needed him to volunteer this information so our relationship could move forward. And by now I knew I wanted that.

He completely ignored my question. "And I was just this skinny teenager, trying to keep everybody else off her, trying to keep her safe, you know?"

He had more to say and I knew I had to let him reveal himself at his own pace. For some reason, I was finding that very difficult at the moment.

"I did the goddamn best I could."

I'd never heard him curse before. "I know you did." I reached over and touched him again. His hand curled up around mine.

What he said next escaped from his lips quickly and in a hushed tone, as if it would hurt less that way. "I left because of the stuff my uncle was doing to me." And as I could've easily predicted, Tristan looked down at his lap and tugged his hand from beneath mine to plow his fingers through his hair. Then all of a sudden, he popped up out of his chair and asked, "Are you finished, Robby? Let's go hang out in the living room."

"What about the dishes? I can do them while you watch TV on the couch."

Tristan laughed, effectively dismissing my offer. "Come on, Robby." He grabbed a few more beers, and I traipsed behind him into the living room.

We sat on either end of the couch, facing each other. "I feel 100 percent better than I did earlier. Thank you."

"It's amazing what a full belly can do for a man." He shifted his ass enough to snap off the lamp over his head so we were sitting in the dull glow from the kitchen. It was nice.

"The food was spectacular, but the company is even better." I reached for his hand before he could use it to hide behind. After giving it a brief squeeze, I let go.

"What happened between you and Mikey?"

"Oh, it was just Mikey being Mikey, I guess."

"He doesn't like what's going on with you and me and Savannah, does he?" It was dark in the room, but I could still feel Tristan's gaze on my face, trying to interpret my expression.

"I'm not going to lie—he hates it. I don't really care what he thinks, but tonight it got in the way of our work."

"It's okay to care how he feels. You guys have been friends for a long time."

My next phrase was grumbled. "Maybe too long."

And then there was silence. Not the Tristan-hesitation kind of silence, either. It was a what-happens-now type of silence.

Surprisingly, it was Tristan who broke it. "Let's go to bed."

"To bed?" I repeated.

"Yeah."

"In the bedroom?" My jaw clenched involuntarily.

"Well, that's where the bed is."

"Y-you go to bed, Tris. I think I'll just stay out here, you know, on the couch." I pulled off my tie and toed off my shoes. "I'll be fine right here."

"Please come with me."

My insides were screaming—a bed, *a fucking bed!* To be honest, something else was running through my mind like ticker tape across the bottom of a television screen: he's a dude and you're a dude, not to mention that there's a fucking *third* person in there sleeping.

"It's just a bed."

If Tristan could manage to overcome the fears of closeness that were lurking in his head for very legitimate reasons, I could get over my stupid fear of facing the truth of who I was and what I wanted. "Yeah, you're right."

He waited in the hallway as I used the bathroom and then he took his turn. Before he turned the hall light off, Tristan said one more time, as if he was also trying to convince himself of the fact, "It's just a bed."

WE LAY there, wearing just our boxers, on either side of Savannah and Runaway. And I would have assumed that my brain would be revolting *big-time* because of that, but strangely, I was totally at peace.

"You okay, Robby?"

"Mm-hmm. You?"

"Really good." There was no hesitation, either. "I like it. Just us three."

"Yeah. Me too." Savannah's presence was Tristan's safety net, and maybe she was my safety net too. I felt a soft tap on the very top of my head. Then those delicate fingers of his started tentatively wandering through my hair, scratching a bit and then rubbing a little; soon I was flying. I'd never been so powerfully affected by another person's touch. "Tristan."

As he moved his hands through my hair, he was quiet, and for some reason I knew that what he was going to say next would change things between us. "I've never made love, Robby. I've only...." I thought he wasn't going to finish his thought, but he did. "You should know, I've only been what you might call *used* before... in bed."

And I found myself searching for the right words, as this was certainly the most profound moment we'd shared since the day we'd met. "You'll never be used that way again, Tristan. Trust me on that." I lifted my hand to my head and joined it with his. And in the cool, gray darkness of a bedroom that wasn't mine, a woman and her large cat sleeping between us, we connected as partners.

CHAPTER 18

Robby

I HAD absolutely no one to talk to about this.

It was quite possible that I was falling in love for the very first time. And I wanted to share it, to discuss it, to talk about it until it made sense, to bask in its thrilling yet nonetheless terrifying glory. But I couldn't very well do those things with the four unadorned walls in my lonely Harvard Square apartment. I needed an actual person with functioning ears.

Lindsey, that's who I could talk to. Linds, the only woman I'd ever connected with.

After a last glance around my impersonal, fully (but very sparsely) furnished shoebox of a studio, I grabbed a sweatshirt and headed to the street where the Jeep was wedged into a too-tight spot that I'd been lucky to get, my thoughts consumed by my older sister. Both of us were tall, athletically built, light-haired, and blue-eyed, but the similarities ended there. Well, we had also both been "popular" in high school; my athletic prowess had been well respected whereas she had actually been well liked. Lindsey was of a gregarious nature, funny and open. I tended to be more of a loner, seemingly aloof and truly very wary. She had always been a tell-it-like-it-is sort of person in terms of her relationships, and because of that people were drawn to her. I'd always been more interested in pleasing my very few buddies, suspecting that if I didn't please them, they'd just dump me on my ass. But despite and maybe because of our differences in character, I loved and respected her above everyone else.

Currently, Lindsey Dalton Clark lived the life of the quintessential suburban housewife. She, however, was not planning to focus singularly on that endeavor for the long haul, but just until her kids were in elementary school. Then she'd return for at least part of her waking hours to her other passion: teaching high school English.

After getting married to her longtime college boyfriend, now a partner in a small Boston law firm, she'd moved back to the town in which we'd grown up. It was "a good place to raise kids," or at least that's what everybody had told her when she'd become pregnant with Madison, my three-year-old niece. But now, two-thirds of the way through pregnancy number two, she'd confided to me that she missed the random craziness of living in the city. Mom and Dad wouldn't be pleased when she and Brandon informed them of their decision to put their quaint country Cape with the huge tree-lined backyard on the market in favor of a compact condo with barely enough sidewalk space for Madison to play four-square. So she was holding off on telling them until after she'd given birth to baby number two. If luck was on her side, she'd manage to have a baby boy in the hopes that the birth of my father's much longed-for grandson would dull the blow of his daughter's family's relocation twenty minutes south to Boston.

"Look, Maddy! It's your Uncle Robby!"

"White Jeep! White Jeep!" Maddy looked adorable in her bright-green fall sweater with this huge red apple embroidered on the front of it and her blonde curls bouncing on her shoulders, as she ran across the yard toward the driveway.

"Hey, Maddy! How's my baby girl?" I climbed from the Jeep.

She stopped midrun, stared at her sneakers, and pouted. "*Not* a baby!"

Lindsey grasped her protruding belly and laughed boisterously. "Looks like you still know how to piss off a girl!"

"Funny." I picked up the rake that Lindsey had dropped in her spasms of laughter. "Are you sure you're supposed to be raking leaves—in your condition?"

More snickering. "I'm pregnant, not dangerously anemic."

I busied my hands by picking up where she'd left off with the leaves. Maddy also grabbed her pink plastic rake and started back on her own pint-size pile.

"So, to what do I owe this unannounced visit from my little brother? Not that I'm not thrilled to have a distraction from the mess Mother Nature has made of my yard."

I started raking faster. "Can't a guy visit his sister anymore without being given the third degree?"

"Listen, Robby, I'm ready for a break. I need to get off my feet for a while. So come on, let's go sit at the picnic table and you can talk to me. I have a little snack waiting there for Maddy and me, and I know how to share cookies much better than I did when we were little." With obvious effort, she lumbered toward the picnic table in the side yard. "Maddy, sweetie, are you ready to eat your animal crackers?"

Maddy dropped her rake and then ran to me. I scooped her up and carried her over to the picnic table. "Uncle Robby, Mommy says we gots to wipe off our hands 'fore we eat." She pulled a little wet wipe out of a bright-green box and presented it to me. "I'll do mine, you do yours."

Obediently, I cleaned off my hands and then we sat down for juice boxes and crackers. Maddy, concentrating intently on specifically which body parts of the different animal shapes she was biting off, slipped into the head space that kids so often go to—wherever that was. It soon grew quiet.

"What's on your mind, Robby?" One thing I loved about Lindsey was that she was always direct. Maybe that was part of the reason I'd initially been so interested in Savannah; she was as no-nonsense as my sister, who I'd always held in high esteem. "I can't weigh in on what you're dealing with if you don't tell me what it is."

I sighed.

"It can't be that bad."

I smiled sheepishly. "Yes, it can. In fact, it can be worse."

She lifted a handful of crackers and dropped them all in her mouth at once. "God, I'm starving. I have to eat for two, you know?"

"Mommy's not supposed to talk when she gots food in her mouth, Uncle." Maddy sent her mother a stern glance.

I tousled my niece's curls a bit and replied, "Then I guess it's my turn to talk, huh?" Both girls nodded at me before Maddy once again got distracted, this time by the picture on the back of her juice box. "Linds, I met somebody."

Lindsey looked up sharply from her next handful of cookies. After all, I was twenty-six and had never brought a girl home for the family to meet. "Holy shit, bro! That's not exactly a problem, is it?"

"Dad's not gonna approve."

"If she's got big breasts and wears a short skirt, Dad'll love her." She rolled her eyes and then picked up a juice box and put the straw between her lips.

"Um, there are no big breasts or skirts involved here, I'm afraid."

"Oh, so you found yourself one of those flat-chested, spandex-shorts wearing, granola-eating types? Well, Dad will have to adjust."

I stood up and turned away from the picnic table. It would be easier to say this if I wasn't looking at her. "Which do you want first—the startling news or the super fucked-up news?" After all, she was pregnant; it was only fair to prepare her for a shock.

"I'll go with door number one: go ahead, Robby, startle me."

"Okay. Lindsey, let's just say there are no breasts or miniskirts involved because 'she' is a 'he.'"

I heard some throaty sputtering and then a couple of deep coughs.

"Are you all right, Mommy?"

I turned around to see Madison patting her mother's arm, looking very concerned. And her mother was absolutely gaping at me, looking *far more* concerned than her daughter. "Yes, honey, Mommy's fine." Then very quietly, she added, "But your Uncle Robby's not going to be fine when Grampa gets wind of his big news." Somehow, however, Lindsey's expression had already shifted from one of worry to one of amusement.

I turned back around to face the next-door-neighbor's house. "Thanks for the encouragement, Linds."

Her voice grew soft. "Are you saying that you're gay, Robby? Because truthfully, I can't say that I ever saw that one coming."

Suddenly I found myself needing to look at her. For comfort, for acceptance. "Lindsey, I never saw it coming either. And I don't really feel *gay*, per se, but I, uh, it's just *him*. I want to be with *this particular guy*."

"Mommy, can I play in the sandbox?"

Both of us turned abruptly to stare at her. I don't know about my sister, but I'd gotten so wrapped up in my own personal saga that I'd forgotten Maddy was still in the yard with us. It was a good thing I wasn't her mother.

"Uncle Robby, would you please take the cover off of Maddy's sandbox?"

Obediently, I marched right over to the big turtle filled with sand and lifted off its big green back. "There you go, baby. Make me a sand pie, okay?"

Maddy plopped down on her butt into the sand and then she looked at me with an expression that could be described as no less than scathing. "I'm *not* a baby. Aaaand you forgot to say please."

Despite the monumental nature of our discussion, neither Lindsey nor I could stifle our giggles. "I know, I know; you're a big girl now. And I'm very sorry, Maddy. I meant to say please."

Maddy nodded with satisfaction and got to work.

I looked at Lindsey again, knowing it was time to tell her the rest. "Ready for the fucked-up news?"

She honestly looked like she wasn't sure how to answer that question, but she managed to squeak out, "Do tell."

"You promise you won't go into labor right here on the picnic table when I tell you?"

"I'll try not to, but Robby, you're really freaking me out. You didn't kill someone, did you?"

My own laughter eased my mind slightly. If Lindsey could still joke, maybe the world wasn't going to come to an end. "Let's see, how should I phrase this part? Okay, here goes: Tristan, the guy I, uh, the guy I like, and I are involved in a—Jesus, this sounds kinky—we are part of a sort of threesome." I figured I owed it to Lindsey to shut up for a minute to allow the "threesome" concept to sink into her brain.

"Um, three guys?" I could tell by the disconcerted expression on her face that she was actively fighting off the visual images of her little brother locking lips and other body parts ever-so-passionately with *two* burly dudes. And then suddenly, she looked skeptical. "You aren't trying to pull a fast one on a poor pregnant lady, are you?"

"I only wish." I stepped right in front of her and gathered up her hands in mine. "No, the third person is a girl. She's the one I originally started dating." I took a few minutes to fill her in on the brief history of our strange little love triangle, adding, "But the part I'm still trying to figure out is how Savannah, that's the girl, fits into our relationship. She's a super great woman, don't get me wrong on that; she's smart and honest and principled. But it seems as if she just wants Tristan and me to be her best pals, and her *big* concern is getting us together."

"Maybe that genuinely *is* her big concern. Maybe she's a matchmaker, and from what you've told me, it looks like she might have made a love match between you guys." I felt my face grow hot with embarrassment because this certainly was a strange conversation to be having with my sister; however, I didn't interrupt her. "But are you, and Tristan, of course, both willing to be 'just friends' with her?"

"I know I'm okay with being just close friends with Savannah, because it's Tristan who I feel, you know, like, *romantic* for. I'm still trying to figure out her relationship with Tristan. But I do know they've lived together for more than four years and they aren't, well, they aren't lovers. She says they never have been."

"Robby, from what you've told me, Tristan and Savannah seem to be more than slightly dependent on each other. Maybe she…. Okay, so here's what I really think: I think it's very possible she believes he won't go along with engaging in a romantic relationship with you unless she's right there beside him."

"And exactly how fucked up is this situation, in your humble opinion?"

She hesitated, reminding me of Tristan. And then with a tilt of her head, she asked, "You want to know what I think? Do you really want to know?"

I nodded. I really did want to hear her opinion of this shit-hole in which I'd found myself buried up to my neck.

"I think that today is the first time I've ever seen you fully invested in a relationship with someone other than Maddy or me. And I think it's wonderful!" She pounced forward as delicately as a very pregnant woman could manage and hugged me hard. "Do you really want to spend your life reinventing the farce of a marriage that Mom and Dad have, with a woman who is not right for you? Or do you want to spend your life with a person who you can talk to, laugh with, relate to, and have good sex with, of course?"

Cold chills ran up my spine. I was not at all ready to think about having sex with a man, let alone to have a birds-and-bees chat about it with my sister. "Linds, *that* isn't on either of our minds right now, or Savannah's either, for that matter."

"But you feel attracted to him?"

"I think he's beautiful—incredibly so. And it's not just because of how he looks."

Lindsey was quiet for a moment while she digested my words. "Then I'll tell you this much: I don't give a crap what the gender of the person is as long as he can reach your heart, Robby, and it seems like Tristan has done that. You've been alone long enough. I say, go for it, baby brother!"

"Uncle Robby is *not* a baby!" At that very moment, I was presented with two equally precious gifts: a surprisingly well-constructed mud pie built on a yellow Frisbee from my niece, who'd incidentally just defended my honor, and a candidly satisfied smile from my big sister.

CHAPTER 19

Robby

WHENEVER the Red Sox made it to the playoffs, Mikey, his cousin/buddies, and I routinely got ourselves some "break the fuckin' bank" (Mikey's words) expensive tickets to at least one of the games, and off we'd go to Fenway Park to party. But because of the big chill currently occurring between Mikey and me, I'd decided I'd take my "boyfriend" and my "girlfriend" to the game instead; after all, they *were* a "package deal," right? And incidentally, they were turning out to be the best deal I'd ever made. And being a businessman, I'd made quite a few deals.

Savannah was so bundled up with layers of clothes she looked like she was planning to climb Mount Everest rather than attend a baseball game in Boston. Tristan appeared as excited as a kid on his first trip to Fenway Park, which was pretty much exactly what he was. Wearing the Ortiz jersey I'd given him over his sweatshirt and a Sox cap to top it off, he stood on the sidewalk in front of his building with his hands stuck deep in the pockets of his jeans, waiting for my Jeep to pull up so he could jump in.

Yes, there he stood in front of his apartment—all flush-faced and foot-tapping—and if I hadn't known how psyched up he was to be going to the game today, I would have thought he'd downed one too many cans of Red Bull. As usual, Tristan hopped in the back, allowing Savannah the front passenger seat. And on the short drive from Somerville to Kenmore Square, he must've asked me at least ten times how much farther it was. I was also very well aware that Tristan knew the layout of Boston like the back of his hand; he was just truly excited.

When we arrived, we didn't spend too much time on Yawkey Way because my dates were eager to get inside the park to catch their first glimpse of the famous Green Monster. We wasted no time in finding the lines for the Fenway Franks, popcorn, and beer, and I got Tris a program so I could help him to keep track of the game on the scorecard inside it. Armed with our feast and Tristan's precious program, I led the couple to our seats, which just so happened to have been pretty decent, down by first base. I sat in between them and turned to Tristan, ready to teach him the scoring shorthand.

"Awww! How fucking romantic!" I didn't even have to turn around to know who the owner of that grating voice was. But nonetheless, I glanced up and saw that Mikey and his cousin/buddy were sitting about six rows behind us. "I see you took your two lovers to a ballgame, Dalton!"

I felt the stares of the people around us burning into my back. On both sides of me, Tristan and Savannah had suddenly become completely fascinated by the cement underneath their seats. "At least I've got a date, who're you with up there, your boy, Eddie Martini, again?" Knowing poor Eddie, he'd probably just turned red as a beet, but I had to fight fire with fire.

"Well, we were good enough for ya last year, asshole!" Several parents sent him "watch your language" glares, so Mikey sat down.

But Tristan, ever the gentleman, stood up and turned around to face him. "It's nice to see you again, Mikey," he called. "I'd love a chance to buy you a beer today."

Mikey jumped back to his feet. "It'll be a cold day in hell when I drink a beer from outta your dick-fondling hand, you faggot!"

"Come on, loser! I didn't take my kid to Fenway to hear your crap!"

"Yeah, man. Sit down and shut up!" The crowd seemed to know how to keep Mikey in line much better than I ever had. As they ranted at him, all I did was sit there with my head pretty much up my ass, steaming with fury.

"I guess I'll leave you three to your ménage à trois. Have a ball, homos!"

Tristan blushed and then lowered his head, off came the ball cap, and before I knew it, his hand was in his hair.

Yes, Mikey and I were pissed at each other. He could treat *me* like shit until the cows came home, but Tristan had not done a fucking thing to deserve that kind of treatment. I gently pushed Savannah back and started to slide down the row toward the aisle. I'd teach that asshole some fucking manners! One more fistfight at Fenway Park wouldn't be big news, anyways.

"Don't do it, Robby." Tristan immediately had his hand on my forearm, and he was pulling me back to my seat.

Right then I could only see red, and I wasn't talking about anybody's socks. "He insulted you."

Savannah's mittened hand was suddenly caught up in my own. "There was no harm done, Robby. Let's get our minds back on the game. Look, the teams are coming out."

"He called me and Tris *gay*—you heard the slur."

Tristan immediately interjected, "So suggesting that we're gay is a *slur*? Is that how you see it?" He stared at me as if he didn't even know me, his eyes colder than I'd ever seen them. "I thought you were cool with, *with things*."

"No! No, that's not what I meant, Tris…. Please, man, just listen to me. It was *how* he spoke that pissed me off!" At this point, I had completely turned my back on Savannah and was basically ready to fall to my knees to beg. I didn't care who the fuck saw me do it, and for that matter, I didn't even know what I was going to beg for. I just wanted another try to make Tristan's day picture-perfect. I searched his face, but for the first time ever, I couldn't read his expression. And that in itself really threw me. It seemed I had disappointed the person I most wanted to please.

"This is our very first Red Sox game, you guys. Let's make memories we want to keep, hmm?" I heard Savannah's calm voice behind me. She reached right across my chest and took the popcorn from out of Tristan's white-knuckled grasp. "Now, could the two of you go and buy me another beer? I seem to have spilled mine in all of the excitement." Her eyes meant business, so Tristan and I slid from our seats like two obedient children.

As we headed down the aisle, I placed my hand on Tristan's shoulder; it felt stiff to my touch, probably from the effort it took for him to hold it so rigidly. "I'm sorry, man. I wasn't thinking too clearly."

He looked at me, his deep brown gaze softening slightly. "You think being gay's a crime or something? Because I don't."

In his own reserved way, Tristan was as honest and direct as Savannah. And in order to deserve their affection, I knew I had to be the same. "God, no. No, I really care about you, Tris." As soon as we got to the area near the concession stands, I pushed on his chest lightly and kept on pushing until I'd backed him into a corner. "I just didn't like someone making what we have sound dirty, 'cause it's not."

Tristan nodded sweetly. I could already tell he understood.

"Meeting you and Savannah—*however* we end up fitting together— is the best thing that has ever happened to me." I needed him to nod again, just one more time, so I knew he accepted my apology and everything was okay between us.

But instead of nodding, he walked over to the beer stand and bought three beers. When he returned to where I stood staring at him anxiously, still waiting for a sign that I was forgiven, he bent down to put a beer on the ground. Then he stood back up and handed me one. Tristan lifted his beer between us and I lifted mine in response. "Here's to our first Red Sox game in Fenway Park, of hopefully very many."

I thrust my beer against his and replied with relief, "Now, buddy, we've got a lot of work to do if you want to understand how to score a game. Let's head back." After Tristan picked up Savannah's beer, I escorted him back to our seats, and suddenly Mikey DeSalvo was no longer even a factor for my consideration.

CHAPTER 20

Robby

IT MIGHT as well have been the height of the Cold War in the office of Robert Dalton Builders. I'd have liked to think of myself as the freedom-loving United States of America and Mikey as the tyrannical Union of Soviet Socialist Republics. In any case, my office hadn't exactly been Group-Hug Central lately, and both of us had managed to avoid the place as much as humanly possible. I don't know if it was also true for Mikey, but every Starbucks on the outskirts of Boston had been seeing a great deal more of my laptop and me since early October.

Thankfully, it wasn't entirely necessary for us to do any cooperative strategizing in search of new work, as we already had four small jobs that would keep us busy enough until the spring. I less-than-courageously decided that interviewing for new jobs could wait until the big freeze between us thawed.

If the big freeze thawed.

It was the miracle of all miracles: Mikey had picked up his *own* cup of coffee this morning. Of course, he hadn't stopped to get the boss a cup. Not much of a surprise there; I realized that he was in no mood to make any kind of a peace offering. He pushed through the office door, coffee and briefcase in his hands.

"Hey, we've to go over a few things on the renovations at the McPhee Nursing Home. You got a minute?" I looked up at him gravely as he closed the office door.

"Oh, so you've lowered your standards enough to talk to me now?"

I stood up and walked over to his desk. "Look, man, we work together. And if we want to keep it that way, we have to be able to get a few things done. You don't have to be my best friend and I don't have to be yours, but we need to at least be civil enough with each other to talk business."

Surprisingly, my statement seemed to shock him. And hurt him. He glanced down. "So we're not best pals no more, huh? Easy come, easy go, I guess."

"Come on, Mikey."

He dropped down into his seat. "I get it, D-man. You met some people who can give ya something I can't. Don't know just what the fuck that *something* is, but it seems like you're happy enough getting it." He raised his eyebrows, as if what I was getting from Tristan and Savannah was being given between the sheets. "I don't have to like it to work wit' ya."

"When have I ever commented on *your* love life, Mikey? You sleep with girls like they're going out of style; you tell me every fucking detail of what you do with them in the sack. Have you ever even considered that I don't necessarily *like* everything *you* do?"

Mikey once again appeared shocked by my revelation. He looked at me strangely, as if he didn't know who I was. "So sorry for sharing."

"My point is, Mikey, I stay the hell out of that stuff. It's *your* business—not mine to judge."

"Whatever you say, big guy." He allowed a big yawn, as if I was boring him with my useless chatter. "I can be civil. How 'bout you?"

I nodded and pulled out my iPad. It wasn't going to be pretty, but it looked as if the two of us would be able to function together in the office, which was a huge relief because the last thing I wanted was to have to fire Mikey. But if I was going to be brutally honest with myself, firing Mikey was the *second*-to-last thing I wanted to do. Because the *last* thing I wanted was to do anything to hurt Tristan or Savannah. "So break out your notes from the last job meeting at McPhee. Any changes in the plans?"

CHAPTER 21

Tristan

"IF THINGS had been, like, say, *different* for you when you were a kid, I think you would've turned into quite an athlete."

"Yeah? You think?"

Robby smacked my rear end kind of sharply the way *real* athletes did on TV as he passed by me on his way to where Savi sat on a bench watching us. I just stood there overwhelmed by my stupid and most likely underserved feelings of pride in how well I'd played. He didn't look back at me, but I could still hear him yell before he spiked the football hard, "You heard what those guys said. They wanted to know what high school we played for?"

He was right; those two teenaged athletes, all dressed in their royal-blue-and-gold school jackets and sweatpants, had watched us toss the football back and forth for a while, and then had sauntered up to us wanting to know where we were from. And seeing how giddy I was at even the suggestion of having played on a *real* team, Robby had bluffed. "It's pretty far away from here, in Rhode Island. You've probably never even heard of it, but this guy"—he'd given me another one of those butt whacks—"is the QB."

For several weeks now, we'd been going to the park a couple of afternoons a week when I was off work and when Robby could manage to escape his office, for what he called "football boot camp." It seemed I was his prize, if not his only, student. Savannah came to watch us whenever her class schedule allowed.

I glanced over at Robby and Savannah, sitting on the bench under a huge leafless oak tree, all wrapped up in a lively chat. Whenever I saw them together, laughing and teasing each other like they'd been friends forever, I couldn't help but think, *My family.* But usually I wasn't thinking in terms of specific roles within the family; right now as I approached them, they were beaming at me eerily, as if they were my proud parents and I'd just won the Student-Athlete-of-the-Year Award.

All excited, Savannah grabbed Robby's hand, but she was still looking at me. "I didn't know you had it in you, Tris."

"That's because he never had a chance before. But seeing as I'm nothing but an overgrown high school jock, he's gonna get plenty of chances to be *this threesome's* star athlete." Savannah and I turned to stare at him, unsure of how to react. Robby had never referred to our relationship as a "threesome" before. "What? You guys think we're *not* a threesome?"

I had absolutely no plans to put my foot in my mouth, so I said nothing.

Savannah, direct as always, cut straight to the heart of the matter. "You know, you're right: we really are a threesome. So tell me, how do you feel about it, Robby? You know, being part of a *voluntary* love triangle?"

I couldn't believe she'd asked him that.

Robby stood up, covered his even features with one large palm, and then wiped his other palm on the front of his sweatpants. "I feel better, *happier,* than I ever have before." He dropped his hand from his face and began to study the way the toe of his left sneaker was digging into the dirt, so I still couldn't see his eyes too well.

But Savi wasn't finished with her little fact-finding mission. "We haven't been sexual, beyond a kiss or a hug or a touch. This must be strange for you." It was one of those statements that was really much more of a question. I wondered if Robby would take the bait.

He shook out the big plaid blanket that he'd stuck in the back of the Jeep, laid it down on the grass, and then he plunked his backside on one side of it, stretching out and inviting me with his eyes to lie down next to him. I hesitated, unsure as to what was coming, but Savi grabbed my hand, led me to the blanket, and sort of pushed me down between them.

"It's not strange. Well, maybe at first it was a bit confusing. But I think I'm figuring out how we fit together." I noticed that my partners caught each other's eyes over my head. Then Robby looked right at me. "Tristan, can I kiss you?"

I sat up quickly and instinctively checked all around me to see if anyone was within earshot, or even eyeshot. And we were alone. Not a single soul was at the park, just the three of us. Savannah gently but insistently pulled me back down.

"Robby asked you a question. Aren't you going to answer him?" Her voice was smooth, cool. Unsurprised.

I turned to Savannah, my lifeline; I was completely panic-stricken. But she was smiling at me as if everything was okay. Then I turned to Robby. He didn't appear as freaked out as I figured he would be, since what he was suggesting was kind of groundbreaking for all three of us, in more ways than one. His blue-eyed gaze was so soft and hopeful, and I realized quickly that I'd never been looked at in precisely that way before.

"Only if you want to, Tris."

If *I* wanted to?

Nothing sexual had ever happened to me by *my* choice.

Did I want to?

In the past with Savannah, I'd desperately wanted to make love, but I just couldn't make it happen. Between us there hadn't been fear, and there *had* been love, certainly, and a level of attraction, too, but it had all been there except *this*. This certain something, maybe you could call it a fascination, or maybe more an infatuation, that existed between Robby and me. But until now, it had always been so very easy to blame my lack of drive, I guess you could call it, on impotence resulting from all of the unresolved sexual issues left over from my messed-up childhood.

This was now, though, and the person who wanted to kiss me was Robby. It was time to figure out what I wanted, wasn't it? Not that I didn't already know that I wanted to kiss Robby, because I did, beyond a doubt. But this one small kiss would change things, and I didn't know what those things would be changed into.

What about Savannah? What was she supposed to be doing when I was locking lips with our boyfriend? And what about the easy-going, no-pressure, happy-go-lucky relationship we'd built? "What do you say, Tristan, baseball or football this afternoon?" "You up for a game of Monopoly or Clue, Savi?" "You choose, Robby, *Die Hard with a Vengeance* or *Rocky II*?" "Chinese or Italian, you guys?" Until now, those had been our only concerns.

It was truly amazing how many thoughts passed through my mind in what amounted to probably no more than a couple of seconds. And somehow I managed to hold myself back from making excuses as to why I couldn't kiss him. I didn't come up with any manipulations to convince Robby he shouldn't kiss me, either.

Instead, I said, "I want to." *Did I just say that?* What I really should've said was, "You *can't* want to kiss me—I'm all used and ruined." But no, I'd just proclaimed out loud to these two people, individuals I cared about more than myself, that I wanted to kiss *one* of them.

Thankfully, what happened next unfolded very slowly. Slow enough for me to be able to deal with it. Savannah sort of pushed on my shoulders so that I was lying on my side, facing Robby. And she did not let go of me; her small hands remained firmly pressed to my shoulder and the side of my neck, each of them rubbing just a little bit. And then Robby reached, and I'm talking as slow as a sloth, for my hands, which were definitely shaking at that point. First, he lifted them to his lips, as if he was sampling what it was like to kiss another man's skin. I watched as his lips touched the back of my hands, and his eyes closed like he was concentrating. Then his hands let go of mine and they rose gradually to my face, where one of them somehow joined up with the hand that Savannah had pressed to my neck, and Robby leaned in for a kiss.

The tender touch of his lips to mine completely shattered me. My body, and I mean my entire body—from my lips to my toes—tightened and tingled and nearly burst apart with the pure thrill. And my heart, well, my heart wasn't unaffected by that thrill, and that's a fact, but there was also something else there. Something I'd never known and had never sought out. This puzzling feeling was safe, yet scary. Comforting, yet disturbing. Yeah, the kiss was powerful in the same way as an earthquake—frightening yet exhilarating all at once. In fact, I couldn't have reasonably bet my life as to whether or not the earth had actually shaken when our lips met.

And when that extraordinary kiss was over, four loving hands remained on my body, calming and stilling me with their presence. When I opened my eyes, Robby was looking at me with the very same soft sweetness in his eyes. He was okay; he was fine.

I turned to study Savi's face. She wore an identically soft, sweet expression to Robby's; Savannah was okay too. Looking back at him one more time, the fall afternoon sunshine brightening the slight smile on his strong jaw, I realized that the kiss had been right for all three of us. Today's kiss had moved our uncertain little group in a definite direction, although I had to admit I was far from prepared to examine our new course very closely at this point.

So I just took a deep breath and moved so that I was again on my back between them, looking up at the blue sky and bare trees. Then I reached for my partners' hands and tried to smile.

Looking back.... Savannah

I GUESS what had happened next had been predictable in the way a made-for-TV movie was predictable. You know how they always went; the boy found the girl, the girl fell in love with the boy, the boy sacrificed himself for the girl, the boy lost the girl, the girl found the boy, and then came the happily ever after. But this had been real life so I hadn't expected any of that. And the fact was, what I'd found that day had been merely the tattered remnants of the person I'd met years ago. I'd hated to admit it back then as much as I hate to admit it now, but since I'd always tried to stick to a pretty firm tell-it-like-it-is policy, I had. What had been left of Tristan hadn't been pretty. I'd realized I had a lot of work to do if I was going to achieve that Hallmark movie happy ending I so desired.

I'd only been working at my job at the S-Squared Diner for two days, mostly shadowing Lil as I learned to be a waitress, when Gus had asked me if I could do him a favor and go down into the basement and get another tub of mayonnaise. He'd explained exactly where it could be found, and had warned me that he had a boy working down there, cutting up cardboard with a box cutter, and he was a "good kid" who'd been doing odd jobs for him off and on for years, so I shouldn't be startled when I saw him. I'd stepped down the creaky basement stairs, on the lookout for rats and roaches, and I'd stumbled right into Tristan.

For as long as I live, I will never forget Tristan's expression when he saw me and recognition set in. My old friend had looked like he'd seen the face of God. And I'm fairly sure I'd looked the very same way. His bloodshot dark eyes had narrowed and then quickly widened. When he'd opened his scraggly, bearded lips to speak, I couldn't miss a wide gap where a good portion of a side incisor was missing, but no sound had come out except for a nasty cough. After his brief coughing spell, he'd just let his jaw drop and his mouth had hung open.

I had tried to approach him, but he'd stepped back each time I'd gotten closer, hurting my feelings deeply, but at the same time giving me a better perspective of his alarmingly bony frame. And finally he'd spoken. "Just stay there. Stay where you are and don't move. Please don't move."

When I'd stared back at him in wounded disbelief, now fully taking in his disheveled hair and frayed clothing, Tristan had rushed to explain. "I'm afraid that you're not real, Savannah, and if I try to touch you, you might disappear." His voice had been rough and raggedy, a perfect match to the rest of him. He'd looked like a street person, and it had dawned on me quickly: it was very likely he was still living on the street.

And so I'd immediately set my mind to proving to Tristan exactly how real I was. I'd flung myself into his smelly and gangly arms and then had hung onto one of his trembling shoulders like it was a lifeline. Because he had, indeed, long been my lifeline: the memory of how he'd put me first when I'd needed someone the most had truly kept me going through my lonely teenaged years. Tristan had swayed away from me a bit when I'd run my fingers through his dirty, tangled hair, as if the familiarity of my reassuring touch had been too intimate for him to endure, and so I'd dropped my hands, stepped back, and allowed him to use my shoulder to steady himself.

"I told you I'd find you. I told you, Tristan."

By then, I'd been crying and he'd been crying, and I'd gone back to clinging to him, to his wrists this time, my grip now desperate and clawlike.

"Savi, I never expected to see you again." As he'd put words to his utter shock at seeing my face in this dank and chilly cellar, I'd mentally summed up his condition the way a social worker might have done. Tristan had been close to starving and filthy and sick with a cough that he couldn't seem to suppress. "I can't believe you're really here. How long can I have with you before you gotta leave?"

"Leave you?" And that had been the moment that I'd made a promise to myself and to him. "You're not alone now, Tristan. And you'll never be alone again."

And finally, I'd felt his wrists twist out of my grasp and his hands had closed possessively around mine.

CHAPTER 22

Tristan

THE only person who would understand this was Sandy.

I mean, it wasn't as if I was kicking Savi to the curb as my number-one confidante, but she was just too close to this situation for me to separate her feelings and her needs from my own. In fact, Savannah's heart and mind and soul had been completely wrapped up with mine ever since the day she'd found me in Gus's basement.

"Sit down, T, and tell me what's got you acting as serious as a heart attack, instead of your usual goofy self." We stood together outside near the loading dock. Sandy lit up a cigarette and puffed in.

It was cool but not too breezy, even though we were near the water, so I knew it wouldn't be too cold to stay outdoors and talk for our full break. Outside near the busy street, I could relax a bit and stop clutching onto my feelings with such a tight fist. "I've just been thinking a lot about, well, about how—you're gonna think I'm nuts to ask you this—but how did you know *for sure* that you wanted to be with women?" I reached up and ran my hand through my hair. "No, no, that's not really it. I *know* my sexuality, even if I don't broadcast it. What I *really* want to know is more like how did you know without a doubt that you wanted to act on it with a woman, you know?"

"Why? Do you think you're a lesbian?" She smacked me hard with her free hand, and then pulled the red lipstick-smeared cigarette from her lips to laugh at her own joke. "I'm just kidding, honey, you know that."

"Seriously, Sandy, I need to know." I didn't even smack her back. "How do you know when you're ready? I mean, when it's the right time to *do something*?" I blushed, knowing that these questions must've sounded extremely naïve coming from the mouth of a twenty-three-year-old man who'd started having sexual intercourse when he was barely eleven.

"Okay, Tris, I've told you before, I always knew I liked girls. Back in grade school, before I even knew about sex, I just wanted a lot of closeness with other girls. As I got a little older, I had these minicrushes on some of my friends, if you know what I mean. I was ready to act on it, and I actually *did* act on it at the end of high school. And I've been acting on it ever since!"

This was a perfect example of what I loved about Sandy; she put my needs first. Her curiosity over why I was asking her all this stuff took a backseat to her desire to help me by providing me with the answers I needed. Often, in more detail than I wanted. "Well, Sandy, I *don't* really know anything about how normal sexual relations play out, that's why I'm asking. My grade school years didn't offer me much of an opportunity to reflect on who I was or what I wanted, that is, beyond food and a corner to hide in. Mostly, I was trying to survive the ride with my family. And with my Uncle Ben."

Sandy dropped her cigarette and ground it into the cement with her sensible black waitress's shoe, which she absolutely despised. Then she raked brightly painted fingernails through short black spikes of hair that she kept gelled into a single point. "And your teenage years out there on the street weren't exactly introspective years for you either, were they?"

"Not even slightly. And since I've been with Savannah, it's been so easy to shut out the whole sexual side of me. You know, to say that I'm just not a sexual person and be done with it."

She threw her arms around my neck and whispered into my ear. "You've been too comfortable living as brother and sister with Savannah, honey, that's all. I think it's time to break out of your comfy little box, hmm?"

"But I never felt much sexually—I mean, I've never really felt *anything*—before I met *this person*." God, could I sound any more cryptic? She already knew I was talking about a guy. "Sandy, up until recently, I really didn't think I was a sexual person at all. I thought I'd lost all of that when all those things happened when I was young."

Sandy was on the small side, but she was still sort of a bruiser. She put her hands on the collar of my coat and pushed me backward until my back was pressed up against the building's brick siding. "How could you have expected to feel anything when you were just an object for assholes to use to satisfy their lust?" I winced at her words because they were so blunt, and she saw me do it, but she still pressed on. "That doesn't make you asexual, Tristan. You just never got a chance when you were growing up to feel safe enough to figure it all out. Now you do." She was studying me so intently I could almost feel her gaze on my face.

"Yeah, I guess, but it's so weird. Feeling this way."

Her cherubic face split into a grin. "You're falling, honey, ahh yes, my boy is falling in love." And she didn't ask about who he was, because she knew I'd tell her when I was ready. "Don't worry, T.... This may sound cliché, but just follow your heart." She slid her hand over to where my heart was. "You have a beautiful heart, hon, and it won't steer you wrong."

"Okay, Sandy, talking to you about this helped. I guess I owe you some good advice now."

"Don't worry about it, kid. I'm always glad to help, and you know you're the first person I'll come to when I need to get my own ducks in a row."

CHAPTER 23

Robby

"ROBBY, what are you doing here?" Savannah looked a bit surprised, but she'd asked me with a smile so I knew she wasn't pissed off that I'd more or less snuck up on her.

"Figured that my number-one girl would be here getting her Tuesday night mocha latte. And I wasn't wrong."

Savannah slid over in the booth and patted the place beside her. "Sit down, Robby." Then she flagged down Lil and ordered for me. "Lil, can you get Robby a cup of coffee, a bit on the dark side? And how about a piece of Gus's apple pie with just a single scoop of vanilla ice cream? Oh, and don't forget to warm up the pie." Lil nodded and was rewarded with one of Savannah's sweet, gap-toothed smiles. Then Savannah redirected her attention to me. "So how did you come to be in this neck of the woods tonight?"

"Well, the head of maintenance from the university called and asked me to meet him at the end of his work day. Seems that they liked the job we did on the classrooms and they have a few more projects in mind for Dalton Builders."

Clapping her hands together, she squealed, "Oh, Robby, that's awesome!" Then she sipped her mocha and said more seriously, "Good things happen to good people. You must have some excellent karma, hmm?"

I shrugged at her and placed my hands on my lap as Lil served my coffee. "Thanks, ma'am."

I could tell by her crooked expression that Lil wasn't quite certain whether to like me or to be suspicious of me. "I'll be back in a couple of minutes with your pie."

"So, will you give me a ride home? Then you can come in and see Tris if he's home from work." She looked hopeful, as she always did when she was trying to arrange for Tristan and me to get together.

"Sure, but Savannah, I thought that maybe *you and I* could spend some time together. You know, maybe we could hang out here for a while."

First, she looked perplexed, followed immediately by an expression of deep concern. She was worried I was still more interested in her than in Tristan.

So I set her straight. "Don't worry, Savannah, I'm into him. That's what you wanted all along, isn't it?"

Her expression didn't change. But she nodded once.

"You have nothing to be concerned about, then. Tristan is amazing. It's like since I've gotten to know him, I can finally feel *that way* for someone. Really feel it, you know?"

Savannah's tight expression loosened into one of relief. "Oh God, it's so good to hear you say that!"

"But you're an important part of this equation too. You mean a lot to both of us."

Before Savannah had a chance to respond, Lil stopped in front of our table and sort of slung the plate of pie across the table toward me. The ice cream was already melting over the top. Savannah pushed the ice cream off the pie with her fork.

"So what's your plan, Savannah?"

She pulled the plate in front of her and took a tiny, genteel bite of the pie, as if she was just sampling it. "I don't know what you mean—*my plan*?"

I ignored her protest. "I'm ready to take things to the next level with him. I need to know what you want—how you want to fit in—with us."

"You ask too many questions, Robby."

I grabbed my own fork and allowed myself to be distracted by the delicious pie. While I was doing that, Savannah showed her cards, I guess you could say. Her nervousness was betrayed in the way she twirled her finger in her hair and by how she repetitively shifted her weight, leaning side to side. So I did what I'd learned to do with Tristan; I waited for her words to come.

When they came, they were in her straightforward, I-mean-business manner. "Let's just allow things to just fall into place, hmm? A 'relationship of three' isn't necessarily modeled after an equal-sided triangle."

"You mean an *equilateral* triangle." My fork clattered onto the half-empty plate. "Are you comparing our relationship to an *isosceles* triangle?"

"Only if isosceles is the kind with only two equal sides."

"*Congruent* sides."

"Whatever, Robby. Equations, congruent, isosceles—we're not in geometry class. And you know what I mean. I told you that it was okay if you and Tris got close in ways that I'm not necessarily a part of, remember?"

"Yeah, that's a pretty difficult thing for a guy to forget." I took her hand into mine. It was cold, despite the fact that she'd been holding a hot drink. "I'm falling for him really hard, Savannah. I didn't know that I could feel like this. But you, *you* are part of us too."

Strangely, Savannah didn't seem at all shaken up by my confession. "I want you to do what feels right with Tristan, and we don't have to have a formal discussion about it. So don't worry about me—this is exactly what I'd hoped would happen with you guys. And yeah, I'll admit it, maybe I *did* have a plan."

"Why? Why would you do this? What's in it for you?"

"Just don't hurt him." She'd become quite skilled at dodging my questions. "You know how innocent he is."

Many people wouldn't refer to Tristan as innocent. He'd been having sex since he was a boy, he'd been gang-raped as a teen in an attempt to protect Savannah, and it was not unlikely that he had even sold himself when he'd lived on the streets. But he was still so innocent. "I know how innocent he is, Savannah. Much more so than me."

She smiled at me with satisfaction because she knew I understood.

"I never was interested in the pure and innocent type of girl, you know. Maybe I knew deep down inside that I couldn't take a girl's innocence, seeing as I wasn't planning to keep her. But it's different with Tris."

Savannah studied my face, in the mood to listen now, so I didn't disappoint.

"I know he's had sex before, probably more times than I have, but he's never experienced sensuality. You know, he's completely innocent to the pleasures of the flesh."

"Robby, that sounds almost biblical." She smirked and then squeezed my fingers. "But I know what you mean."

"I want to show him all of the flirting and the thrill and physical pleasure that can come with sex."

Savannah's face scrunched up a bit, once again revealing signs of concern. "Yeah, Robby, satisfying sex is great and all that. Just don't hurt him."

Realizing that she'd already given me that exact same warning before, I took her chin in my hand and said evenly, looking directly into her eyes, "I promise it won't hurt him. I'll go slowly. Very slowly."

"Oh, Robby. Don't you get it?" Her eyes were wide and intense. "There's more than one way to hurt someone."

That's when I realized she was referring to his heart not his body. She was pleading with me to never break Tristan's heart. "I won't. I won't hurt him *that* way eith—"

"I don't know if he could stand it." Her eyes had filled. There was no question of her love for Tristan. None whatsoever. Only my love for him was in question now.

"Put that worry to rest, Savannah. I'm in this with Tristan for the long haul. But that doesn't answer my question from earlier. So just tell me, what do *you* get out of all of this? What exactly do you want from Tris and me?"

A tear trickled down the side of her face but she brushed it away irritably as soon as she'd shed it. "All I need is to know that you guys will always be my family and that no matter where I go I'll have a home to return to. A home where I know Tristan is safe and happy." She looked down at where our fingers were entwined on her lap. "I want you guys to love me and welcome me home when I've been away and save a place for me at your table."

It was becoming quite clear. "But not in our bed?"

Savannah shook her head slowly but emphatically. "No."

"I think I understand." I leaned forward and hugged her firmly. "The place you want with Tristan and me is in our hearts, and I can promise you that you will always have a home there, Savannah."

"Then let's not talk about this anymore. And we shouldn't tell Tris about this conversation, at least not until he's ready to hear about it, okay?"

I nodded.

"Don't hold back from Tristan. Just go where your heart takes you."

She looked so solemn and earnest that I found myself nodding again.

"And Robby, I trust you to never hurt him."

Chapter 24

Robby

So THERE we sat. Savannah, Tristan, and me. With all of them.

"Where's the goddamned cranberry sauce, Martha? You can't expect me to eat turkey without any goddamned cranberry sauce!" My sputtering father sat at the head of the table.

"Oh my, I'm so sorry, John. I left it in the refrigerator—it's not the canned kind, you know. I made it from *real* cranberries, just the way you like it." My groveling mother, who had been sitting to his left, started to rise from her chair.

"Sit back down, Mom. I'll get it. And take a chill pill, Dad, it's only cranberry sauce, not the Holy Eucharist." My sister was really the only one in our family who was allowed to put my father in his place. Which she did quite frequently and with enthusiasm.

"Did you know that a single serving of cranberries provides you with 25 percent of your daily requirement of Vitamin C?" As expected, my brother-in-law, Brandon, who sat at the opposite end of the table from my father, was trying to distract everyone from this afternoon's bicker-fest, otherwise known as the Dalton Family Thanksgiving Day Meal.

"C is for crayon, Grampa." Madison was not one to be left out of a conversation.

"Yes, Madison, C is for crayon, and it is also for cranberry sauce, which is still conspicuously absent from this table!" Yes, my father was still waiting impatiently for his condiment.

Looking across the table to where Tristan and Savannah sat on either side of Lindsey, I expected to see classic "your family is nuts—where is Dr. Phil when you need him?" expressions on their faces. But I actually felt the need to rub my eyes and take a second look, because both of my partners sported equally serene smiles. Catching my eye one by one, they each shrugged at me tolerantly, as if my bickering family at the dining room table was no more irritating than a bunch of play-fighting kittens in a wicker basket. *Whatever.* If behavior that seemed humiliating to me appeared entertaining, or even endearing, to my partners, who was I to complain? Apparently, they were both still quite pleased to be here.

Now, the reason Savannah and Tristan were both sitting here in the Daltons' formal dining room patiently listening to us squabble was because on the Saturday before Thanksgiving, I'd received a rather timid phone call from my mother. "Rob? Is that you, Rob?"

"Uh, you dialed my number, Mom. Who did you expect?"

"Oh, yes, of course. You're right." A self-conscious giggle.

"So what's up?"

"Well, dear, I was just calling you to check in about Thanksgiving. I wanted to invite you over at two o'clock."

"Since when have you been so formal, Mom? Of course I'll be there. At two, like always."

"That's nice, dear." She stopped talking and I could hear her suck in a deep breath. "And by the way, your friend Mike DeSalvo stopped by last night. It seems you have a young lady friend you've neglected to mention to your father and me."

Immediately, perspiration broke out on my forehead. I wondered what else Mikey had told her.

"Rob, you *do* have a new lady friend, *don't you?*"

Wiping my sleeve across my forehead, I answered curtly, "Well, yeah, but what was Mikey doing over at your house?"

I could hear the smile in her voice. "Mike's been stopping by a lot lately with cookies from his mother's bakery. And they are absolutely to die for! I haven't been buttoning my pants so easily since he started visiting, come to think of it." I knew she had stopped talking for a moment to consider her growing waistline. Dad always told her that he wasn't attracted to fat women, so being a rather large-boned person, she'd always watched what she ate almost obsessively. "That boy is such a sweetheart."

"You think?" I wasn't happy with the news that Mikey had become a regular participant in my parents' lives. And the part about Mikey being a sweetheart, well, that was definitely debatable.

"He told us your girl was quite attractive, though he used words that I wouldn't repeat, being a lady. He said she's blonde, like all of us."

"That's right, Mom. Savannah's very pretty." I was feeling more uncomfortable by the moment. "Did Mikey say anything else?" If he'd said anything twisted about Tristan and me. Well, he better not have, that's all.

"Not too much, dear. Except he mentioned that you have not been spending much time with him lately. And I think that's a shame, Rob. You shouldn't allow your friendships to slip away just because you met a woman."

I really didn't need to be lectured by my mother about the finer aspects of my friendship with Michael DeSalvo. "Right, Mom."

"So anyways, I would like to invite you and your lady friend to our house for dinner on Thursday."

The moment of truth had arrived. So naturally, I hesitated. "Uh, Mom, you see, Savannah has this roommate—he *seems* like a nice enough guy—and he doesn't have any family in the area and is it alright if he tags along with us to dinner?" So much for my moment of truth.

"Oh certainly, Rob. There's always room at our table for one more."

And at that moment I had felt an incredible sensation of relief because I knew the three of us would be together on Thanksgiving Day.

"Do you need to have your hearing checked, son?" My father's demanding voice brought me right back to the dinner table. "I asked how you met Savannah."

"Oh, sorry, Dad. I guess my mind was on business," I lied, reaching up to unbutton the second button of my shirt, as if that would make it any easier to breathe. "I met Savannah after a job meeting at Somerville University, she's a student there." I shifted my ass on the stiff cushion of the dining room chair in a futile effort to get more comfortable.

"Somerville University?" Dad repeated the institution's name, his nose wrinkled with distaste. S.U. wasn't exactly a country club of a college; it was schooling at its most basic level, designed to educate those who hadn't been born with a silver spoon anywhere in the vicinity. "What are you studying there?"

Savannah did not appear even slightly daunted by my father's arrogance. She spoke to him patiently, as if he was a child. "I'm a graduate student, Mr. Dalton, in the School of Education. I want to be a high school guidance counselor."

"Education?" Dad coughed a few times, rather forcefully. I half expected a pea to come rocketing out of his throat, shoot midair down the length of the table, and hit Brandon in the forehead. "You won't make any money in that field, young lady."

In response, Savannah's jaw dropped. Coupled with her bulging eyes, she really made quite a picture. Before she told him off, I stepped in. "Dad, Savannah isn't pursuing counseling for the money. She wants to help teenagers in crisis."

My father continued to examine Savannah critically, but directed his words to me. "Like I always said to Lindsey when she was in school, it isn't easy to make a living in this economy." He didn't look pleased at all, and he demonstrated that by wrinkling his nose again. But finally he conceded. "I guess *somebody* needs to do that sort of work, though. And you *are* both women, so you'll end up raising families, not being breadwinners."

Lindsey rolled her eyes, as she was accustomed to Dad's chauvinism as well as the complete lack of value he placed in social services, but Tristan and Savannah both appeared flabbergasted at my father's attitude, which I'd honestly never questioned until that very moment. In fact, I'd constantly strived to prove to my stockbroker father that my chosen field of construction management was a worthy one.

Buttering a roll, Dad turned his thick neck to look at Tristan. "So, Tristan, Rob's buddy, Mike, tells me that you are a *waiter*." He might as well have said that Mikey told him Tris was a serial killer. His tone of voice would have been identical.

Warily, and for good reason, Tristan lifted his gaze from his dinner plate and looked at my father. "Yes, sir. I work at Michael's on the Waterfront, on the Boston Harb—"

"I know exactly where it is." Dad cut him off curtly, midword. "How *did* you get involved in the practice of *that* type of work?" Again, the same disgusted tone that sounded as though he wanted to say, "How *did* you get involved in the practice of tossing live kittens from moving vehicles?"

And then there was silence. Yes, it was Tristan's thinking kind of silence that I had become accustomed to, but I knew my father would have no use for it. Everyone at the table gawked at Tris, as he dipped his head and ran his hands through his hair. "I guess one thing just led to another and I found myself working at Michael's. I really like it there, sir. I love to serve people and see them enjoying themselves."

My father's expression shifted rapidly. From distaste to disgust to disbelief in a mere second. It was record-setting. "Didn't you even go to college?"

Tristan's head fell further and I knew what was coming next, because I also knew he'd barely managed to get his GED. He raised both of his shaking hands to that silky dark hair at once and began to move them around in agitation. It was clear that Tristan was in dire need of rescuing. And who was it to come galloping in on a white horse, ready and willing to sweep him up and save him from this terrible interrogation? Yes, it was Savannah.

"Mr. Dalton, Tristan is a very *good* waiter." She spoke with pride. Tristan glanced up just slightly and caught her eye. I could see his pain—it was right there, bubbling out of those sensitive brown eyes.

And she may as well have said, "Mr. Dalton, Tristan is a very *good* male stripper." Her sweet compliment did absolutely nothing in terms of raising my father's opinion of Tristan. Open, honest, caring Tristan, who'd dressed with such care today in his best shirt and tie and fancy slacks in an effort to make a good impression on my family. But no, my dad had not been even slightly impressed by any aspect of Tristan Chartrand. He abruptly turned away from Tristan as if he was no longer worthy of his attention.

"Brandon took me to Michael's for Mother's Day. God, it was amazing!" Lindsey was clearly stepping in to assist Savannah in Tristan's liberation from my father's oppression. "I had the seafood chowder first and then the Lobster Alfredo."

Tristan lifted his head a bit more and spoke quietly. "Those were excellent choices, Lindsey. We *are* rather famous for our seafood chowder." I sincerely hoped that he was oblivious to my father's rudely rolling eyeballs. "Next time you are going to Michael's, have Robby tell me. I'll take good care of you."

Lindsey smiled and even blushed, because she could tell he meant it. And then my mother chimed in with, "That sounds heavenly, dear. John, maybe the four of us could go together? I'd love to try the Lobster Ravioli. I've heard it is wonderful."

Dad simply looked at her blankly and then dove into his meal, predictably spouting his stocks and bonds discourse between bites.

AFTER dinner, we all gathered in the living room to view the newly decorated Christmas tree. My mother always managed to have it set up for our Thanksgiving celebration because she loved to have us eat our pumpkin pie beneath its lights. And Savannah was decorated as festively as any holiday gift that would go beneath that tree. A forest-green velvet dress, a perky red satin bow at the small of her back, and a ribbon of green velvet holding her golden ringlets off of her face. Yes, she looked like a gift most men would be in a huge rush to unwrap. And although I appreciated her beauty, I was much more interested in unwrapping all of the secrets that enfolded the man who sat on the floor by her feet, leaning against the couch.

While Savannah chatted enthusiastically with my sister about the lack of crisis programs for at-risk teens in local high schools, Tristan sat silently, seemingly taking in the aura of a real family holiday. Probably for the first time in a long while. Maybe ever. It was nearly impossible for me not to stare at his delicate face in order to study that wistful expression. But I knew I had to hold back; the others would surely notice me gawking at my "girlfriend's" roommate and it would raise eyebrows.

But Jesus, it was a challenge to drag my gaze from his face. And it was even more of a challenge to restrain myself from moving to his side, just to feel the warmth of his body against mine. Or better yet, to reach up and loosen his tie, to smooth my hand over the silky skin of his face, to stroke my fingers through his hair so softly, like he'd once stroked mine. I found my fingers itching to do those things, and honestly, the list of things I wanted to do didn't end there.

I needed to distract myself from the intensity of what I was thinking and feeling for Tristan, from what I was now fairly certain was Robby Dalton falling in love for the first time. "Tris, you love a good game of Go Fish." I shuffled the deck of cards that I'd picked up off of the bookshelf. "Come on over here and we'll show Maddy how it's played."

"Uncle Robby, I already *knows* how to play Go Fish. And even Daddy can't never, ever beat me at it." Nonetheless, she'd dropped her baby doll right where she was standing and was on my lap in a split second, all ready to play.

Crawling over to the coffee table where I was already dealing the cards, Tristan wore the sweetest smile. He truly did love to play children's card games and I knew he was going to love getting to know Maddy even more. That was when the front door burst open and Mikey DeSalvo, towing this year's nameless Thanksgiving date behind him, barged his way through the front door.

"Mista and Miz Dalton, I brought ya family a nice big platter of cannoli. My mama just put 'em together 'specially for you." Smiling widely, he hugged my mother and then lifted up the hand of the bimbo. "This here is, uh, Monica, yeah. We're just on our way to the bar at her hotel and we wanted to stop by wit' these." He nodded to the dessert platter he held in his other hand.

"Why, thank you for the treats, Michael. I'm sure we'll all enjoy them." My mother was suddenly fluttering about, placing the cannoli on the coffee table, and then she scurried off to drag a bench in from the hallway. "Sit down, sit down, you two, and have a cup of coffee and some pie with us before you go."

Mikey approached the couch where my very pregnant sister sat beside Savannah. He leaned over and hugged her like a brother would. Then he quickly stepped over to where Brandon sat and put his hand on the man's shoulder. "You's looking damn good, have ya been hitting the gym, my man?" Mikey completely avoided my eyes as he crossed the room, but he did mumble something like "hey, man" as he passed by me. My father stood up and shook his hand heartily, and then they exchanged more than a few quiet words under their breath. After their little chat, Mikey whirled around and directed his attention to Madison, who was still seated on my lap. "And you, my little princess, I brought you a pretty ring. It's in this here velvet box. And I got me a secret; it's the same color blue as your eyes." He bent down to hand her the box.

"You are not s'posed to tell secrets, Mr. D. 'Cause if you tell them, then they isn't secrets anymore." Nevertheless, she reached for the velvet box and was soon sporting a shiny blue plastic bauble on her index finger.

"Madison, you are supposed to say thank you when someone gives you a present." My sister didn't let her get away with too much. "I'm *waiting*."

"Thank you, Mr. D.," Maddy replied obediently. She was a very rule-oriented child.

"And you, baby, have got yourself the prettiest ring in town."

I waited for what I knew was coming, and Madison did not disappoint. "I am *not* a baby."

Yes, Mikey was quite charming, bearing sweets and gifts and secrets and hugs, but he did not once so much as acknowledge the presence of Tristan and Savannah. I wondered if my family had noticed his slight.

"Please, Mike, sit down and make yourself at home." My father's voice was friendlier than it had been all night. "You too, Monica."

"Nah, we ain't here to impose. Just stopped by to wish a happy Turkey Day to my good friends."

"At least let me walk you two kids out to the car." Dad was on his feet in a flash, grabbing his zip-up sweatshirt off of the back of his chair. And he was eager. Much too eager.

When I looked over at Tristan's downcast expression, I decided I'd had enough of our family holiday. So I got to my feet as well. "See you later, Mikey. And nice to meet you, Monica." I still had manners. "I think it is time that we started getting ready to head out too."

My mother headed for the kitchen to pack us each a plate of leftovers. That left Tris, Savannah, and me alone with my sister's family.

"Well, there was certainly a chill in the air when Mikey came in the room, huh?" My sister hadn't missed Mikey's snub of my partners. She looked squarely at Savannah. "He doesn't seem to care for you two very much at all. Why is that?" Yes, Lindsey was very observant, and even more direct.

But then, so was Savannah. "Well, Lindsey, I can't say that I'm particularly fond of him either. He has not shown himself to be very polite and respectful in my presence." Savannah did not dip her head shyly as Tristan would have. She held her head high and stared right back into Lindsey's eyes. "His rudeness tonight was to be expected. Not a surprise at all."

My sister nodded and then looked to Tristan for his response. As predicted, Tristan was hiding behind the hand he'd placed on his head. "What do you think about Mikey's behavior tonight, Tristan?" Lindsey alone knew my feelings for Tristan. I'm sure she was very interested in his response.

"I, um, I can't help but feel sort of bad for Mikey. I mean, he thinks that because of us, he has lost his best friend. He's hurting, you know?"

In my opinion, the man was far too good-hearted. I shook my head.

"You think that maybe he's jealous of your relationship with Robby?" Brandon interjected. "Robby has really never been close friends with anyone but him."

"Oh, yes, I'm sure Mikey feels jealous. Who could blame him? And although we love spending time with Robby, we would be more than happy to share him." He glanced at me and bit down on his bottom lip, his entire face suddenly blushing to a bright pink. "I meant that *Savannah*, I'm sure, wouldn't mind sharing him." Tristan was becoming emotional. I wasn't sure if it was because he feared he'd slipped up and said too much in front of my sister, or if he was simply upset that my friendship with Mikey was so strained. His pretty eyes had become red around the rims. "I really hope Mikey and Robby can figure out how to fix their friendship. I really do."

At this point, I'd had more than enough family fun for today. I needed to take my partners home and get them settled in their apartment. I wanted to make sure Savannah wasn't angry and Tristan wasn't upset.

I had to take care of my family.

Brandon retrieved our coats and my mother returned from the kitchen with a few filled-up Tupperware bowls. After quick hugs and other pleasantries with my mother and my sister's family, including a reminder from Madison that Tristan and I owed her a game of Go Fish, I led Tris and Savannah to my Jeep, noticing that my dad still stood with Mikey beside his car, deeply absorbed in conversation. So deeply absorbed that he didn't even notice us leaving. Or he just plain didn't care.

I, however, noticed Tristan waving good-bye to my completely oblivious father from the backseat of my Jeep. And then I heard him ask quietly, "Do you think they liked us, Robby?"

Tristan

"COME on over here, buddy, so we can be a little closer." Robby patted the place beside him on the couch and his hopeful blue eyes met mine. "If you're cool with it, I mean."

I got up from my chair and slowly crossed the room, sitting down lightly beside Robby on the couch, when what I'd truly wanted to do was to lunge right over the coffee table and flop myself gracelessly into his arms like a puppy in desperate need of affection.

What was happening to me? I'd lost my ability to set boundaries, to keep my cool, to put Savannah first. Wasn't I supposed to be dating Robby strictly for Savannah's sake, so Savannah would date a man who could give her all that she needed and deserved as a woman? But here I was, all ready and willing to cuddle up on the couch with the very man who could give her all that.

"I'm so confused, Robby. I just want to do what's right and…." I hadn't even realized I was speaking out loud until I'd heard the words ringing in my ears.

"This *is* right, Tristan. You being close to me *is* right. Something inside me won't stop screaming just how right it is." Robby looked at me with such an expression of certainty that I wondered if maybe I actually could believe him. "And Savannah, well, I think she wants this for us too."

So maybe just for tonight I'd let myself believe him. Hadn't Savannah told me over and over again that she wanted me to listen to my heart when it came to Robby? And hadn't Sandy told me the very same thing? I closed my eyes tightly and just pushed all my worries about Savannah out of my mind for the time being.

I turned toward him and then shimmied a little bit closer. Robby lifted one strong arm onto the back of the couch and tentatively wrapped the other around my shoulder. He pulled me against his broad chest, tilted his head until it leaned softly against mine, and gave me a gift that I'd never before admitted I needed. "I feel safe." I'd spoken without thinking again.

The arm that had been waiting patiently on the back of the sofa wound around my other shoulder. He squeezed me firmly. "You *are* safe, Tristan."

My breathing sped up. No man had ever held me this way before. Savannah had tried to hold me, but with her slight arms around me, I'd never felt completely safe. And when Savannah was in *my* arms in bed at night, I wasn't as much holding her as I was clinging to her.

This was different. Not only did I feel protected, but I also felt needy in a way I'd never expected. The sensual feeling was almost too much for me to deal with. I hadn't thought I could feel this way about another person, mostly because women didn't arouse me, and men, well, most men rather terrified me. I squirmed a bit until I was still closer to Robby, feeling even more secure now than ever. I had to smile; he probably thought I was trying to climb into his lap, which actually didn't seem like such a bad idea.

And then there were moist kisses on my neck. Not breathy and slurpy and selfish, but tiny, delicate, almost experimental kisses, that felt like the fluttering of a hundred teeny butterfly wings against my skin. The only problem now was that I knew only too well where necking led. Because yes, a former now-and-then call boy knew things like that. And I waited for Robby to lewdly express his body's physical need, accompanied by the expected rush of fear that would bowl me over.

But neither came.

"You are so sweet." Robby's deep voice was murmuring into my ear. "You are the sweetest thing." But he was still speaking very quietly, not panting with the sort of need that had always led to pain.

Knowing just how far what he'd said was from the truth, though, I kept on waiting for what would surely come next, what had *always* come next: the suggestive words, the wandering hands, the huffing and puffing and humping that had *consistently* been a precursor to me giving a man what he wanted. But surprisingly, even shockingly, all Robby seemed to want was to hold me, to soothe me, to shelter me.

It appeared that he wasn't here simply to use me.

"Everything that has always seemed wrong for me is right with you."

I wanted to shout, "Yes! I know! I feel that way too!" but I couldn't make myself speak. I was still so afraid he'd turn into one of those heated-up, lustful monsters from my past.

"What happens if I fall for you, Tristan?"

Turning my head just slightly, I pressed my lips softly against Robby's throat, the only way I could think of to show him that I'd catch him if he fell, because I'd fallen weeks ago and I was already waiting for him down below. His skin felt rough and stubbly and honestly, fantastic, against my lips. Another first for me.

"What if I've *already* fallen, baby? Tell me, what then?"

And that's when I pushed him back enough so that we could look directly into each other's eyes, and I replied, "I guess I catch you, and then we pick each other up and dust each other off and keep on going, Robby, because I'm pretty sure I've fallen too." I stood up and took Robby's hand in mine. "Let's go to bed."

He stood and followed me down the hall, and as we had done once before, we silently took turns in the bathroom. When we were in the full darkness of the bedroom, we stripped down to our boxers on either side of the bed. In the bed, Savannah had positioned herself all the way on the right edge, so I climbed in the middle, ran my fingers lovingly along the skin of her arm, and then Robby climbed in beside me.

Robby said, "I want to hold you all night." His words didn't scare me.

His words didn't scare me.

And this time, it was *me* who wrapped *my* arms around Robby's bulky shoulders, and I wasn't merely clinging onto him for dear life, but I was giving him what strength I had, and in turn, I was taking his strength into me.

"I think I love you, Robby." Yeah, I just blurted it out.

Robby chuckled softly, and I could feel the skin of his bare chest vibrating a bit against my own. "I can do you one better, Tristan, because I *know* I love you."

He'd said it. Robby loved me too.

"But, Robby, I'm not sweet, you know, like you said before. I've been *used*. You've gotta know that w-when times got really t-tough, like when it was freezing cold outside, or when I was starving, sometimes I sold my *body*. It was all I had to sell. And I think that you have the right to know this." My confession just escaped. It seemed I hadn't spoken a single word tonight that hadn't caught me by surprise. But still I repeated my message so he would understand. "I'm not sweet, not at all."

Suddenly, Robby's hands were on my face, holding it in place, and they were not soft and gentle like before, but instead their grasp was firm, almost rough. Hands that had a purpose. "That's not who you are, it's what you had to do. You did what you had to do and you survived, and I'm just so thankful for that." That's when his lips covered mine, at first tentative, but soon more insistent. And when he stopped kissing me long enough to take a breath, he told me, "I love you, Tris. So much. And believe me, you just can't help it, you're so damned sweet. You *are* the sweetest thing."

And I didn't want to run and hide. I wanted to stay exactly where I was, in Robby's arms, kissing Robby's lips. Safe and loved.

Looking back.... Savannah

IF I'D *thought I had my work cut out for me in locating Tristan, I'd soon learned that finding him had been the easy part. Getting Tristan's life into some semblance of order, now that had been the real challenge.*

Above all else, he'd needed a place to live. A place to feel safe. Lately, Tristan had been staying more or less regularly in the shoebox of a storage room over the S-Squared Diner in exchange for doing odd jobs for Gus. In the corner of the room was a couch that had seen plenty of better days, on which he slept. At the end of the hall was a tiny bathroom with no more than a sink and a toilet and not much else in the way of amenities. But Tris had told me that it had seemed like a castle to him. Since I was eighteen and had aged out of the system, the time had come for me to step out on my own. I'd decided to forgo university housing and find a place that Tristan and I could pay for from the wages we earned at the S-Squared, where we now both worked full-time hours. And we could live together. It hadn't taken us very long to find a small one-bedroom apartment near the square, where Tristan could finally, at long last, make a home.

But there had been so much more to do.

Tristan's physical health had needed addressing; there'd been no question about it. He'd been sick when I'd found him, and it took several courses of strong antibiotics from a local Health Stop to fix that. But I'd had other more serious concerns in the wellness department than his bronchitis. Tristan had been living on the streets for the better part of a decade and he'd confessed to me that he'd done "whatever it took" to stay alive. "Whatever it took," he'd explained flatly, had included turning tricks when he'd found himself in dire straits. That news, coupled with him having had no access to healthcare during that time, had been my incentive to get him to a health clinic ASAP. I'd located a free clinic just south of Boston, where Tristan had undergone a complete physical, including a barrage of blood tests for STDs and HIV, and the doctors there had addressed a whole host of other health concerns as well.

Tristan had faced all of the poking and prodding with little outward emotion. In fact, he'd barely spoken a word during the doctor's appointment or in the days that followed as we'd waited for results. And even when he'd received the phone call that had given him a clean bill of health, he'd said nothing but "Yes, this is Tristan Chartrand speaking." I'd had to take the phone from his loose grasp and finish the conversation with the doctor, who suggested that he repeat certain tests, which he did six months later. His teeth had been a total wreck. Tristan had needed four appointments just to clean things up, and he'd needed more work to fix a broken tooth, but we'd had to save up for almost a year to get that done.

It had not been as simple to repair Tristan's mental health. Though never sullen, Tristan had become extremely withdrawn. Having spent the majority of his time in no one's company but his own, he hadn't ever become accustomed to sharing his thoughts or asking for help. No amount of cajoling on my part had been able to convince him to see a counselor to help him deal with what life had dealt him. Or, more truthfully, how life had cheated him. His mistrust of society had just been too huge. Very gradually, though, Tristan had opened up to me. He'd told me how broken he'd felt, how lost and alone he'd been. Until I'd found him. And I'd changed the course of his life.

And when I'd felt that Tris had been well on his way to good mental health, or at least better mental health, I'd tutored him. Math, English, reading and writing, and even current events. I'd actually been very good at tutoring and successful too. It had been so incredibly rewarding when Tristan had received his GED. When I had seen his face as he grasped his diploma, I had known for certain that helping people was what I'd been born to do.

It had taken nearly two years to complete the bulk of project "Rebuild Tristan," but it had been worth every bit of effort. Out of the discarded fragments of a person I had found, I'd molded Tristan into the healthy, well-adjusted, competent, and loving man I knew he could be.

CHAPTER 25

Tristan

SANDY came up behind me and pinched my side playfully. "Hey, handsome. You've got a phone message at the bar. Phillip asked me to tell you."

"A message? I can't remember the last time I got a call at the bar, Sandy. It must be important. Can you bring water to table eight for me? I'll be right back."

"That is absolutely not a problem, T."

I wondered if Robby had called. Maybe he wanted to pick me up tonight or meet me somewhere after work. Those thoughts had me sort of race-walking to get my message, a stupid grin on my face, no doubt.

"Hey, Tristan." Phillip stood behind the bar hanging wine glasses. "Some dude called you. Hang on, I wrote down a message." He turned around and grabbed a small scrap of paper off the counter. "Yeah, Mike D. is gonna be at the bar here at 10:30 tonight and he wants you to meet him for a drink. Says he wants to talk about 'shit with Rob.'"

"Thanks, Phil. You have a good night, okay?" I headed back to my serving section feeling happier than if it *had been* Robby who had called. Because it was clear from this phone call that Mikey wanted to make peace with Robby. Which was not to say I hadn't experienced a momentary chill of suspicion in regards to Mikey's intentions for wanting to meet me tonight, because, yeah, I was suspicious as hell. I guess mistrust was just how street kids reacted to kind gestures like this. But I forced myself to swallow hard and to push back my overabundance of caution; I was not a street kid anymore, and Mikey was simply a close friend of Robby's who wanted their friendship to move forward in a positive manner.

But the single factor that most swayed me to overlook any sense of wariness I felt in regards to Mikey was that lately, I'd sensed that Robby was truly affected by the breakup of his friendship with his longtime buddy. Not that he said much about it, because he barely ever mentioned his old friend's name, but I could tell that trying to get anything done at work with Mikey had become very stressful for him. And the times when he and I had seen Mikey together, like at the Red Sox game and on Thanksgiving night, Robby couldn't hide his tension. Finally, as he and Mikey were becoming more and more distant, his father and Mikey were growing closer and closer. All of this spelled out d-r-a-m-a, which took a heavy toll on Robby. Above all else, I wanted his happiness. I knew that this was my opportunity to help him. I wasn't going to let it slip past me.

Luckily, I'd wrapped up all of my tables by quarter past ten, so I had a chance to wash up and change my clothes in the men's room before meeting Mikey at the bar.

MIKEY was late. It was almost eleven and the bar was about to close to the public, so I decided I'd just stand outside in front of the restaurant and wait for him there. I still really hoped he'd show up. I wanted to get this whole thing straightened out so Mikey would know how important he was to Robby and they could be friends again.

And I refused to give in to my sheer sense of relief that he hadn't showed up. As I crossed the empty bar, I reminded myself once again that Mikey, however unlikeable he might have been, was a law-abiding business man, and people of his social stature didn't engage in street fights.

"I thought you were meeting somebody at the bar tonight." Phillip was wiping down tables, starting the closing process. "You get stood up?"

I looked down at the floor, a bit embarrassed because it seemed that Mikey was, indeed, a no-show. "I, uh, maybe. I mean, it's starting to look that way."

"Shit, Tristan, if you want to wait around for a half hour or so, I'll be ready to get out of here, and you and me can go get a drink somewhere."

"Thanks, Phillip, but I think I'm gonna go out front and wait for him there. Are you working tomorrow?"

"Nah, got a couple days off."

"Same here. Well, I'll see you later."

I grabbed my jacket and put my tips in the pocket. Then I went out the front entrance, the door locking behind me. It was a cold night so I threw on my wool blazer, which was fairly thin and didn't go very far in the direction of keeping me warm. I decided I'd wait around for another thirty minutes or so; maybe Mikey got caught up with business.

But it wasn't even ten minutes before he pulled up in a jazzy black sedan. He leaned over and opened the passenger door for me. "Get in."

I slid inside; the strong leather scent coming up from the seats was not enough to distract me from a sense of impending danger. "Nice car, Mikey."

"Yeah, sure." He didn't look at me. "Whatever you say."

"The restaurant's bar is closed now. Should we maybe go somewhere else?"

At that point, he looked at me for a few seconds but didn't answer. His expression could only be described as confused.

"If this isn't a good night for you, Mikey, we can talk some other time."

As if my words had snapped him out of a trance, he broke into a wide grin that showed his mouthful of even white teeth. "No, tonight's the fucking perfect night for what I got in mind."

That was an odd answer, I thought, and I experienced a definite urge to dive for the door handle, but I rationalized with myself. I told myself that Mikey obviously wanted to get things straightened out with Robby sooner rather than later.

Now, there was no way I would bring up the topic of Robby and me and what was going on between us. I knew for a fact that was the last thing Robby would want. So my plan was to act as if Savannah was Robby's girlfriend, and I was just their sidekick friend. In fact, I'd pretty much decided I'd continue pretending to be the third wheel as long as Robby needed me to. I had nothing to lose by coming out; *he* did.

"I'm gonna park out back. We can deal wit' all the bullshit there."

Deal with all the bullshit? Must be Mikey's way of saying, "We can have a conversation." "Okay, that works." I already knew I was fooling myself, but I kept on going with the charade.

Mikey pretty much put the pedal to the metal and we were out in the back of the restaurant near the loading dock in a less than thirty seconds. "Get out. I'm gonna have me a smoke."

I did as he ordered, thinking he surely wasn't the friendliest guy in the world and I honestly had trouble imagining that the man had any redeeming qualities at all. And I continued to ignore my gut feeling to run and hide.

My taste in friends is not what is in question here tonight.

It was Robby and Mikey's friendship I was here to save. So against the better judgment I'd gained from a decade on the streets, I got out of the car and met him in front of it. Mikey had left the car running, probably so that we could see each other in the glow of the headlights, but other than that it was pretty much pitch-black outside.

"I'm glad you waited around for me." He lit his cigarette and took a long drag.

"No problem, I want to help you and Robby work things out."

You are not safe, Tristan. And you know it.

I thought I heard soft laughter. When Mikey leaned forward toward me, I got a good look at his face. He was not smiling, nor was he sporting the serene expression of a man preparing to discuss a peace treaty. I experienced no shock at that realization. "Well, princess, sorry to disappoint, but there ain't no fucking way that's gonna happen."

And that's all it took for me to know for a fact that I was in big trouble.

"So it seems that you and Robby been spending a lot o' time together these days, huh?" He dropped what remained of his cigarette and stomped it into the ground.

If I want to, Mikey De-fucking-Salvo, I can stomp you into the ground until you're flatter than that smoking butt beneath your boot.

I nodded and faked a half smile, not yet ready to throw in the towel on helping to fix Robby's oldest friendship.

Mikey sauntered to the back door of his car and reached into the open window. When he pulled out a bat, I knew I was up shit's creek. Glancing around instinctively, I searched for my best escape route. Finding the nearest path to safety was a habit I'd developed and used often during my homeless youth. But surrounding me was what seemed to be miles of parking lot, which spelled "No easy way out."

Mikey spoke again. "You a big Red Sox fan?" He didn't wait for an answer. "Me and Robby used to go to Fen—fuck, never mind that. Ya see this bat? Your boyfriend gave it to me last year, for Christmas."

"We're just *friends*, Mikey. And Robby still wants to be friends with y—"

"Yeah, that's right. Mistah Generosity, himself, bought this for me at an auction. Look here"—he moved to my side, lifting the bat for my inspection—"it's got the whole goddamn team's signatures on it."

I replied quietly, "That's an awesome bat." It really was. Apparently, I was going to be beaten with a collector's item.

"Ain't it? And you know what?"

I shook my head slowly. In all honesty, I had no clue what Mikey was going to say next. I hadn't taken the time to consider it as of yet. Because my mind had been busy.

Our eyes connected, and I can't say exactly what he saw in mine, but I know I saw a hell of a lot of jealousy in his. "Well, I thought, since you two lovebirds are so fucking into the Red Sox, that I'd give this here valuable souvenir back to ya. Ain't I considerate?"

I'd lived out here on these cold harsh streets for years and years. These streets had taught me every trick in the book. I knew exactly how to take him down and how to snuff him out. Or, at a minimum, to make good and fucking certain he was no longer a factor here tonight. But I already knew I wasn't going to fight back.

So to his last question, I didn't respond, unless you considered just standing there and staring a response. And before I had a chance to blink, Mikey was holding the bat as it was meant to be held. He took a single practice swing in midair, and with the very next one, he slugged me hard, right in the belly.

And I took it.

Sure, I could've run, or I could've force-fed the asshole his prized bat. But I didn't. Like I always had in the past, I just stood there, slightly bent over from the pain that ripped through my stomach, and I took what was coming to me. The next hit was to my chest; it had been a homerun swing, and that Big Papi T-shirt Robby had given me flashed before my eyes.

Big Papi swings like that.

Then I fell to the pavement, the pain now searing around my heart. Knowing I couldn't take another hit to my chest if I wanted to stay conscious, I rolled onto my stomach. The third swing of the bat made a thudding sound when it hit my lower back. In what was left of my awareness, I heard echoes of my Uncle Ben's voice from years ago when I was a kid. *"Boy, if you make a sound, I'll hurt ya a helluva lot worse'n this."*

So I stifled my groans.

"Pretty impressive bat, huh?" Mikey's voice brought me back. He sounded winded.

I curled up so I could protect my head. A swing like one of those to my head would kill me. But still I wasn't gonna fight him.

Mikey is Robby's friend. I can't hurt him.

I just had to get through this.

"Not gonna cry, pansy-boy? Not gonna beg me to go easy on ya?" He nudged my side with the bat. "Well, listen here, cocksucker. You ain't worth no more of my effort than I already gave ya. I think you get what I'm trying to say."

I really wasn't all that certain exactly what his point was, other than that he was pissed off. And I really couldn't afford to spare too much energy worrying about it. The pain in my stomach and chest and back was blinding, deafening, and even nauseating. I thought I might pass out, but I tried as hard as I could to hang on.

"So here's the deal. I want ya to give this fancy-ass bat back to your lover-boy wit' my compliments. Got it, faggot?"

I just lay still, trying not to even breathe, and praying that he'd leave me here alive.

Mikey poked me with the bat again, harder this time. "I asked if ya got it, faggot?"

I think I nodded, but I couldn't bet my life on it. The world was getting hazy.

"Oh, yeah, and a coupla more little thingies. First off, no cops, ya hear? And second, tell your *boyfriend* that I plan on keepin' my job at Dalton Builders, and if he even *thinks* of firing my ass, I'll come after your sweet little Savannah. I got more baseball bats at home."

Within a couple of seconds the car door slammed, the headlights faded, and I lay there alone on the cold blacktop. I'd be lying if I didn't admit that it brought me back to days long past.

"Is THAT you, Tristan?"

Oh, God, he'd come back for round two.

"Hey, dude, Tristan? Are you okay?" Not Mikey's voice.

I lay there in the exact same position as when I'd blacked out, all curled up like a baby in a fetal ball. I groaned softly, assuring whoever was here with me that I was still alive.

"Hey, man, it's me, Phillip." I heard a loud clatter as he dropped the trash bags he was carrying onto the ground. "Shit, dude, you are definitely not okay!" I could feel his hands on my side, gingerly lifting my shirt and coat, surveying the damage.

"Phi-Phillip.... Phillip... help me up... please...."

"Shit, man, somebody sure did a number on you. You okay?" His voice was shaking.

I had to help him calm down. This was not Phillip's problem. "S-sure... sure I'm okay. At least I think I'm okay." My entire chest was on fire. My back throbbed.

Nope. Not okay.

"Hey, listen, I've got my car parked on the side of the building. Let me take you home—or do you need to go to the hospital, you think?"

With Phillip's help I struggled to my feet. "No, no, I don't think so, but could I just have a ride to the train station?" He placed his arm beneath my shoulder, and we started in the direction of his car. I used the baseball bat as a makeshift cane and slowly we hobbled along.

"So dude, there's no way I'm putting you on the subway tonight. I'll take you home. Not another word about it. I'm taking you home."

I DON'T know exactly how I managed to climb the stairs to our apartment, but eventually I found myself standing in front of my door. I don't think anything had ever looked more welcoming. I knocked quietly, so as not to alarm Savannah. But I just couldn't deal with searching for my keys right then. I wasn't even sure I still had them.

"Thank God, you're home—you're an hour later than I expected and I was starting to get really worried."

Savannah went to throw her arms around me but I gently pushed her away. "I'm not feeling good. You shouldn't get too close to me." I dropped my coat and the bat on the floor by the doorway, toed off my shoes, and shuffled down the hallway to the living room.

"What's wrong with you?" She tried to take my face in her hands but again I shoved them away. "Tristan, look at me!"

"No—I just can't do this right now—I'm really sick." My voice was quiet, but sharp. I dropped to the couch. "Sorry, honey, I'm sorry. I just need to sleep." When I curled up on my side, with my back to her, I knew she was suspicious. "Could you grab me a blanket? And a couple of Advil. Please."

"The Advil's in the bedroom and Robby's sleeping in there. I'll be really quiet and I'll go in and get it."

"Robby's here? Jesus, no, not tonight. Just listen to me—forget the Advil and just go back to bed. *Don't* wake him up. Please." With supreme effort, I managed to roll over to lie on my back so I could see her. She was looking down at me and shaking her head, a world-has-come-to-an-end sort of expression on her face. "I'll be better tomorrow, honey. I promise."

Without saying a word, Savannah reached for my shirt and started unbuttoning.

"Don't."

She looked at me with a pointblank stare and said flatly, "You're not sick; you're hurt." I didn't have the energy to resist any further. I let her unbutton my shirt to the waist and push it open. Although her eyes widened at the sight of Mikey's brutal handiwork on my torso, her voice betrayed no emotion. "Who did this to you?"

Now that she knew, I figured I wasn't going to be sleeping any time soon. I decided I'd be more comfortable if I got undressed. I struggled with my shirt until it fell to the floor, and then I unbuttoned my jeans and started to pull them off, unembarrassed, since after this many years I was used to Savannah seeing me undressed. And soon she was on her knees by my feet, tugging on my jeans until she succeeded in removing them. When she was finished, she stood and looked down at me, her face stern. Again she asked, "Who did this to you?"

"I don't want Robby to know about it. He'll feel responsible."

"It was that DeSalvo guy, wasn't it?" She already knew the answer, so I didn't bother to nod.

By then, I was starting to feel really cold. Maybe it was from shock, maybe it was from sitting there in nothing but my boxers. "Can I have a blanket?"

"First things first." She knelt back down to examine the wide purple welts on my chest and then my stomach. "Do we need to get you to a hospital?"

"I don't think so. I don't think anything is broken, worst case a couple ribs... not too sure." I lay back down and curled up as I'd been before. "But I'm pretty sure I'll know tomorrow." I felt her fingertips tracing the throbbing welt on my back.

"Did you even *try* to stop him, Tristan? Because I've seen you fight on the street, and let's just say you could've taken that big-mouthed jerk without even a slight problem. Or did you just lie down and take it because...." As she pulled the blanket off the chair, her words trailed off, but by the time she'd turned back to tuck it in around me, I could tell by her expression that she'd gotten the complete picture of what had happened behind the restaurant tonight. "You took it because he's Robby's friend, didn't you? You basically *let* him do this to you!" I don't remember her ever looking at me with this much frustration. And disgust. "God, Tristan, at least you could've run." Savannah shook her head. "I'm gonna go get the Advil."

Before I could protest, she was stomping her way to the bedroom. Within five minutes, she had given me painkillers and water and had settled herself on the end of the couch, pulling my feet onto her lap. "I'm sleeping out here with you tonight." By now she was beyond frustrated; she had worked herself into a state of silent fury. There was no way I'd be able to change her mind and make her go to bed. And to be honest, I didn't have the will or the desire to change her mind. My body felt like someone had hit me hard a couple times with a baseball bat.

Despite the pain, I found myself drifting off.

Robby

"WHAT the hell is going on out here?" Tristan was curled up on his side on the couch, his blanket-covered body rocking forward and backward very slightly, and Savannah was asleep, sitting up, down on the far end. Savannah opened her eyes slowly and just looked at me without any expression at all, offering no explanation.

"You guys, what's going on?" I'd come out of the bedroom because I had sensed something was wrong. And now they wouldn't answer me. "Why aren't you two in bed?"

The lump under the blankets moved. "I'm sick."

"You're sick?" I went over to the couch and sat down on the edge. When I tried to pull the blanket back to look at him, Tristan clung to it. "Tris, if you're sick, you need to be in your bed, not out here. Come on, buddy, let me help you." I pushed on his side a little bit to let him know I meant business, causing him to yelp like a kicked puppy.

"Just let me be!" Tristan started moaning as if he was in pain. Then he rasped, "Go to bed, both of you, and I'll be better in the morning! *Please just go!*"

Now I was certain something was more than a little bit wrong here. First, I examined Savannah, whose guilty eyes were staring up at me, as round as golf balls. Then I took in the rest of the room. Tristan's pants and shirt had been dropped in a rumpled ball beside the couch. There was a glass of water and a bottle of Advil on the coffee table. Down the hall, I could see Tristan's black blazer on the floor beside a baseball bat.

A baseball bat.

I walked down the hall without a word, picked up the bat, and immediately recognized it—this bat was one of a kind. "What did he do to you?" I roared with a rage so fierce I thought my brain might come unglued. Then I actually ran back over to the couch, leaping over the coffee table in the process, and tore the blanket off him with one swift yank. On the smooth light-brown skin of his back was the indisputable imprint of where he'd been hit by a baseball bat. "Christ, Tristan!"

When he turned to face me, struggling in a futile attempt to cover his bareness with his hands, I saw the rest. Two more thick purple welts had been left by that one-of-a-fucking-kind bat, the first diagonally across his chest, the other horizontally across his stomach. Wide and swollen and furiously inflamed. What shocked me even more than those contusions, though, was that he instinctively reached his arms out to hold me, to comfort *me*, when *I* was the reason he was experiencing what had to be excruciating pain. "Robby, I'm okay. Please don't worry about me. I just need some sleep." He sounded every bit as shitty as he looked.

"Sleep isn't gonna do a fucking thing for what happened to you." I rushed into the kitchen and returned with a tray of ice cubes and a couple of dishtowels. Savannah had gotten up and was hovering around by Tristan's head. "I'm gonna ice these bruises down. Then we'll go to the hospital, and after that you can make a statement to the police."

At those words, Tristan shot upright. After a grimace and a groan from the pain that came from the sudden movement, tears starting to stream down his face, "No, I can't! H-he said… if I tell anybody anything, he'll go after Savannah and… and… just n-no. *Please*."

Before I knew what I was doing, I'd grabbed Tristan by the shoulders and was staring down into his eyes. "What the fuck did Mikey say to you?"

"No cops, okay?" Tristan was crying. I'd never before seen a man quite this devastated. "Just no cops, please! Or he'll go after Savannah."

I dropped my ass onto the floor beside the couch. My thoughts were jumbled. All I knew for certain was that I wanted to kill the bastard I used to call my best friend.

Savannah, at this point, was kneeling beside me on the floor. "He won't hurt me, Tris. And we need to report this—it's a criminal act!"

Tristan was inconsolable, now writhing around on the couch so violently I thought he was going to further injure himself. "No. No, you guys. Promise me, just promise there will be no cops!"

Savannah looked over at me, completely speechless.

"I can't let him get away with this, Tristan." That was the truth.

At those words, Tristan started to get up off the couch, which obviously pained him greatly. "Then I'm leaving. You guys promise—no cops—or I'm fucking outta here!"

"Okay, okay, Tris. We won't tell the police. So now, lay back down." Savannah's voice had become soft and crooning. "We promise, no police."

He looked up at me for my assurance and I nodded too, not knowing what else I could do at that moment. "But I'm going to fire his ass from Dalton Builders."

Tristan started up with more of the same moaning and twisting that had just ceased. "No, Robby! He'll come after her—he told me so! You can't fire him either...." His voice trailed off and his body became still. But after a few seconds, he added with a sniff, "He said he'd hurt her if you fired him." Silent tears continued to rain down his cheeks.

I had to make Tristan's crying stop. And I would do whatever it took to comfort him, to help him find peace so he could get some rest. "All right. I won't fire his ass, but I'm not gonna just drop it with him. I can't."

My words seemed to soothe Tristan slightly. He took a deep breath, which served to make him grimace in pain. "Thank you. Thank you, Robby." His eyes fluttered closed.

I needed time to think this through. At the moment, I was completely overcome with feelings of powerlessness and guilt, as I knew my presence in Tristan's life had brought all this pain down on him. And on Savannah, because sure as shit, Tristan's pain was her pain. "I've caused this pain to the two people I care about—the two people I *love*—the most!"

And right then, in the midst of our pain and anguish, the three of us actually took a moment to stop and study each other. Tristan's eyes popped open, and he looked first at Savannah for her reaction to my words of love, and then at me. Savannah came to my side, hugged me hard around my neck, and looked at me with an expression of reverence that I knew I didn't deserve. It was as if we'd gotten caught up in a tornado of emotion, all of us flailing around helplessly in midair, and the only thing that could bring us back to the ground was the sight of each other's faces.

"Let's just wrap up this ice inside the towels and take him to bed, Robby. You can help ice his stomach and chest and I can ice his back, and we can hold him between us and keep him warm. And we can talk about this situation more tomorrow."

"That's good, a real good idea." Tristan voice was weak, crackly, and exhausted.

"You guys go to bed. I've got to take care of something really important right now." There was no way on earth Mikey was gonna find comfort on his soft mattress and pillow tonight if I had my say. Not while Tris was suffering. Because no, I couldn't let it go, not even for just this one night.

"No, Robby. I don't want you to do it tonight." Tristan again looked up at me, and it wasn't difficult to read the plea in his eyes. "I need you now."

"I just can't believe he did this to you! I'm so sorry, baby." Once again, a tidal wave of anger and guilt flooded over my head, not a pleasant mix to drown in. I found myself on my knees next to the couch, my head pressed to the unharmed side of Tristan's chest. And I realized I was now crying, or more sobbing, as Tristan had been before. "I'm so sorry this happened!"

Tristan rose unsteadily to his feet, and then, very ironically, he attempted to help me to *my* feet, as if *I* was the one who could barely stand. I'd never known a man so completely selfless. "Come on, Robby. Let's go to bed. It'll all be better in the morning." He was actually comforting me like *I'd* been the one who'd been beaten senseless tonight. I shook my head to clear my brain.

All three of us clung together as we slowly made our way down the hall.

When we got to the bedroom, I pulled down the covers and Savannah helped Tristan into the middle of the bed. Then we pretty much fell on either side of him, each of us icing our designated parts of his body. After fifteen minutes, Tristan was shaking with cold and fear and shock, so we dropped the wet towels onto the floor beside the bed. Tristan curled up on his side facing me, with Savannah spooned up against his back. I took him in my arms and cradled him to my chest like the treasure that he was to me. Then somehow we all fell asleep.

NONE of us slept well. At one point in the early morning hours, a disconcerting sense of being watched woke me from my fitful sleep. In the dull light of dawn, from deep within the narrow slot between Savannah and me where he was tucked, Tristan's haunted dark eyes stared up at me. And when I caught him looking at me, so completely absorbed in my face, he didn't do the "embarrassed Tristan" thing that I was used to. There was no dipping his head down to escape my regard. Instead his gaze intensified. And as he continued to stare at me, I began to squirm. What thoughts were passing through his mind? Was he looking for something in *my* expression? Was he searching for answers in *my* eyes? I was not enough of a man. I would never be enough to deserve a person like him.

But as quickly as the possibility had entered my mind, I knew I had to dismiss the concern that Tristan was searching for something inside me. Because that wasn't it at all. His expression seemed too pensive for that type of scrutiny. Tristan, I decided, was gazing at my face with hope. He was trying to muster the courage to believe he'd already found what he was looking for in me. This realization prompted me to move. I hunched my shoulders a bit, pressed a single kiss to his forehead, and said, "I love you, Tristan, and I'll be here for you."

I hoped like hell I wouldn't let him down.

And after sending me a tiny melancholy smile, he closed his eyes.

CHAPTER 26

Robby

"DAMN it! I knew we should've iced it more last night." Perched on the edge of the couch, I held ice packs to the swollen purple welts that rose on Tristan's chest and stomach. I tried to swallow back my disgust at the entire situation, but I couldn't seem to rid my throat of the lump that had firmly lodged itself there. "I don't know what the hell I was thinking. I know all about how important icing is from all of the football injuries I had."

Tristan tried to pull the ice from my hands, but I held fast to them. "Stop babying me. I'll be fine. I've had worse." From the little hitch in his voice, I knew he had just revealed a small but painful truth of his past.

"Judging by the size and color of these welts, some of your ribs have got to be broken. Are you sure you can breathe okay?" I ran my fingertips lightly over the distended skin, knowing that I was every bit as responsible for his beating as Mikey was. I'd practically led Mikey right to the guy and placed the bat in his hands. My stomach twisted with regret and guilt, a sensation with which I was becoming quite familiar.

"I'm fine, and I really think you should go to your meeting—"

"I've already cancelled it. Business can wait." *Huh?* The Robby I used to be would never have considered putting business on the back burner for anything. I admitted to myself that I liked this part of the new Robby much better. "You talked to your boss when I was in the shower, right? He's going to give you some time off?"

"Yes, for the hundredth time. And when I go back, he's gonna put me behind the bar until I can lift trays." He was trying to calm my worries, but I'd had a high school football injury in which I'd broken several ribs and I knew it was no fun at all. "So you don't need to—"

Just then, Savannah, her small frame still enclosed in a pocket of frigid December air, pushed through the front doorway. "Breakfast sandwiches and coffee for everybody." She was trying so hard to sound chipper, but one look at her told the story of how she was really holding up: not well. Tristan had been her entire family for a long time. She had nursed him back to health once before when she'd found him again after years of homelessness, and her haggard expression spelled out the fact that she'd never expected to have to do it again. But thanks to yours truly, her gentle roommate was writhing in pain on the couch, unable to work. Unable to move. Probably struggling to even breathe, but too kind to admit it to me.

And I was champing at the bit to find Mikey. Despite what I'd promised Tristan, I wanted nothing more than to fire him, and then to call the cops on him, and while we were waiting for the cops to come, to beat him until he couldn't remember his own first name. Then I'd remind him that his name was Mikey, and I'd beat him until he forgot it again.

A bag of warm breakfast food from the S-Squared Diner was dropped lightly onto the table and Savannah removed the coffee cups from the tray. "Go ahead and open the bag. And help Tris sit up a bit so he can eat." She clearly had no interest in eating, and I could relate. Food had no appeal when I knew Tristan was suffering right there beside me. Taking a cup of coffee, she plopped into the chair and leaned back, still not looking at us.

I did as she asked, fully aware of Tristan's wincing when I helped to reposition him on the couch. I unwrapped his sandwich and held it to his lips.

"Uh, I can feed myself." He tugged the food from my hand and took a tiny bite. "Thanks for getting this, Savi." His voice was shaky.

Across the room, Savannah sat up in the chair and looked directly at Tristan. "We need to talk about a few things."

We both looked over at her, wondering what was so important.

"Tris, I've decided that until you are better, I'm going to pick up a few shifts at the diner." She took a long sip of her coffee but kept her gaze fixed on the floor. "I already talked to Gus this morning, and he said it would be no problem whatsoever."

I felt Tristan's shoulders straighten, and then I heard the short gasp of pain that accompanied his involuntary movement. "No. You aren't going back to work. We've discussed this. I work, you study."

A loud huff of air escaped from Savannah's lips. "Be reasonable. You aren't going to be able to work for six weeks and we have bills to pay!"

"Six weeks?" For a second, I thought Tristan was going to bounce up off the couch and get into her face. "I'm not gonna be outta the game for no six fucking weeks, Savannah!" I turned sharply to stare at him. I'd never before heard him curse like that. Then I looked back at Savannah questioningly, but she only had eyes for Tristan.

Behind me on the couch, Tristan's body began a gentle rocking. "No. No, you can't work. No, no." He almost sounded like he was chanting.

Savannah got up and crossed the room. Unsure of what to do, I stood and allowed her an unobstructed path to the couch. She knelt on the floor beside Tristan's head and raised her hand to his hair. "Tristan." She said his name softly as she worked her fingers over his scalp, and I noticed that his rocking motion gradually stopped. "You need to rest so you can get better. You won't heal if you start lugging those trays and running around the restaurant too soon."

It had been a long time since I'd seen a face so grief-stricken; the man was dry-eyed but clearly distraught. "*I* take care of *you*, Savannah. *I* take care of *you*!"

For a moment it was quiet. Savannah bent down to press her cheek to the side of Tristan's face, mumbling something about how they didn't have enough savings to live on for very long, and that it was okay, she'd wanted to take some time off school anyways.

"Let me help."

In unison, my partners' heads snapped in my direction.

"I want to help. I have savings. I-I...." I was stuttering.

Savannah sat up. Her eyes suddenly filled with tears and her face went a ghostly white. And Tristan, as a matter of fact, appeared exactly the same way. "You'd help *us*?"

I nodded. "Of course I would."

"But why? *Why?*" His voice was hoarse. And very skeptical, I should add. It appeared he didn't trust my good intentions.

Knowing I should be highly insulted in the face of their reaction, I felt the blood drain from my face. "Because I love you guys." I guess it was really that simple. We all stared around in a circle, and it once again seemed like the simple sight of each other's faces possessed sufficient power to pull us safely out of the raging floodwaters. "My lease is up January first, and it's mid-December now, so I could just write off the rest of December as a loss and move...." Christ, I'd almost invited myself to live with them.

"Yes, Robby, yes! You can move in with us and then we can share our expenses and—" Savannah was absolutely overjoyed. The look on her face matched her jubilant voice.

I hadn't fully absorbed the enormity of what I'd apparently requested and Savannah had apparently agreed to, until I heard Tristan's voice.

"And then we can be together."

And *that* was what it really boiled down to, wasn't it? Yes, if I moved in, Tristan wouldn't have to rush back to work before he had healed, and Savannah wouldn't have to cut down on her studying to get a job, because I could pick up the financial slack. But we all knew what it really came down to was that we would be together. For meals, for game nights, between our jobs and classes. We would sleep in the same bed every night and wake up in each other's arms every morning.

Like a family. An untraditional one, but a family, nonetheless.

"Yes, then we can be together," I said with a smile. Our little group of three had turned something awful into something beautiful. But that did not mean that the magnitude of what Mikey had done escaped me for so much as a split second.

IT WASN'T until late in the afternoon, when we all crawled back into bed for a much-needed nap, Tristan again wedged snugly between Savannah and me, that we finally talked about just what had happened with Mikey. I had bided my time, waiting patiently all day to receive this information I simultaneously dreaded and craved. The facts I needed with which to confront Mikey.

In a monotone voice, Tristan had briefly explained about the phone call he'd received at the bar and how he'd agreed to meet Mikey to discuss mending our friendship. He hadn't gone into much detail when it had come to specifically what had happened with the bat, but then, he really hadn't needed to. In fact, he'd told us very succinctly that Mikey had "hit" him, but his voice had slurred a bit when he'd said it and he'd kept shaking his head, as if to stay focused. It was like he could somehow force his brain to detach from his physical pain so it could only affect his body, not his mind.

"Tristan never started fights when we lived out there." Savannah glanced toward the window, and I knew that she was referring to the city streets. "Robby, he really never did. And he was usually clever enough to avoid a fight to begin with, but if he had to, he had the street smarts to turn things around in a fight. I mean, I saw him do it plenty of times." At first it seemed that she was speaking to me, but she switched her focus onto Tristan. "What I don't get is why didn't you take Mikey down when you knew he was going to beat you, or maybe even *kill* you. I just don't get it." She broke into a sob that seemed to rise from her fear of what could have happened as well as frustration at Tristan's inaction.

But it appeared that Tristan had nothing more to say. He closed his eyes as if to close the subject.

I ran my fingers through his dark silky hair. "Why didn't you knock Mikey on his ass, even just long enough to get out of there? 'Cause God knows he deserved whatever damage you could've wreaked on him. Tell me the reason."

For a while Tris stayed quiet, but eventually his mouth curved into a slight smile. "I just couldn't hurt him, Robby." He licked his lips to moisten them. "I could *never* hurt a friend of yours."

My insides, from my throat to my heart and all the way down to my gut, clenched like an enormous, angry fist. According to Savannah, Tristan could have easily made Mikey *very* sorry for having even considered hurting him, but he didn't out of his regard for Mikey's friendship with me. "I'm gonna kill him."

"No, you're not." Tristan moved his hand lightly down the length of my arm. "And you're not going to call the cops or fire him either."

"But what he did to you, I can't let it slide. *I can't.*" I pounded my fist into my palm.

Savannah leaned up on her elbow and sent me a perturbed look. "You can't fix everything with your fists."

"But I told Tristan he'd be safe, and then he got hurt because of me. And what did Mikey want from you, anyways?" I was trying to stay calm, but I already knew that I was on a direct path to losing it. "*Exactly* what did he say to you?"

"It doesn't really matter, does it?" With some effort, Tristan turned his aching body away from me to face Savannah. Feeling a bit as if I'd been dismissed, I glanced down at his lower back where the T-shirt he wore had lifted, exposing the thick purplish-black raised stripe. Another overwhelming surge of anger flooded into the veins in my arms and my neck and my head.

"Yes, it matters to me! What did he say? Tell me! Jesus, Tristan, tell me now!" I'd lost my cool.

Without turning back over to face me, Tristan replied flatly, "He just wanted you to get 'the message,' whatever that is. Okay? That's all. And now it's over and…." I heard him exhale loudly before he finished his thought. "I don't want you to fight him or fire him. He'll go after Savannah."

"But, Tris—"

He was insistent. "You know how the saying goes, Robby. 'Keep your friends close; keep your enemies closer.' We can't afford to completely alienate him because we need to know what he's up to."

I wasn't sure how to respond to that.

"Well, this is *not* your fault." Savannah was looking at me now, even if Tristan still wouldn't. "Maybe you could just talk to Mikey. You know, tell him you got his message. Find out what else he wants from you."

"He wants me to dump you guys." I lifted my hands and pressed my thumbs hard against my temples. "And if I did just that, you guys would both be safe."

At those words, Tristan flipped over, his penetrating gaze centered on my face. "You can't leave us. I need you to stay. Please don't go, Robby." The way he was clutching my wrists emphasized his pleading. "I feel *so much* for you. Don't leave us." Eyes as dark and sweet as chocolate melted into mine. Tristan needed me. And I needed him even more.

"Okay, baby, I won't leave you, but I'm still going to talk to him. I have to at least talk to him about this." God knew he deserved firing, and worse. And luckily, Tristan had never technically asked that I promise not to throw a punch or two (or ten) in Mikey's direction. This time, I didn't give a shit if I rocked the boat that we were floating on, even if it launched us both into the sea.

Tristan yawned widely. "Just keep it civil when you talk to him. Try to be nice." Another yawn. "And Robby, stop worrying. I'm okay."

He curled against my chest, and I wrapped my arms around him. "Go to sleep. We'll be here when you wake up." I think he was already asleep as I spoke. Then I looked over at Savannah, and she reached out her hand to me, her eyes wide with concern over our partner.

I didn't deserve to have either of these people in my life. I wasn't sure I'd ever be worthy of them. But I *was* sure that Mikey DeSalvo was gonna get a taste of his own medicine, and I could hardly frigging wait for tomorrow to come so I could feed it to him. I guess some things were more important than keeping the status quo.

CHAPTER 27

Robby

I COULDN'T fucking believe that the asshole was actually sitting behind his desk in *my* office, sipping calmly on a cup of coffee, and punching keys on his computer as if it was any other ordinary work day. I slammed the door so hard that the framed panoramic photograph of my college campus rattled against the wall.

For one of the first times I could remember, I was gonna rock the boat.

"So, Dalton, it seems ya got my message." He didn't even have the good grace to look up at me.

I threw down my briefcase and coat on my desk. "Yeah, I got it. Loud and fucking clear." Perspiration rolled freely down the sides of my face. The effort of holding myself back from snapping the bastard completely in two was already taking its toll on me. "Now, you're gonna get *my* message." I stepped over to his desk and bent right down into his face.

Only then did Mikey grace me with a brief glance. "You don't look too good, D-man. Now, don't ya go straining ya-self or anything." He was taunting me.

"Listen, DeSalvo. The only reason you still have a job right now is because Tristan asked me not to fire you."

"Well, then, you *must* remember to thank him for me." Looking up again, Mikey batted his eyelashes. "That boyfriend of yours is such a frigging sweetheart and a looker too, huh? But what I like best about him is he's fucking great to use for batting practice."

My fists clenched into balls so tight that my knuckles whitened as a surge of hot fury rushed through my veins. And I knew for a fact that Mikey DeSalvo wouldn't walk out of this room today. If the asshole was damned lucky, when I was finished with him he'd still be *alive* to crawl out of here. "Stand up and face me like a man, DeSalvo!"

So Mikey calmly stood up, stepped aside to push his chair under his desk as if he had all the time in the world, and directed his eyes to mine. Then he asked me mildly, "Is there anything else you wanna get off your chest there, Dalton?"

At that moment, I found him more infuriating than ever before, which was certainly saying a lot. I wanted to go straight for his throat, but I couldn't resist the urge to smack my fist very hard into those smug lips and then swing once more and flatten his big nose against his ugly face. So yes, his face is where I started. When I was satisfied he wouldn't be able to bite into or smell his mama's home cooking for the better part of a month, I went for his gut. The dude worked out, and he put up a little bit of a fight after he recovered from the whole nose thing, but I had him doubled over on the floor beside his desk in a matter of minutes. I'd seen Mikey fight before—in fact, I'd stood beside him in a few physical disagreements. So I knew his tricks, I knew his weaknesses, and I knew exactly how to take him down. Before five minutes was up, I was looming over him, and "in a fetal ball" would be an accurate way to describe his position.

"Since you asked, there is one more thing I'd like to get off my chest." Blood streamed from his nose, but the overall damage would have been much more severe had I not been respecting Tristan's wishes that I not kill the guy. "Next time you're pissed off, take it out on the person you're pissed at—and that's *me*."

Tilting his head sideways as if in deep thought, he replied somewhat groggily, "Maybe that's what I shoulda gone and done, Rob. But it sure felt good to see that pussy crumpled up in a pile on the ground."

At the visual image of Tristan lying helplessly on the ground, I again came unglued. I grabbed the asshole by his now mostly bloodred collar and gave him a shake he'd remember well into middle age. "You are never, fucking ever, to so much as look at, let alone touch, Tristan Chartrand again. You got that? You got it, asshole?"

My employee actually had enough spunk left to smirk at me. "Why don't you scribble that li'l thought down on a piece o' paper and stick it in my suggestion box, huh, boss-man?"

"And stay the fuck away from Savannah too. You hear me?"

I might as well have been talking to a brick wall. Mikey let his head roll back, shut his eyes, and asked, "We done here?"

I was speechless. Somehow, while trying to teach the asshole a lesson he wouldn't forget, I had managed to let Tristan, Savannah, and myself down, and I didn't even know precisely how I'd done it. I just knew that what had happened between Mikey and Tristan was wrong and I had done nothing at all to make it right, except take a few swings at the asshole and shake him around like a rag doll. I hadn't done enough. I was still furious, and now I felt guilty on top of it. I pounded my fist hard into my palm and said, "Get the fuck out of my office for the rest of the day. It's your turn at Starbucks."

Chapter 28

Robby

"So, since your father's company holiday celebration is being held on Christmas Eve this year, we thought the family would just get together on Christmas day, in the early afternoon."

"That sounds doable, Mom." At long last, I had the luxury of being alone in my office since Mikey had gone up north skiing for a few days. To say I was enjoying my solitary work status would be an understatement; I sat back in my leather chair, sipping coffee, my cell phone on speaker. "I'm going to bring Savannah and Tristan again, like on Thanksgiving. That a problem?"

"Oh. Oh, well, let me put your father on, dear."

That didn't sound promising.

"Rob, about you, er, about you having guests to Christmas dinner, son...." My father rarely stumbled on his words. In fact, I'd say it was a first for him. "Well, I was thinking it might be nice if it was just family this year."

I hadn't seen this coming, not at all. I couldn't think of anything to say.

"You know, we don't have a problem if you bring that pretty little gal, Savannah, is it? But...."

"But no Tristan—is that what you are saying? Don't bring Tristan?" I noticed that my voice still sounded vaguely confused, but his point had already become crystal clear to me. "Are you saying Tris isn't welcome in our home, Dad?"

"Damn it, Rob! It's just one day—can't you separate yourself from the boy for just twenty-four fucking hours?"

My blood froze. I wanted to scream at him, but cowardice held my tongue still. Maybe I let loose on Mikey, but things were completely different with my father.

Dad lowered his voice. "Besides, I've invited Mike DeSalvo over for dessert on Christmas night. He's such a fine young man. But poor Mike has expressed to me that he is uncomfortable with homosexuals."

"*What?* What are you talking about, Dad?" This was getting just a bit too close to the heart of the matter for comfort.

"Jesus Christ, Robert, do I have to spell it out for you?" I could tell my father had left the room my mother was in because his voice returned to its typical booming volume. "Mike confided in me that you'd mentioned to him that your girlfriend's roommate is a fa—is a *gay*."

"I never said that Tristan was gay, but what difference would it make if he was?" Already, I'd started sweating rather profusely. I got up and went to crack the window to let in some cold December air. "What are you trying to say?"

After a brief pause, he replied, "Look, Rob, personally I don't care if the boy is gay, straight, green, or blue. But I-I'll just say I didn't appreciate the goddamned *love-struck* way he looked at you on Thanksgiving. No, I didn't like it one bit. And Mike, well, if I'm going to put it plainly, Mike told me that he is very uncomfortable with what he considers to be Tristan's deep *feelings* for you."

"Mike is talking crap—Tristan is my *friend* and Savannah's roommate, and that's all," I lied like the complete coward that I was. Amid the intense irritation I was feeling toward Mikey at that very moment, a stab of personal guilt found its way to my gut.

"Well, Mike DeSalvo is a close family friend, and he's already been invited, so I feel I need to respect his wishes. Understood, son?"

I had nothing to say. There was absolutely no way anything I could possibly say would help me please my dad, as was my usual goal, let alone please myself, so I kept my mouth closed.

"I'm glad you understand, Rob." He cleared his throat. "So, I'll see you and Savannah on Christmas Day, and that's just four days away now, so you'd better start your shopping." I heard his laughter before I ended the call.

It took me less than a split second to know that I wasn't going to be going home for Christmas this year. Maybe I wasn't yet ready to come out and declare my newly found love of a man, *of this man*, to my father, but I would not hurt Tristan by leaving him alone for Christmas. Not that Savannah would ever even consider doing such a thing, because she wouldn't.

And not only was I refusing to hurt Tristan, but I was doing what I wanted to do for once. I wanted to exchange gifts with Tristan and Savannah *together* on Christmas Day. If that couldn't happen in my childhood home in the presence of my family by blood, then it would happen at my new home with the family of my heart. And that was exactly what I planned on doing. The rest of the Daltons and that sack-of-shit, DeSalvo, would just have to survive without me.

I briefly wondered how he was going to explain the condition of his nose to my family.

But I had to figure out how to explain the situation to my new roommates, as well as to my family. But there was no real rush to tell Tristan he'd been barred from my family party and my family that I was going to be a Christmas Day no-show for the very first time in twenty-six years.

I had four whole days to get those distasteful duties done, right?

IT TURNED out that I had no explaining to do. Two days after I'd engaged in that extremely disheartening conversation with my father, Mom called to inform me that Dad had very suddenly come down with a horrible flu and they were not going to be able to host Christmas dinner this year after all. In fact, my father would probably not even be able to get out of bed that day to eat his Christmas ham.

Some may call Dad getting sick right before Christmas a case of very bad luck, but I preferred to call it karma.

What goes around comes around, Dad.

CHAPTER 29

Robby

WHAT I saw when I looked across the room, Tristan and Savannah sitting cross-legged beside our scraggly Christmas tree like a couple of excited little kids, was everything I'd ever imagined the joy of Christmas could be. And yes, I realized that my thoughts at that moment were sickly sweet and sappy, but I didn't give a shit. For the first time, I was *really* home in every way for Christmas. Although I'd been living out of suitcases stacked up at the bottom of the bed for the past several weeks, I knew I was exactly where I belonged.

"I think we should start our own Christmas tradition," Savannah suggested brightly, her eyes shining in the soft glow of the tree lights. "Let's exchange our gifts tonight, on Christmas Eve, when it's just the three of us here alone. It'll be nice."

Tristan didn't need to answer in actual words; his huge grin informed us that he liked the idea very much. So, I crawled down off the couch and joined them by the Charlie Brown tree. "Sounds like a plan."

The two of them scrambled to grab the presents they'd wrapped and placed under the tree several days before. And I have to admit, I did the same thing. I was truly thrilled with the prospect of putting smiles on the faces of these two people I cared for so much.

"Can we go first, Robby? We have some small stuff for you here, but first I'll have to go down into the storeroom for the big one!" Tristan hopped to his feet, tugging up those loose gray sweats when he was finally standing, and before I had a chance to answer, he was out the door.

Savannah smiled sheepishly. "We planned your gift together and, uh, he's a little bit excited."

I returned the smile and we waited while Tristan retrieved my gift. I was definitely surprised and rather alarmed when he staggered down the hall with a huge box in his arms. I had to force myself to shove the worry about him damaging his healing ribs to the back of my mind. "Did you guys get me a refrigerator?"

"How'd you guess?" Savannah laughed, but she appeared very eager as well. "Go ahead, what are you waiting for? Open it!"

And if I was going to level with myself, I was pretty excited to see what kind of a gift these two had come up with. So, none too slowly, I pulled off the giant red bow and the colorful paper. "Oh, guys, you got me a bureau! I need this so much!"

Tristan's face was pink with pleasure, his eyes sparkling. "We want you to feel like you're really at home here, and you can't feel at home living out of suitcases."

"We already know exactly where we're gonna put it in the bedroom, and guess what else?"

I just looked at Savannah, waiting for her to spill the rest, knowing I wouldn't have to wait long.

"We cleared out the smaller bedroom closet—it's all yours. For your suits and stuff." Had anyone ever appeared so pleased to give me a gift before? If someone had, I couldn't remember it.

"Come here, you guys." I held my arms open to them both. "Thank you. You got me just what I needed and I love it, but honestly, I already feel like I'm at home just because both of you are here."

Savannah and Tristan climbed into my arms and clung to me for a moment, both of them near tears. Certainly, they had each experienced rough times in their lives, but they were still so pure of heart. Unjaded, really. After our group hug, they presented me with a few things that I'd been missing since I'd made my rather hurried move: slippers, my own deodorant, a bottle of my usual cologne, and a special construction-themed mug for my morning coffee.

"So, how about I spoil one of you next?" I reached for a box. "First, Savannah." I handed it to her.

She glanced down at the box in her hands, and then at me rather shyly. "Okay." With her tiny, delicate fingers, she tore off the paper. "Oh,

Robby, an iPad! I can take it with me to classes! My laptop breaks my back when I try to carry it! This is so great! I never expected it!" And again they were both in my arms, Savannah for obvious reasons, and Tristan because his joy at seeing Savannah so happy was too great for him to stay still.

Once they'd climbed off me, I handed her an envelope. "This one is for both of you, and me too, I guess."

With wide eyes, she opened it as Tristan looked on. "Tris, look— season's tickets for three—to the Red Sox! Oh my God, thank you, Robby!"

I was fairly certain, judging by the way Tristan was looking at me, that he was going to cry. He opened his mouth to speak, but no sound came out. Then he gently took the envelope from Savannah's hands and held it to his heart. Nope. No verbal thank you was necessary. "I got something else for you, buddy." I handed him a separate envelope.

"Y-you didn't n-need to get me anything else, R-Robby."

"I wanted to, baby. It was my pleasure, okay? Now open it."

Tristan hesitated, dipping his head down and rubbing his hair fleetingly in an attempt to collect himself, and then he pulled out the little card I'd placed inside the envelope. He looked at it like he wasn't sure what it was.

"Now you belong to the Rose Gym, too, bud. And you and I are going to get plenty of use out of that membership, believe me." Tristan seemed to be in a daze, staring at the hand that held the membership card I'd purchased for him. "We're going to be permanent workout partners from now on. Sound good?"

Still staring down, Tris choked out what I thought was "Yes, Robby" and the next thing I knew he was crying. "No one has ever been this good to me, besides Savi, and I don't know what I did to deserve it and…."

I pulled Tristan back against my side, right where he belonged, kissed his lips briefly, and said softly, tears in my eyes now as well, "You're my partner, and I love you. I love *both* of you." I caught Savannah's glance. "You two, like you told me once, Savannah, are 'a package deal,' and believe me, this deal has given me all the friendship and love that I'd always wanted and could never find. What we have may be unconventional, but it's ours, and it works."

In less than a split second Savannah was pressed against my other side and was kissing my cheek. "This is a family. *We* are a family." She said it with conviction. Her eyes were somehow still dry, unlike Tristan's and mine, but her expression was impassioned.

We stayed close together, embracing one another, until Savannah remembered that she and Tristan hadn't yet exchanged gifts. So, then we got back to the business of Christmas.

WE WENT to bed at midnight after what was likely the best Christmas Eve any of us had ever experienced. As had become our habit, Tristan climbed in first, always in something of a rush because he was still a bit shy about me seeing him in just his boxers. When he was settled, Savannah climbed in, usually in an oversized T-shirt (more and more often now the T-shirt she wore was one of *mine* that she'd swiped from the clean laundry, which I really liked), and she and Tristan hugged and kissed each other good night. I was always the last to get in bed, as I had become the one officially designated to turn off the lights.

Tonight, when I slid into bed beside him, Tristan turned to face me, and in the darkness he tried to study my face, his eyes wide. "Tonight was the best night of my entire life. Thank you so much, Robby." He spoke the words like a prayer.

"Don't thank me. We gave *each other* this special night." God knew I wanted to kiss him. I wanted to take him in my arms and show him how I felt. And I wanted to cover his mouth with mine until he was gasping for breath, and then explore the lean lines of his pounding chest with my hands. But I didn't know what he wanted. I didn't know if he was afraid of intimacy, or if he was uncomfortable because of Savannah's presence. I just didn't know what came next for us.

Then I heard a sleepy, feminine voice coming from the other side of the mattress. "I just want you guys to know that I hung mistletoe on the ceiling, directly above where your heads are at this very moment, as a matter of fact."

Tristan and I froze and waited for her to say more.

"I'd be extremely disappointed if you broke the 'mistletoe rule'—in other words, I expect you two to be locking lips within the next couple of seconds." After another brief silence, she said, "I love you guys. Good night."

Savannah had virtually been paving the way from me to Tristan ever since our first date. So who was I to question her, let alone the cherished tradition of kissing beneath the mistletoe? I didn't fully understand why she was doing it, but I knew she'd also encouraged and embraced Tristan on every step of his journey toward me. So, I took Tristan's delicate face between my palms and I pulled his mouth in toward mine.

I couldn't help myself; I kissed him with a need that stopped just short of forcefulness. Never before had a person awoken my heart and my body in such a powerful way. There was something I found irresistible in the paradox of his person, in his soft and gentle, even yielding, masculinity. Inexplicably, I wanted to make him mine as much as I wanted him to make me his. And this wasn't mere affection or simple lust I was feeling; it had gone well beyond that. I was talking about real passion, a thirst for his love that needed to be satisfied. Simply because my heart responded to him with such fervor, I believed that my body, likewise, ached with need.

Before long, I had climbed on top of his slim frame, my lips never leaving his even for a second. An urge to know him in every way, and I mean in ways I'd never before conceived of knowing a man, was the only thought my mind could entertain. At this moment, I longed to be as close as I could be to Tristan Chartrand, to be *inside* him, to know I'd made him mine in the most intimate way I could perceive.

I found his tiny nipples with my fingertips and teased, trying desperately to entice this man to need me with the same desperation with which I'd come to need him. In fact, I knew beyond a doubt that I had to have him; how could I possibly wait? And then I felt the weight of his hand between my thighs. He moved his flat palm tentatively up and down my length, trying to let me know that he was okay. That *this* was okay with him. But already my concern for Tristan's mental health had shifted to the forefront of my mind, effectively pushing back my burning lust. Tristan's emotional safety was, and would always be, my first concern.

"I love you, Tristan, and I can wait for this."

Between heavy breaths that led me to suspect he was in no way unaffected by our contact, he murmured, "I… we won't need to wait too much longer. I'm almost ready…."

Our lips met again and we moved together with fervor, our passion only enhanced by the depth of our mutual respect. "There's no rush, Tristan, whenever you're ready, baby." I dared to reach my own hand down and pressed it to the front of his boxers. And there I found the proof; he wanted me in the same way I wanted him.

Since our lovemaking was not going to progress any further tonight, I gentled down my kisses and started to use my hands to soothe him rather than to inflame him. Tristan responded to my calming touches like a cat would. He raised each and every part of his body upward to meet my hands. Tristan was a very sensual man, and I supposed that as of right now, I was too. Because now I was with him.

"I never thought I'd feel this way." He pushed his crotch against my thigh in repetitive, subtle thrusts, probably hoping to relieve some of the pressure of his physical need. I didn't think he even knew how seductive his movements had been.

I stilled his recurring thrusts by placing my hand firmly on his ass. "There's no rush to make love, baby. We have all the time in the world. And tonight was perfect just as it was. Let's go to sleep now and wake up to our first Christmas morning together."

"First of many, right?"

As I nodded, the light stubble on my jaw brushed against Tristan's smooth forehead. It shocked me how much I wanted a hundred Christmas mornings with this man.

CHAPTER 30

Tristan

THERE was a definite love connection between Robby's niece, Madison, and me. First of all, I have to admit, I'd never been close to a child before. Once in a while a kid came into the restaurant, but most of the time the parents spent the whole meal trying to keep him quiet and occupied. Tonight's gathering was definitely not designed to keep little Madison's behavior under wraps. All of the adults present seemed to share the "Christmas is for children" philosophy. They asked her questions about whether she'd been a good girl this year and what Santa Claus had brought her and which kind of cookie she was going to eat first when she finished her dinner. And Maddy wasn't shy about answering questions, as long as you in no way suggested that she was a baby.

And I couldn't stop looking at her. She had clear blue eyes, a junior version of Robby's, a devilish little smile, and adorable blonde curls that bounced around on the puffy sleeves of her shiny, cherry-red Christmas dress. When she took me by the hand and pulled me over to the Christmas tree to show off all of her brand new toys, I was tongue-tied at first (what does a twenty-three-year-old man *say* to a three-year-old girl?), but that didn't seem to bother Maddy in the slightest. She talked enough to make up for my silence, and pretty soon her incredible toys had me almost as enraptured as I was with her.

"Play-Doh has definitely come into its own since we were kids, huh?" Robby crouched down beside the place where Maddy and I were making Play-Doh burgers, fries, and strawberry frappes.

"I guess so. I, uh, I don't think I had any Play-Doh when I was a kid." Madison looked up at me, completely scandalized by my confession. "But I think I made some silly putty in my first-grade art class." That comment seemed to have gotten me out of the doghouse.

But Robby tilted his head and looked at me strangely. Then he pushed up his sleeves and dove into the Play-Doh right along beside us, making a pretty good replica of a double cheeseburger with pickles and ketchup on a bun. It was fun.

"Now eat it, Mr. Tristan." She lifted Robby's cheeseburger and shoved it to my lips. I froze and must've looked like a deer in the headlights, not wanting to eat it but at the same time not wanting to disappoint a sweet little girl. In the nick of time, Robby mouthed the word "pretend" to me, and I did my best imitation of a man sloppily eating a burger.

It appeared that Madison was pleased with my performance. "Funny!" She clapped her chubby hands. "Do it again!" The giggle that followed was truly heartwarming. I would've eaten a dozen Play-Doh cheeseburgers to hear it again.

"Hey, you two, come join the big kids for a while." Robby's sister, Lindsey, called us over.

"But Mr. Tristan is playing with me right now, and you and Daddy aren't big kids, Mommy. You are *growed-ups*." Madison sent her mother a scornful glance. Lindsey was on her feet in no time at all and was soon speaking sternly into Madison's ear.

"Oh, o-o-o-kay. You can have Mr. Tristan and Uncle Robby back for a while." Madison stood up and then tried to help me to my feet, pulling at my arms with her plump little girl hands. "Mommy says I gots to say thank you for playing with me, and now it's time you gots to go sit in a chair and talk growed-up talk."

"Well, I want to thank you for playing with me too." I looked down at the little girl as she tried her very hardest not to pout. "And I brought you a little something for Christmas. I'll meet you in front of the tree after dinner and you can open it." Thankfully, the prospect of receiving a gift restored the grin to Maddy's face.

This afternoon's Christmas get-together had turned out to be just Robby's sister's family, Savannah, Robby, and me. Sadly, Mr. and Mrs. Dalton both had terrible cases of the flu and couldn't make it. Tonight, though, I wasn't nearly as nervous as I'd been at Thanksgiving; I didn't feel as much like Savi and I were being analyzed under a microscope. Not to say that Lindsey wasn't very aware of everything I said and did, because she was. And she actually seemed far more interested in me than she was in Savannah, which made me wonder if Robby had said anything to her about our growing feelings for each other.

"So, Tristan, how about a beer?" Lindsey approached me boldly, an open beer already in her hand. "Here, this Bud's for you." She laughed.

I took it from her with a nod. "I'd like to thank you for having us over tonight, Lindsey."

She didn't reply right away, and I could tell she was thinking. "Aren't you at all close to your own family, Tristan? You've spent Thanksgiving and Christmas with us." I could tell by the way she spoke that Lindsey wasn't trying to be cruel; she just wanted answers.

"Well, I... no, Lindsey, I'm not close to my family." After that admission I scoured my brain for a way to regain her decent opinion of me. "But I consider Savannah to be my family. And there is nothing I wouldn't do for her."

I received a smile. "I know what you mean. That's how I feel about Robby."

"Your daughter is very sweet too. And she knows how to tell it like it is." I hoped that was all right to say.

I guess it was, because I got another smile from Lindsey. "Well, I want Madison to be a polite young lady, but it is most important that she feels like what she says matters to us and that she grows up knowing and liking who she is."

I was tongue-tied for the second time tonight. Nobody had cared if I'd even grown up at all, let alone grown up with a positive self-image.

"You okay, Tristan?" Lindsey touched my arm. "Did I say something wrong?"

Suddenly, I felt like an imposter. Here I was, enjoying a Christmas celebration in a beautiful home, eating delicious food with quality people. And even if *they* didn't know who I was, *I* knew. I was a no-good runaway prostitute, whose own mother hadn't cared enough to keep me out of her brother's bed.

Worthless trash doesn't belong in a classy place like this.

I glanced around desperately for my lifeline. Where the fuck was Savannah? I needed her to save me from this moment. I shifted my weight back and forth from one foot to the other in discomfort, trying to calm my nerves.

"Hey, buddy, my sister is cool." I felt Robby's hand come down steadily on my shoulder and stay there. "Lindsey knows that not everybody gets an equal start in life. She was a high school teacher until Maddy came along, and she's seen a lot."

I managed to clear my throat and say, "Oh, yeah?" But I knew my eyes had swelled up and reddened. Only then did I notice that Savannah was watching this exchange from across the room. Couldn't she see my dismay? Why the fuck hadn't she come over to bail me out? I could feel the thirteen-year-old boy in me panicking.

"Now, Tristan, never worry about things like where you came from or how you were raised. You are a very kind person, I can tell, and I think my Maddy would agree." I glanced over at Maddy, who just so happened to be sitting cross-legged on the rug, her face in her hands, staring at me like she was in love.

Robby looked at his sister and smiled widely, his hand still on my shoulder. "Believe me Linds, human beings do not come any kinder than this man right here." He looked at me for a long moment. "I'm lucky I found him. Or that Savannah found me and introduced us, I guess I should say."

With his warm palm on my shoulder and his words of support, I felt my muscles loosen up a bit, and I began to relax. "Sorry I clammed up there for a minute, Lindsey. It is strange for me to see how, um, how much everybody cares for Madison. Kids in my family weren't treated, well, with such respect."

"Hey, it's no problem, not at all. Come on, Tristan, Robby tells me you like to cook and I want you to try my artichoke dip. I'm looking for a brutally honest opinion, okay?" As I followed her into the kitchen, I caught Savannah's eye from her high stool at the little bar in the corner of the family room. She smiled and winked, and I knew she had just taught me an important lesson.

I'd just learned that Robby could be my lifeline too.

CHAPTER 31

Robby

NOT to overuse a cliché, but on a scale of one to ten (ten being the best) our first Christmas as partners scored an eleven. And after a Christmas that good, how could New Year's Eve possibly not be a letdown?

One night several days after Christmas, the three of us were hanging out on the couch with all of the lights off just watching the snowflakes fall in the darkness outside the living room picture window, when I brought up the topic. "So, to start off the New Year right, should we go out to dinner and then go dancing, or should we rent a bunch of movies and get Chinese food delivered?"

Tristan lifted his head just slightly from my lap to respond. "I say we stay in. We can open up the sleeper sofa, put lots of blankets on it, and get movies and games and Chinese food. And beer. Plenty of beer and fruity wine for Savi. And we have to get champagne for midnight."

I had to smile because this plan sounded like so much more fun than my past ten New Year's Eves had been, nights I'd spent at parties and clubs and bars, pretending I'd wanted to be there. But before I had a chance to get too excited, Savannah, down on the other end of the couch, lifted Tristan's feet from off of her lap and stood up. Seeing the serious expression she wore, Tris shot up to stand beside her, unable to hide his concern. "We can do something else if that doesn't sound like fun to you, Savi."

Savannah took his hand, pressed it to her cheek, and looked up at him. "No, no, that's not it."

Tristan's face twisted; he was panicked. "What do you mean? *It?*"

Savannah sat back down and patted the place between us for Tristan to sit. "Tris, listen, I-I want to do something different this year on New Year's Eve. Something that is very important to me."

Tristan appeared nothing short of shell-shocked, clearly needing to know what Savannah had on her mind, and if he was included in her plan.

"What do *you* think we should do, Savannah?" I decided I should pipe up before Tristan had a coronary. "We're game for anything."

At my words Savannah looked distinctly uncomfortable. "The thing that I want to do is… well, it's kind of for, um, for girls only."

I glanced at Tristan; he was white as the fallen snow. No joke.

"A couple of the Boston area Big Sisters want to take our Little Sisters on an overnight tubing trip to Gunstock Mountain in New Hampshire. You know, when you ride a rope tow up the mountain and slide down on a huge inner tube, for a New Year's celebration. There's been loads of snow, and it'll be a once-in-a-lifetime trip for most of these girls and I really would like to do this." She exhaled sharply, seemingly relieved that she'd managed to spit out those words.

Tristan remained speechless, staring at the wall, his jaw hanging down.

"That sounds like a really nice thing to do. The girls will love it." It really was a terrific thing to do for young girls who didn't have all of the opportunities in life that kids like me had enjoyed.

"I think so, and I love to make my little sister, Lani, feel like she's important to me." Savannah addressed her words to me but was staring straight at a still-stunned Tristan. "She doesn't have anyone else to make her feel that way."

Tristan blinked. Savannah's request was apparently sinking into his brain.

"Don't worry, Savannah. Tristan and I will keep each other company." I leaned over toward him and hugged him tightly around the shoulders. "Right, Tris?"

Tristan turned to me slowly until those gorgeous brown eyes met mine. "R-right, yeah… Savannah, you go on ahead and hang out with the girls. I'll be fine h-here with Robby." This time his words were directed to Savannah, but his gaze did not waver from mine.

It seemed as if Savannah collapsed a bit onto the arm of the couch after Tristan let her off the hook, most likely in relief. "Thanks, you guys. I'll really miss you, but there are some things I need to do, you know, there are things I need to do to help the kids who need it." She nodded at Tristan. "Kids like *we* used to be."

Tristan blushed at her pointed comment, and we both chose to ignore the plural word "things." We would deal with one "thing" at a time, as far as Savannah separating herself from us went. And like clouds parting to allow the sun's rays to shine through, it became clear to me at that very moment exactly why Savannah had been so motivated to get Tristan and me together. She loved Tristan so deeply and she felt she owed him such a debt of gratitude, that she couldn't leave him to pursue her own goals in life until he was safe and secure in the arms of another person who loved him. She'd found that person in me.

And in no way was Savannah being selfish. She didn't require time away from Tris to travel the world or to date rich and successful men or to live in the lap of luxury. No, she needed time and space to accomplish important tasks, to prevent more teens from becoming lost like Tristan and Savannah had been. Or maybe to right the wrongs that had been done to them. Helping other teens in crisis was how she would deal with her own past, a past that had also been filled with pain and loss. Right then, I loved her more than I had ever loved any other woman. And I would do my part; I would stay with Tristan and love him and comfort him and be what they both needed me to be. Not because I had to, but because I wanted to.

Looking back.... Savannah

"*I'M SORRY, Savannah. I just... I just can't.*"

On the last night that we'd tried, I'd known pretty quickly that it simply wasn't going to happen with us. I mean, we'd been together for more than two years at that point. We'd become extremely close; we'd come to love each other beyond reason. And in this time together, Tristan had grown much healthier in mind as well as in body. There'd been no valid reason why we couldn't be intimate.

Our lack of success in the bedroom had a rather drawn-out history. The first time we'd tried and failed, we had attributed his inability to perform on the sexual trauma of his childhood, which was a very legitimate reason for impotence. The second time, we'd credited the effects of the gang rape when he was sixteen years old for his incapability, and the next time we'd agreed that he hadn't recovered sufficiently from the emotional toll of having been, at times, a child prostitute, to be sexually close to me. All of those had been valid reasons.

And there had been more attempts to be intimate, which had all started with frenzied kisses and had consistently ended with Tristan's head hanging, frustrated and humiliated by his inability to make love to me, and equally distraught by his inability to explain it. Or understand it.

But I'd eventually come to understand that Tristan's problem had not been with sex; the problem had been sex with me. I'd realized that though he'd loved me deeply, it was the sort of love a brother held for a sister. At first that knowledge had shattered my girlish dreams (no, Tristan and I were never going to get married, have babies, and live the white-picket-fence kind of traditional happily ever after). And soon, it had been my ego that had felt the devastation. I'd asked myself over and over why I hadn't been able to make Tristan want me. Hadn't I been pretty enough to attract him? Womanly enough? And that particular question had set off in my brain a slow process of realization.

So after a few weeks of observing him and speculating on his each and every word and movement, I'd just come right out and asked him, "Tristan, are you gay?"

CHAPTER 32

Tristan

THE night was here. I'd waited for it with a sort of annoyed impatience. I'd also wished it would never arrive. But it was here. And there wasn't much I could do about it now, was there?

"Savannah looked pretty happy to be climbing into that minivan with the girls, huh?" Robby and I had just returned to the apartment after having dropped Savannah off for her overnight trip to the mountains. I pushed the door open and both of us hung our coats on the hooks on the wall.

"She sure did, Robby. I'm glad she went. And Lani was having a pretty hard time acting as angry at the world as she usually does." I walked down the hall into the living room. "Hey, come here and look at this." On the coffee table was a small bouquet of red and white roses, and beside it a bottle of champagne and a card addressed to Robby and me.

Looking stunned, Robby said, "So this was what Savannah was doing when she came back upstairs to get her 'forgotten mittens.'" He leaned down and picked up the card. "You want to open it?"

"No." I shook my head. "You do it."

I watched as Robby opened the envelope and took out a pretty floral watercolor greeting card. "Savannah wrote, 'To my two favorite guys, Be each other's tonight.'" His voice broke on the last word. "There's a slip of paper in here with your name on it." He passed it to me.

Goosebumps rose on my skin as Robby's fingers pressed the note against my hand. Silently, I unfolded the paper and read.

Tristan-

You know I will love you and need you forever. We are, and always will be, each other's family. But now it is time for you to lean on Robby. And it is time for Robby to figure you out by himself. I want this for you, both of you. And for me, Tristan, I want this for me as well. So, now is the time for you to become each other's, in every sense.

Be my family and a home I can always return to.

I love you.

Savi

"I think I'm ready now, Robby."

Robby

I'D BEEN intimate with a handful of women. Maybe a bit more than that. Certainly not buckets full, though. But enough so that I knew what I was doing between the sheets. None of that less than plentiful (but surely sufficient) amount of experience was of any help to me tonight.

We lay shoulder-to-shoulder in the big bed, both of us highly aware of the fact that there was no Savannah present to act as our sexual buffer. Tonight we were alone and we were in love and we had Savannah's blessing—if not her direct command—to consummate our relationship. Stripped to the waist but still wearing my boxers, I'd never felt more naked and exposed before. As Tristan pulled the sheet up to his neck to cover his bare chest, I was fairly certain he felt the same way.

"I'm scared."

"Don't be. You know I would never hurt you, right?"

Tristan turned onto his side to look at me. "I'm not worried about *physical* pain, Robby. You *do* know that there's more than one way to hurt someone, right?" His voice was breathy as he threw my words back in my face.

I had to think about that for a minute, and when I did, it brought back words Savannah had said to me not too long ago. "Of course I know that. Why do you think I'd hurt you, anyways? I love you, Tristan."

He continued to study my face with a scrutiny with which I was almost uncomfortable. "Then I'll try not to be scared."

I turned to face him. "I'm as scared as you are, just for different reasons."

"Then tell me why."

God, Tristan was so fucking beautiful, so desirable. His dark hair fell over his forehead and rested like strands of silk on the pillow, begging me to run my fingers through it. And no eyes had ever been more compelling to me than his. But beneath his perfect face was a *man's* body, which complicated things. "H-how do we know, y'know, how do we know who goes on top?" I felt my face heat and a line of perspiration form above my top lip. I was out of my league here.

Strangely, where Tristan had seemed anxious about the emotional side of intimacy, he was far less uncomfortable with the physical aspects of it. "Well, when you think about us being together, how do you picture it? How do you fantasize about it, I guess is what I'm asking?"

My forehead joined in the rest of my face's perspiration party. "Uh, the only way I've ever, um, *been with someone*, is by being inside them. So, I guess I picture myself being inside you."

He didn't look at all scandalized, though I felt almost weak from the magnitude of my confession. "Is that how you want it, then?"

"I-I suppose so, if it's how you like it too."

Tristan placed a palm softly on my cheek and shrugged. "I've never been asked how I liked it before, but that's okay with me. I mean, it's good with me." Then he reached over me to the bedside table. "I'm gonna need to be ready for you, Robby. It's been a long time since, well, I'll put it this way, it *will* hurt if I'm not ready." He grabbed a small tube and a condom that he'd placed there before we'd gotten into bed.

"Let me. I want to get you ready myself." I took the tube from his hand but allowed it to drop onto the bed. "But first...." I shifted his slim form beneath me. "First, I want to kiss you."

And that is when the awkwardness of our preamble-to-sex discussion simply dissipated, because kissing Tristan plucked me right out of my head and transported me to a place where all I could do was feel. As my lips devoured his, my body responded quickly and powerfully, somehow screaming silently into my consciousness, "This is right! This is so very right!" There was no room for doubt; there were no questions. Tristan was the unique combination of strength and fragility that I had never before known but I simply had to know tonight. He was distinctive in my mind, though, not simply because he was a man, and not just because he was beautiful, but because he was pure and selfless, and at the very same time resilient and sturdy.

Because he is Tristan.

The desire I felt for him was matchless; he was forever irreplaceable to me.

I had to have him.

With the haste of a horny seventeen-year-old, I stripped us both of our shorts, and though I'd never seen Tristan's naked body in its entirety, as I ran my fingers methodically over every inch of his skin, I knew that it was perfect.

And when I was finally inside him, filling him with my body, the only quandary I experienced was that I also longed for him to be inside me at the very same time, taking me, making me his, as I was making him mine.

"I love you, Tristan, and you can trust me. *Please*, just trust me." I didn't want him to hold back any part of himself from me. He had opened his body to me; I needed his heart to be just as wide open.

In response to my pleading, Tristan just closed his eyes. "I love you too, Robby." His voice sounded breathless, even shaky. "I love you s-so m-much."

That was when I reached down to touch him in a way I had previously only touched myself. I could tell that he made a considerable effort to stifle the sound of his pleasure at the feeling of my hand on him, but he couldn't do it. Tristan moaned. And within a few seconds, we took each other to a place I'm certain neither of us had ever before been in the company of another human being.

Tristan

GET the fuck out of there, Tristan!

I was experiencing a panicked urge to flee to the bathroom, to find a safe haven to hide in.

Had I actually just loved this man with my body? Had I allowed him inside of every part of me? *Have I truly let him in?* The fight against flight took every bit of strength I had, but instead of withdrawing to a separate room, I curled up tight into a ball, but kept my face pressed flat against his chest.

"Tris? Baby, are you all right? I didn't hurt you, did—"

"No… no, it was… it was great." After a slow, deep breath, I kissed his skin, my lips sweeping the soft blond hair of his chest.

My answer hadn't satisfied Robby, though. He took my chin firmly in one hand and raised it so I was forced to look at him. "What's wrong? Talk to me *now.*"

"Just don't leave me, Robby. Don't leave, okay?" I blurted out those words without so much as a thought. But I couldn't confess the whole truth of what weighed so heavily on my mind—my senseless fear of entrusting my heart to another man. Even if I really did love him.

No man had ever gained my trust. Not even Robby.

I could feel a chuckle rumble up from deep within his chest. "Don't worry, baby. I'm not going anywhere. Not even if you chase me."

I believed that he meant those words, at least as he spoke them. As to whether he could keep that promise, I had absolutely no idea.

Robby

WE WOKE up at about seven minutes before midnight. I scrambled to the kitchen and grabbed the bottle of champagne that we'd put in the refrigerator and a couple of champagne flutes from off the counter. By the time I returned, Tristan was sitting up in our bed, shaking his head slowly as if in a daze.

I popped open the bottle and quickly filled each glass halfway. And I handed one glass to my lover. *My lover.* "Here, buddy, we have to make a proper New Year's Eve toast, and kiss exactly at midnight."

Tristan smiled, still appearing distracted by something, but I had no idea what. He could be a hard man to read, and since midnight was less than a minute away, I didn't have time to wait for him to spill out his thoughts.

"Why don't you make the toast, Tristan."

For a moment, he appeared uncomfortable. "To Savannah who brought us together, and to being each other's." He spoke those words with little expression, watching his hand on his glass rather than looking into my eyes.

"I want to see your eyes, Tristan." I waited for his soulful brown eyes to meet mine. And when our gazes finally connected, after he'd dragged his eyes excruciatingly slowly up the length of my naked body like he was memorizing every inch of me, there was absolutely no awkwardness between us. I felt no strangeness whatsoever when I studied the face of my male lover, a sentiment I suspected that Tristan shared. And our union was still as perfect now, without even touching, as it had been when we were making love. We clicked our glasses together lightly. "To our love, and our *trust*." But it was a fact: I wanted Tristan to know that I was aware of the one thing he withheld from me.

"It's midnight." Again, his voice was soft, even subdued.

And so I kissed him, all the while resolving that I would be the partner Tristan deserved. I promised myself I would not hide our incredible love, this honest and exquisite passion I'd been so blessed to discover, from anyone.

Then I prayed that I had the strength it took to do that.

CHAPTER 33

Robby

BEING in the office with Mikey for any substantial amount of time was close to being completely intolerable. The only small consolation I got for having to look at him came from the grisly sight of his swollen nose. Not pretty at all.

I was just so furious at him, and I felt that my promise to Tristan had prevented me from taking the necessary actions. When Mikey had first arrived this morning, there had been a prolonged period of complete silence. And in such a small office, the lack of Mikey's constant babbling unfortunately allowed me to become aware of so much as every breath the man took. After enduring the painful silence for an hour or so, Mikey started taking swipes at me. You know, verbal jabs.

"So, did you and your two honeys have a romantic New Year's Eve?" Neither of us looked up from our work.

"It was fine." I didn't even know why I answered him.

"Not gonna ask 'bout my New Year's, Rob?" He abruptly stood up and pushed his chair backward with his calves. "Not gonna ask 'bout how I survived my first New Year's Eve since I was a kid wit'out my wingman?"

If I didn't know better, I'd say the tone of Mikey's voice sounded like he was actually hurt by that fact. My absence had sincerely been mourned by a guy who could hurt another human being so badly without so much as a drop of regret. I looked up at him in shock. "You fucking beat an *innocent man* with a *baseball bat*, DeSalvo. I'm having trouble getting past that, okay?"

"That stupid night still on ya mind, bro?" He took a step around his desk in my direction. "You gotta learn to let that kind o' shit go."

That *stupid* night? I clenched my fists, ready to go to town on him yet again.

"So, let's just say for shits and grins, that maybe I was wanting to hook up wit' my oldest pal on, say, New Year's Day. You know, like how that song 'Old Lang Zine,' or whatever it is, says: 'don't forget the good old days wit' your good old friends,' right? So maybe I stopped by your apartment, and what do ya know? No Robby nowhere."

As I added the list of numbers in my ledger, I didn't hesitate long enough to betray any of my genuine concern about what he'd discovered.

"And what *else* do ya know? When I chatted up the building manager, he told me that Robert Dalton'd moved out, what did he say? Oh, yeah, way back in mid-December. Well, wasn't that an interesting little tidbit o' news for me?"

"So? What do you care where I live?" I forced my eyes to stay on the calculations in front of me.

He moved to my desk and then propped his ass on the edge. Bending down to get into my face, he said, his tone matter of fact, "I guess now you're a homo, huh?"

And yet again, he managed to push me over my emotional edge. I stood up. "So maybe I'm living with my girlfriend now," I lied, and it felt so wrong. I was nothing but a piece of shit for betraying my love for Tristan like this. Yet I pressed on with the farce. "Lots of guys live with their girlfriends, Einstein. It's not exactly front-page news."

"Ever think to tell your family 'bout it? I'm pretty sure they got no clue that you changed your residence."

"I don't need their permission to move."

Mikey shook his head and offered me a patronizing smile. I knew he wasn't buying what I'd said about me living with my girlfriend, and honestly I really didn't care what the fuck he thought.

"Right-o, Rob. Whatever ya say."

"I suppose you're gonna run right off and squeal to my father, seeing as you two are attached at the hip lately, and all." I was perspiring, and abundantly so because my father's opinion of me was my only real concern here. Always had been, probably always would be.

"I'm thinking that it's my duty to inform him." His mouth was shaped into a strained grin, but his eyes were dead serious. "As the *son* your father never had."

It was so hard to hold myself back from beating the piss out of him right then. And my anger was only compounded by my guilt, because my biggest concern at that moment was what he was going to say to my father. Mikey had fucking attacked my partner with a baseball bat—Tris still wore the ugly bruises to prove it—and here I was fretting over what the asshole was going to spill to my dad. But I somehow pushed that issue from my mind and took a verbal swing back. "DeSalvo, you've got to go out and get yourself a life so you can stop obsessing over mine. And leave my father the fuck out of your plans for the future, huh?"

In a split second the grin had fallen from his face and the look in Mikey's eyes had grown even more menacing. "I'm afraid I can't do that, D-man. So, I'd say you should be expecting to hear from dear old Daddy soona rather than later. Unless you wanna make a quick change, you know, dump the fag and the bitch and come stay wit' me at my place." Were those dark eyes pleading with me? "And if ya do that, I think it'd be real inconvenient for me make that little tell-all trip to the Dalton household."

He was trying to blackmail me. If I left Tristan and Savannah, he'd keep quiet about what he'd suspected had been going on between Tristan and me. And, yes, I loved my father, and I placed incredible importance on what he thought of me. But I had to hang onto the shred of hope that I could stay with Tristan and Savannah *and* somehow talk my way out of any complications with my father.

CHAPTER 34

Tristan

TRUST was definitely my biggest issue when it came to Robby, as well as when it came to the entire human race, to be more accurate, but Robby was the person in question right now.

He and Savannah kept me company as I cooked dinner. I was trying out a new recipe, chicken croquettes with Creole sauce, that I'd read about in a home magazine I'd picked up to pass the time while I rode the subway to and from work. I hoped it came out as good as it looked in the picture, but we had indulged in several bottles of white wine Robby had brought home to go with dinner, and I was already a bit tipsy.

"I'll make a salad," Savi said, pulling her bare feet from Robby's lap where she'd been resting them. I loved seeing how close they'd grown. It made me confident that neither of them felt insecure, like a third wheel, in our relationship of three, which had become a concern of mine ever since the romance had deepened between Robby and me. Savannah got up and went to get a chopping board. And soon she was talking. "I, um, I took the second semester off from school."

She had her back to us now, so she couldn't see the way we were both gaping at her in disbelief. Being a guidance counselor had always been her dream.

"See, there's this group home for troubled teens in Boston that's looking for a person to supervise the residents for both short- and long-term stays. It would be an excellent experience for me, it'd look great on my resume, and I-I really want to do it."

After a brief but definitely awkward silence, Robby spoke up. "Would it be safe for you?"

Relieved that she had a question to focus on, she rattled off her answer. "Oh yeah. These kids are more troubled in the sense that they have been abused or neglected and have trouble fitting into society. Many of them are runaways and kids who don't have a foster family, or it didn't work out with the foster family they had." She started to chop rather violently at the salad vegetables that I'd put on the counter earlier.

"How will you work this out with school?" Again, Robby being Mr. Sensible.

"My professors are actually encouraging me to do it. They are going to look into whether or not I can get some credits for it, say, if I do a presentation on my experience for the department at the end."

"Will it affect your scholarship?"

"No, I already checked. Everything would just be deferred until next semester. And I'd make a little money doing it—not much, but it would be something." Her voice sounded so hopeful.

Too bad I was going to crush her hopes. "You don't need to work—I take care—I mean, *Robby and I* take care of you, Savi."

Savannah spun around, knife and tomato still in hand. "Don't you get it, Tristan? This is something I want to do—something I *have* to do. Please don't try to stop me."

She looked absolutely panic-stricken.

Have I done this to her? Have I made her feel this anxious?

"Please, Tris."

Right then, Robby got up and came to stand next to me at the counter. So I turned my back to both of them, staring at the croquettes as if the solution to my problems could be found there. I felt Robby move up behind me, sort of spooning me while standing up and rubbing my pounding chest at the same time. He didn't say anything; he just let me feel the comfort of his presence.

Maybe he's trying to show me that I can trust him.

I took a deep breath and then sucked down a gulp of wine. "Go ahead and do it, Savannah. I mean, you should do it. You can really help a lot of people. After all, look what you did for me."

Robby's arms tightened around my chest. He leaned in close and murmured into my ear, "It'll be fine. *We'll* be fine."

And right then I knew I had the strength to face Savannah. Yeah, maybe some of the strength came through Robby, but I think much of it came from inside me as well. Robby released me as I turned to her, and then I had to smile because she'd put down the knife but still clung to that poor, now-squished tomato. Her eyes were dry but very wide, and she held her body stiffly.

"I'm sorry for what I've done to you for the past few years, Savi. I'm so sorry."

"No, you haven't done anything to me except love me and take care of me—"

"Yes, I have," I replied quickly, cutting off her words. "I've been selfish. I've kept you in the same safe little box that *I* wanted to live in. And I shouldn't have, but until now, until *Robby*, you were the only light in my life and I just needed you so badly. I thought I had to clutch on to you tightly, or I'd lose you."

Savannah stepped forward, her expression fierce. "You will never lose me. Never. We are family."

"I know. And I think both of us need to step out of that little box that I kept us in. I mean, I think it's time."

She reached up and I bent down a bit, so she could hug me around the neck. "I will never leave you alone, not in the way that really counts." She touched the place on my chest over my heart.

Robby cleared his throat. "So I guess that's where I came in, huh?"

We both looked at him, and I admit, we did so somewhat guiltily. What could we say to that? He was right. Clearly, Savannah had been looking at Robby to fulfill me, and I had been looking at him to fulfill Savannah. We had both been very selfish.

"I'm not saying that I mind. I'm just trying to add it all up so it makes sense." He actually smiled. "And look what I got out of the deal, the best friend a guy could ever hope for, and a man who I'm in love with."

Emotional overload. I had to sit down. So I pushed past both of them and plunked myself down on the chair Robby had been sitting in. But I wasn't alone for long. Both of my partners came to my side, Savannah hugging me around the neck, and Robby kneeling down at my feet.

And then it hit me. Tristan Chartrand, the lonely teenage runaway/prostitute/street urchin, had everything any man could hope for. All I had to do now was allow myself to fully trust—in the fact that Savannah would always be there for me, as well as in Robby's love. I thought that maybe today's revelation had been a small step in that direction, but then again, trusting men had never gotten me very far.

"So, Savi, tell me, when do you leave for the group home?"

CHAPTER 35

Robby

SO, I guess I was ready for it when he called. I mean, I was as ready as a guy could be. But who is actually ever fully prepared to inform his he-man of a father that he's gay? I held on to the hope that there was a way around that kind of revelation.

"Rob, it's your father."

I had caller ID so that wasn't news to me. "Hi, Dad."

"We need to talk." His voice was gruff. "Today."

I slowly blew out the breath I was holding. "About anything in particular?"

He didn't answer. But he sounded impatient as he repeated himself. "Today."

"Want to meet for lunch?"

"Now. I want to meet you right now."

Sitting at the kitchen table this morning, debating with Tristan the Bruins' chances of making it to the Stanley Cup, I'd sucked down way too much coffee. Three big mugs of coffee, in fact, because I couldn't bear to drag myself away from the man. Way too much caffeine in the veins; that must've been why I was feeling so jittery right then. *Right, that has to be it.* "S-sure."

"You know where the Egg Shell Diner is, in Saugus?"

The Egg Shell? Did that old place still exist? "Yes, I've been there, I think."

"Well, be there in half an hour."

"Okay, see ya soon, Dad."

I didn't receive a "good-bye, son." He just hung up.

MY FATHER had chosen an out-of-the-way diner to hold this meeting. And he was already inside the restaurant when I arrived, sitting at an out-of-the-way booth, way off in a back corner, which further enhanced my already elevated feelings of trepidation. A dark, shadowy corner where there was no chance that anyone, had there been another soul eating in this tacky diner, would overhear our conversation. He was already mostly finished downing a giant plate of scrambled eggs and bacon.

Thanks for waiting for me to order, Dad. Yes, I *thought* that little slice of sarcastic commentary. What I actually *said* was "Good to see you, Dad. How are the eggs here?"

"Sit down." Dad clearly wasn't here to discuss the Egg Shell Diner's greasy home cooking, though. "We need to talk."

Okaaaay....

I knew what he really meant was that he was going to tell me shit and I was going to listen and obey. Perspiration broke out on my forehead. I sat down across from him and nodded.

A waitress, notepad in hand, made an attempt to approach our table in a futile effort to take my breakfast order, but she was brusquely waved away by my father. He took his napkin off the table and roughly wiped his lips, and then he ran his hands through his thick mop of graying sandy-colored hair, in a manner not too different from Tris when he was nervous. The similarities to Tristan ended there. After straightening his thick shoulders, he leaned in over the table, stared right at me with his piercing blue eyes, and jammed a knife into my heart.

"You, Rob, are the biggest disappointment in my life."

No, it hadn't been his actual butter knife with which he'd stabbed me, but I almost wished it had been. I suspected that even its dull blade would have hurt far less than those words.

I couldn't breathe. In fact, I felt as if a giant had poked a long straw into my chest and sucked all the air out of my lungs, leaving a gasping, suffocating shell of Robby Dalton sitting across from his disgusted father in this greasy spoon. "D-Dad, but, Dad...."

"I worked hard to raise you and your sister with proper Christian morals."

I nodded emphatically in agreement, although I couldn't remember ever setting foot in a church when I was a kid. Or being reminded to say my prayers when my parents had tucked me into bed at night.

"I thought I'd done a decent job with *both* of you, until recently." He wiped his mouth with the napkin again, and then rubbed it over each of his fingertips, one by one. "I got a rather, uh, *disturbing and enlightening* telephone call from Michael DeSalvo last night."

Yup. I knew where this was going. I gulped in a big breath. "And what did Mikey have to say?"

My father shoved the plate holding scattered remnants of his eggs and bacon toward the middle of the table with obvious disgust. "I'm not going to mince words with you, son." He continued to look directly into my eyes as he sharpened his next verbal dagger. "Mike told me that you have been, let's say, *overly affectionate* with a *queer*." My face froze, certainly wearing an expression of unmitigated horror, but Dad wasn't finished yet, and not by a long shot. As I struggled to remove his most recent dagger from my heart, he continued his assault. "You've fucking moved in with that pansy, haven't you?"

I'd thought I'd prepared myself to deal with any nastiness the man could possibly shell out. I'd been wrong.

Could one man's mere words possess sufficient power to taint the purity of newly discovered love? At that moment, I found it very likely. The memories of my closeness to Tristan suddenly seemed cheap and dirty. Perverse, even. I shoved the ethereal beauty of Tristan's face from my brain.

"Don't you have anything to say for yourself, Rob? I'm sincerely hoping that you can clear up this little, um, *misconception* that Mike has regarding your, uh, your *relationship* with this... this *person*."

This *person*? Vulnerable, caring, entirely selfless, but not yet trusting Tristan. And apparently for very good reason. "I don't know if Tristan Chartrand is a faggot or not, and I really don't give a shit either, Dad. I'm stuck with him because he's my girlfriend's roommate. What do you expect me to do? Kick him out of his own fucking place just 'cause I want to be able to get busy on the living room couch with Savannah whenever the mood strikes me?" I was the king of cowards; my words had just proved it.

My father smiled, though only slightly. It was actually much more of an ugly, but very satisfied, sneer. "Spending so much time with that *boy* is indecent. It's actually rather revolting, in my opinion, even if that girl *is* around. Am I making myself clear?"

As a crystal, Dad. "Of course, and I already knew I was gonna have to kick those two to the curb at some point; I'll just have to make my move sooner, rather than later."

I'd pretty much given my father every single thing he'd wanted from me every single day of my life. I'd allowed him to run my athletic life all through my school years, to drive my college plans, and even, to some extent, to manipulate my career choice. I'd struggled to please him from the first time I'd picked up a T-ball bat in preschool, to each and every day when I went to work. I'd always tried so damned hard to make him proud. And this morning, without even thinking twice about it, I'd taken my heart, wrapped it up in colorful paper, and handed it to him so he could do whatever the fuck he wanted with it.

Not only had I relinquished my heart to him, but I'd also given up every last speck of my personal integrity. And I'd done it willingly, dragging Tristan and Savannah right under the bus along with me. With my good old friend Mikey's able assistance, my father had won, like always, and the rest of us had lost. But mostly me.

I am the biggest loser of all.

As he stood up and grabbed his overcoat from the chair beside him, he once again looked at me pointedly. "Now, I want you to give that nice young man, Michael, a call, and the two of you can go out together and play like *real* men." Dad chose that moment to flash me a rather jubilant smile.

I watched him stride purposefully to the restaurant's door, poised body language demonstrating his satisfaction with the direction our conversation had taken. He seemed so huge and towering, as he always had when I was a boy.

"I'll fix it, Dad. I will." I spoke softly, knowing he couldn't hear me, but realizing, simultaneously, that he didn't need to hear my oath. My father left the restaurant completely confident that his puppet of a son would do anything and everything to avoid earning his father's displeasure.

I placed enough cash on the table to cover Dad's breakfast and a tip, and then staggered my way to the door in a complete daze, bringing to mind a strong feeling of déjà vu. I didn't exactly have to scour my brain to remember dropping a wrinkled wad of cash on a different table, in a different nondescript diner several months ago, when Savannah had so bluntly informed me of how it was going to be.

And as always, it was clear that I was going to be unable to please all parties involved. In itself, that knowledge tore me apart. Completely preoccupied by my worries, as soon as I stepped outside onto the diner's icy walkway, I immediately lost my balance, slipped, and fell to my hands and knees. The frozen pavement sliced easily through my khakis to my knees, ripping the skin from my palms as well. And I just stayed in that fittingly submissive position, relishing the sharp pain in my extremities that had plucked me from my daze, but still unwilling to move as I had absolutely no clue where I would go if, in fact, I was to get up off the ground.

CHAPTER 36

Tristan

"I MISS you, too, Savi, but what you're doing is important, probably even life changing for those kids." I stirred the pasta and checked the digital clock on the oven at the same time. Robby was late. "So, call me again really soon, and when Robby comes home I'll be sure to give him a big hug from you, 'kay?"

I ended my conversation with what Robby had lately been calling a "brave little shrug" and then drained the pasta in the sink, thinking how it really hadn't been too difficult over the past few weeks since Savannah had moved into the group home. It was true that I missed her, and I avoided dwelling too much on the fact that she wasn't living with us right now, but Robby had kept me *very* busy, probably to distract me. And I had to admit, he had been successful. We had hit the gym almost daily—with Robby's help I'd even worked up the courage to get in the pool a few times and try my hand at swimming—and we'd watched more sports on television than I ever had before. But what did you expect with two guys living together in what Robby had started referring to as our "man-cave"?

And we'd eaten. A lot. Robby had cut out of work to take me out for lots of long lunches—Thai food, sushi, and Italian food (three times). I'd cooked on the nights I didn't have to work, and on the nights I'd waitered, I'd brought home leftover daily specials from Michael's. Those nights, we'd splurged on seafood smothered in buttery breadcrumbs for our midnight snacks.

The first few nights, right after Savannah had left, I'd had some bad dreams. Really devastating ones about that horrible night when I was a teenager—the night I'd been raped—and I'd woken up shouting for Savannah. Wanting to be certain she was safe... *wanting to be certain I was safe*. What had amazed me, though, was that on those terrible nights, there had been no string of relentless questions from Robby, no demand for an explanation of my nightmares. He'd just pulled me against his chest and held me. And feeling so safe in his arms, I'd been able to go back to sleep without too much trouble.

No, I still hadn't opened my soul to him completely. I refused to spill out my deepest fears, my pain. *My story.* But I was getting closer, much closer, to allowing myself to trust him. At least that's what I told myself.

For some reason, a reason even *I* couldn't fully understand, I still held back that one final piece of my heart from Robby. And he knew it. And he wanted more from me. But I just couldn't release it all. Not yet.

Where was he, anyways? It was nearly eight now. I'd gotten off work at five and assumed we'd work out and then eat dinner together. When Robby hadn't returned by seven, I'd gone ahead and put together a simple meal. But it was really strange that he hadn't called to tell me he was going to be late. Hopefully, it was a sign that his meeting at the nursing home had gone better than he'd expected.

I could feel a gentle rocking motion take control of my body, even as I stood by the stove.

Robby

IT HAD taken me almost half an hour to calm myself down enough to be able to drive out of the diner's parking lot. Maybe my life was all screwed up, but I still knew that there was no reason for me to drive when I was so distraught I couldn't see straight, and then possibly hurt an innocent person. When I finally felt fit to start my car, though, I was presented with an entirely new problem: I had absolutely no idea where I should go.

My office was out of the question. I was likely to kill Mikey if I got close to him, because, yes, it would be way too easy to blame the asshole for all of my problems. But these were *my* problems. Created by me, and they had to be owned by me. And suffered for by me. Mikey had merely added fuel to the fire.

Our apartment was off-limits too. I'd betrayed the man I loved. I'd violated the precious little bit of trust that I had practically begged him for. But my misery didn't end there, since I knew that if I went back to our place right now, I wouldn't be able to simply beg Tristan for forgiveness for my weakness, and forge on ahead with him, hand in hand, into our blissful future, because I had absolutely no plans to tell my father to take a long hike off a short pier. In other words, I had already put into action an almost automatic and completely obedient response to my father's demands, hadn't I?

I was in the process of leaving Tristan. I was running away from him, not toward him.

I wondered for a moment if it was time I tucked my tail between my legs and went home to Mom and Dad. No, that was definitely not going to happen either. Sure, my father had laid down the law, and sure, I had spinelessly fallen right into step with his demands, but still I hated it. I hated my weakness. I hated myself. And I hated the home that had created me.

Lindsey. I could talk to Lindsey. But was it right to bring my drama into her home? Into her life? She was due to give birth any *minute* now and I wasn't going to taint this perfect time in her life with my fucked-up, romantic saga.

So for a long time I drove around rather aimlessly, obsessing over the fact that I couldn't move forward into the future I wanted and that I refused to go backward to the old life I'd never fit into. Finally, I ditched my car at a subway stop, hopped on a train, and headed to Boston.

I had come up with an idea that I hoped would help me to find clarity.

Tristan

IT WAS almost midnight and Robby still hadn't come back home. I was seriously worried about him now. So worried, in fact, that when he hadn't answered the half-dozen messages I'd left on his cell phone, I'd actually called his office, risking a conversation with Mikey. And then I'd called again and again. No one had answered.

I felt sick. As I paced around my apartment, my body didn't know whether to sweat or to shiver. And at the same time that I was agitated to the point of nausea over where the hell Robby was and whether he was safe, I was equally worried about *myself*. I wasn't proud to admit that the prospect of being left by both Robby and Savannah had my heart pretty much tied in knots.

Okay, I could easily be referred to as a complete fucking mess.

I was alone.

Alone, like I'd been for all those years.

Because no one had cared back then.

I was alone.

It looked like no one cared now, either.

Because I wasn't worth much, *was I?*

I curled up on my side into a ball on the couch, wrapping my arms tightly around my knees. This position reminded me of the single obsession I'd lived with for so many years while I was growing up: my desperate need to be small. So small that nobody would notice me. So small that I wouldn't even be conscious of me.

I always knew I'd end up like this.

Robby

IT TOTALLY sucked that bars closed at two.

The drinking had helped to lift my mood, or at least it had seemed that way for the first ten or so hours as I sucked down enough hard stuff to detach me from my fucked-up reality. But according to the plan to find clarity that I'd so hastily concocted, I had to ditch my wallet and my already-dead cell phone at some point tonight. I couldn't exactly experience anything close to what Tristan had lived through with a wallet full of cash, a tall stack of credit cards, not to mention a high-tech iPhone at my disposal, now, could I? So, at closing time, I dropped my wallet and phone into a trashcan in the bathroom of the last nameless bar I visited. And I staggered out the back exit of the bar into the night.

It totally sucked that bars closed at two.

Tristan

THIS was turning into a long frigging night. I'd managed to get some sleep, but I was pretty sure my last nightmare had put a decisive end to all that. Getting gang-raped, and brutally so, even if it was just in your subconscious mind, again and again and again, as helpless as a fucking newborn, suffering indescribable pain and humiliation, begging out loud that they'd treat you as kindly as they'd treat their goddamned dog, well, those things were not exactly conducive to a good night's rest.

It was tough to say which one of them I longed for more. When I stretched out on the couch in the dark and Runaway climbed onto my belly and started his usual paw-kneading thing, I had visions of Savannah.

The frigging weirdest memories of her popped into my mind: our first night together back when we were kids, with Savi alternately shivering from cold and crying from fear, and then me rubbing her arms 'til she was all warmed up and cracking jokes to distract her, the two of us trying like hell to get something going in bed, and failing miserably time and again, the way she moved to music, and how she loved troubled kids beyond everything else.

Beyond everything else.

Beyond me.

And then came the images of Robby, the awesome V-shape of his chest when he stood up in the hot tub at the gym, which consistently caused a physical reaction between my legs that genuinely surprised me every time, the way he'd grinned at me like I was a champion that time I'd dived headfirst into the dirt and had come up with the sky-high pop fly he'd hit, and what it felt like to be joined with him in love, wrapped up in his arms, living in each other's eyes, just for a moment.

But he wasn't here with me tonight either, was he? Robby had left me. He'd *abandoned me*, even after he'd promised me he'd stay. Or else he was dead. What other reason could there be for his absence? In either case, I was alone.

I was dealing with this alone. And that was the biggest surprise of all.

Robby

I WASN'T half the man that Tristan was, and I meant that in every sense.

How had he survived this as a boy? How had he lived out here for years on end? I couldn't fathom how he'd managed to stay sane.

For the first hour or so after I left the bar, I just sort of wandered the streets. I wasn't even slightly tired, nor was I hungry; too much adrenaline was flowing through my veins for me to feel simple bodily needs. But I knew that at some point I'd have to crash.

It didn't take too long until the cold set into my bones. And with the cold came panic. How was I going to stay warm? Would I freeze to death on my one night "trying out" life as a homeless person? Whatever the case, I needed warmth. I needed shelter. I had to find it.

So in the pitch darkness of this bitter winter night I began to search desperately, as if my life depended on it (which it very possibly did) for the right place to shelter me. For just a little corner out of the wind. Heat would be a bonus, a luxury even. After less than four fucking hours outside I was already feeling desperate. I marched down a street whose name I hadn't even cared to note, tugging relentlessly on ATM doors and car door handles as I passed.

But beneath my panic, I knew I could pick up any telephone at any phone booth in the city, make a collect call home, and help would be on its way. Warmth, food, safety, and people who cared would be mine in less than thirty minutes flat. Fourteen-year-old Tristan had had no such assurances to bolster him on his desperate journey. He'd been completely alone in the world. If he got too cold, he'd freeze. If he got too hungry, he'd starve. If someone had wanted him dead on the sidewalk, well, I guessed that now I knew what that had meant for him as well as he had known it then. Ask anyone, except for possibly my dad; I was a quick learner.

After a thirty-minute search, I found an unlocked car door and was overjoyed. I may as well have located heaven's pearly gates. Quietly, I slipped into the sedan's back seat, curled up into a fetal position, and tried to relax enough to fall asleep. Which was impossible. I became hyperaware of every sound—there were sirens, gusts of wind, voices in the distance. At every small noise, I jolted upright and looked around, fear of being caught now added to my list of worries. Soon, I was a shivering, chattering, not to mention paranoid, mess. So much so, that I dragged myself out of my safe haven to search for a better place to call my own until the sun was higher in the sky.

My next stop was a loading dock on the back side of a commercial building. As I lay there, my overcoat filthy, my pants ripped and bloody from yesterday's fall, my bare hands bloodied, and now frozen, I reminded myself that I was here by my own choice. I was out here right now because I didn't know where to go. I couldn't move forward with Tristan because of my fear of losing my father's love, and I couldn't move forward in the way I'd promised my father because then I would more truthfully be moving backward. I'd be living a lie.

I closed my eyes and hoped for sleep, which stubbornly refused to come.

CHAPTER 37

Tristan

I'D MANAGED to survive the night without either of them. It hadn't been fun and I hadn't gotten much rest. But here I was. Alive and kicking.

Since I'd taken the day off work, I had to decide how I was going to spend the next twenty-four solitary hours. If Robby had been here, we would have gotten up early, headed for the gym to play basketball, lift weights, and take a long soak in the hot tub. I definitely couldn't face that gym without my workout partner.

I considered calling Savannah and asking her to come home to visit. Which would surely turn into me begging for her to come home to stay. After all, I needed her every bit as much as those kids did, right? But instead, I decided that despite the frigid weather, I'd go for a long walk and then I'd try to eat something at a diner. Because if I lay on that couch for one more minute, I was going to start to think about the reasons that Robby hadn't come home to me and the reasons that Savannah should. I needed that shit like I needed a fucking hole in the head.

And besides, I already knew why Robby hadn't come home last night. He hadn't come home because he'd come to his senses. He'd finally realized he wasn't a gay man interested in being tied down in a relationship with a barely educated, runaway-prostitute-turned waiter. What handsome, successful, educated businessman would want to throw away his life with someone like that?

But a small part of me rebelled against accepting my automatic assumption that Robby had left me to find something better. Maybe Robby hadn't come home because he'd needed to go out and find something much more essential—*himself.*

Yes, a walk was what just I needed. To hopefully keep me from crying my eyes out. And maybe just to find a measure of peace and acceptance.

Robby

I GUESS I did fall asleep, because all of a sudden I was aware of being prodded by something pointy, as well as being screamed at. "Get the hell out of here, you goddamn dirty loser! Go find yourself another stoop to sleep on." Through my open coat and thin shirt, I felt the prickly bristles of a broom poking roughly into my side. "Yeah, you heard me, all right! Now get lost, and try getting a fucking job!"

I stumbled onto my feet and scurried off down the street, glancing back every couple of steps to be sure the storekeeper wasn't chasing me. When I got far enough away to feel safe from the wrath of the man and his menacing broom, I reached into my back pocket, automatically feeling around for my wallet. Clearly, it was time for coffee, right?

And then I remembered. I wasn't Robby Dalton anymore. I'd left him behind last night in an effort to live out this "homelessness experiment" of sorts. So now I wasn't anybody but a nameless street person who had no ID, no money, no phone, and few choices. But this temporarily homeless guy was damn hungry and more than a little bit hungover. Now I had another problem, didn't I? Food and water. How did you go about getting sustenance when you had not a dime to your name?

At first I scoured the filthy city street in search of lost change. This turned out to be painfully slow going. After a miserable hour all hunched over to examine the minutest details of the filthy pavement, I'd managed to find a mere thirty-two cents and my fingers had grown sticky and black with grime. But I was so damned hungry at that point I decided it was time to find out just what thirty-two cents could buy me at a convenience store.

After a quick browse around the next Quick Mart I came across, during which I received several scathingly dirty looks from the man behind the counter, and to top it off, a mother rather fiercely yanked her pretty little ballerina daughter, who happened to be about the same age as Madison, completely out of proximity of my objectionable presence, I came to the conclusion that thirty-two cents would buy me exactly nothing.

Still hungry, I continued my inelegant stroll down the busy street, suddenly overly aware of all of the passersby, nibbling on muffins and breakfast sandwiches, sipping tall cups of coffee. My mouth was watering enough to irrigate a desert when finally I succumbed to temptation. I wasn't proud, but damn, I was hungry, so when a cleanish office-assistant-looking woman tossed the remainder of her donut and bottle of water into a nearby trashcan, I literally pounced.

As I sat on a bench, scarfing down a stranger's leftovers, dreaming about sipping on a cup of hot coffee, I couldn't help but admit how surreal this experience was. Eye-opening too. Yet another flicker of admiration for the man who'd survived this as a child sparked within me, only to quickly die out.

I wasn't ready to analyze it quite yet.

Tristan

I HAD thought that a brisk walk in the winter air would have cleared my head, but that had apparently been wishful thinking. I returned home several hours later, depressed as hell.

The next big mistake I made involved going to bed. I thought maybe if I lay down, I'd end up falling asleep, and I'd get a little escape from missing Robby so badly. But that didn't go as planned either because I started worrying.

Where was he? Was he hurt? Or sick? Had I done something wrong? Had he realized he wasn't gay? Had he come to his senses about what kind of a person I really was? Or was there another reason he hadn't come home?

There was no end to my list of questions. But what was worse than all of the wondering was the way I missed him. Until then, I hadn't realized how thoroughly Robby had become a part of my life. And being in our bed reminded me of the thing I missed more than anything else; I missed waking up all warm and snug against his chest. When I was in his arms, the world felt more or less like a good place. A place where I was safe. Robby had given me a sense of security that I'd never before even known existed. And I wanted it back.

I couldn't say I took it for granted, because I hadn't, but another thing I cherished about our relationship was Robby's patience in teaching me things, like how he'd taught me all about sports. He'd devoted as much time and energy into teaching me the rules and skills of baseball, basketball, football, and lately, hockey, as any father had ever granted to his school-aged son. When Robby had been teaching me everything I ever wanted to know about sports but had never had anybody to ask, he had always been enthusiastic and encouraging. I'd felt smart when I'd learned and talented when I'd played. I truly loved that aspect of Robby.

Come to think of it, there was so much about him that I loved, but I wouldn't neglect to recognize the way he made me feel sexually. All I could say was that being intimate with him felt perfect—in every way. Somehow, through his unique blend of masculinity and sensitivity, Robby was able to excite me and soothe me, both at the very same time, which, I realized, was how I needed to experience my sensuality.

I was never afraid he'd hurt me physically, as so many had done before him. Robby was always incredibly gentle, although his body possessed the power to do whatever damage he wished. And I'd pretty much come to worship that powerfully muscled body. It was heavenly to run my fingers over all of those sculpted grooves, as well as to study every perfect inch of him with my eyes, knowing that he would only use his strength to love and shelter me.

Why had I never allowed him to see me naked? Why had I withheld those very same pleasures from him? I shook my head, bitterly regretting my unwillingness.

Ultimately, the question I needed to ask myself was not why he had left me, but rather why had I never fully allowed myself to be his? Why hadn't I fully trusted Robby Dalton? Maybe it was because I'd been certain that he'd been holding something vital back from me. Maybe it had been because I'd been scared of having to deal with exactly what I was going through right now.

Maybe it was because I'd been just plain scared.

And since it had been almost twenty-four hours since he'd been expected to come home and hadn't, I allowed myself time to cry.

I needed to cry.

Robby

I WAS pretty sure they were going to mug me. And I suspected that after the fact they'd be damned disappointed with what they'd gained.

Somehow, I'd managed to get cornered in a back alley, behind a big dark-green dumpster, by three gangly, but nonetheless tough-looking young men. Had I been in my element, well fed and well rested on the streets of suburbia, I had no doubt I could have taken at least a couple of them down without too much trouble. But I was not in my element, was I? These street punks had home-field advantage.

"Ya wallet, man, cough up ya wallet."

"'Fore we have ta hurt ya, dude."

I automatically reached into my back pocket, again feeling around for my wallet. "I, uh…. I lost it, uh, last ni-night." My voice actually had the nerve to crack like a teenager's.

"Fuckin' hell. Ya sayin' we have ta fuckin' cavity search ya for it? If I find it, man, you is fuckin' dead." The largest of the three stepped forward. He turned me around like I was an eighty-pound weakling and shoved me hard against the dumpster. Then he proceeded to reach into each of my coat pockets and all four pockets of my pants. He patted my chest and ass, none too gently, ignoring the few coins in the bottom of my pocket, and then whipped me back around to face him. Out of his pocket he popped a small but sufficiently threatening blade. He held it to my throat and I saw my life flash before my eyes.

Where the fuck had big, strong, athletic Robby Dalton gone? And who was this cowering loser who had just removed his wristwatch and was holding it out rather desperately to three skinny teenagers like it was some sort of a peace offering? "Take this. It's all I've got."

The smallest of the three got right up in my face. "Shit—man, this ain't nothin'—we oughtta fuck you up real bad." Nonetheless, he snatched the watch that dangled from my fingers. "We want yer coat, yer belt, and that fancy-ass tie ya got there." I didn't even have to move; they helped themselves to what precious few belongings I had left. And after a couple of quick punches to my jaw and a few kicks to my gut for good measure, I suppose, the little gang made a stealthy exit onto the adjoining avenue.

I sank down to my knees on the pavement beside the stinking trash receptacle. Immediately, I felt a sting as gravel came in contact with the open sores on my knees. A torrent of new terror engulfed me as I knelt there, the first and most primary being renewed fear for my safety, and secondly, a rather widespread sense of distrust for the world in general. But in addition to that renewed distress, I admitted that I felt shamed, even humiliated. I had proved myself to be a coward in the face of my fear. On the tall side and athletically built, I had easily forked over everything I possessed, without so much as a defiant word. I'd sunk that low in less than twenty-four hours.

And this wasn't even real life for me, was it? This nasty experiment could be over with the mere dropping of a quarter into the change slot in any phone booth. But these had been the facts of life for Tristan. Being on his own on the streets, as a skinny teenager no less, this had been his sole reality for nearly seven years. And he had survived. What's more, he had risen above the scars that the streets had left him with; he'd grown into a sweet, loving, compassionate man who had chosen *me* to be the one he loved. And it was no fucking wonder that Tristan still struggled with the ability to trust.

Yes, it was time to think this through. I was ready.

Tristan

"I DIDN'T expect you, Savannah. Why are you here?" I stood in the open doorway, gazing blankly at her as if she was a complete stranger, rather than the person on whom I'd built my entire adult life.

"Well, aren't you going to invite me in?" She squinted up at me, looking more or less perturbed. Okay, *more* perturbed.

"Oh, Savi, y-you don't need an invitation, honey." I led her inside and helped her remove her jacket. "This is your home always, right?"

She didn't answer. I trailed behind her as she plodded down the hall. "What's going on, Tristan? Tell me what's wrong." She dropped heavily on the couch beside Runaway and glanced around her. "Where's Robby? I thought you told me that both of you were taking the day off from work today."

Not sitting down, I grabbed my own coat off the coffee table where I'd dropped it earlier. "I'm starving. Want to go get an early dinner somewhere?"

In response, I got another harsh glare. "I asked you something. Where is he?"

Time for the truth. "I—I don't know." Shaking my head, I flopped down beside her on the couch. "I don't know where he is."

The most ferocious expression I'd ever seen on a woman twisted her pretty features. But somehow she managed to hold her tongue.

"It's okay, honey. I'm okay...." I realized I had nothing more to say on the subject.

Savannah huffed noisily. "Well, I thought it was strange that neither of you picked up your cell phones all day. I just knew." She popped back to her feet. "I found someone to cover for me at the group home tonight. So, that means I'm all yours until tomorrow night, Tris."

We sat staring at each other for a few awkward seconds. Then she said, "I haven't had a home-cooked meal in two weeks; what are you gonna make me, huh?" She stood up and tugged on my arm until I got to my feet too. "I'm having a big time craving for crêpes. So maybe you should start...."

"Your wish is my command. Crêpes, it is!" I supposed that the first step in genuinely smiling was making the shape with your lips, so that's what I did. And it wasn't easy to do because, yeah, I was super confused. And scared. And I was starting to feel a little bit angry as well.

But what it came down to was that Robby had made a choice and I had to learn to live with it. And learning to live with it did not mean begging and pleading with Savannah to give up on her own dreams so she could run home to babysit me. She'd sacrificed her goals for far too long already. So if keeping her on her current path meant faking a smile, that's what I'd do.

Robby

IT WASN'T perfect, but it was the best I was going to get right now, so I settled into a corner booth at a fast-food joint, hovering over the precious cup of coffee that the woman at the counter had allowed me to buy with my thirty-two cents and some additional change from her tip jar. Her generous action brought to mind the sad smile she'd sent me as she'd dipped her hand silently into her tips to subsidize my purchase. I guess it was more or less a "been there, done that" kind of smile, if I had to label it. And she reminded me so much of Tristan. Compassionate, in a quiet way.

Streetwise, but somehow still so pure of heart.

Tristan.... My father.... *Tristan*.... My family.... *Tristan*.... My way of life.... *Tristan.*

It all came back to Tristan, didn't it? A man so beautiful that he'd literally stolen my breath away from the very first time I'd seen him. A man so selfless that he always thought first of others. A man who completed me as no one had before—sexually, as well as emotionally.

A man who held back his trust from me since no man had ever earned his trust. And still, *still* no man, myself included, had ever walked the walk for Tristan Chartrand. My actions had proved that he'd been right in his decision to hold back his trust from me. That thought stung the lining of my brain.

Taking tiny sips of my small coffee so as to make it last, I spent a few minutes reviewing the slow course of our romance and how it had shaped my life as a whole. That meant first thinking of Savannah and how devoted she'd always been to Tristan. For him, she'd opened her heart and her life to me, which couldn't have been easy for someone with a personal history such as hers. I recalled the promises I'd made to her to take care of Tristan, to love him, never to hurt him.

Promises I'd clearly broken.

I thought of Mikey and how he'd wronged me and, far more importantly, how he'd hurt Tristan. And then I remembered the way Tristan had been so eager—without a doubt more eager than I'd been—to preserve my friendship with Mikey, because he considered friendship a precious gift. I realized I'd probably hurt Mikey, too, by replacing him so easily.

Then there was my family. That was where the real problem lay. Well, actually, saying "my family is a problem" was a lie, a cop-out, in that it was an overgeneralization. Lindsey, Brandon, and Madison—they would love whoever I loved, as long as he was a kind and decent person. Lindsey had already told me as much. And if it weren't for my father, I was fairly certain that my mother would just be happy if I was happy.

So, that left my father. *Just Dad.*

God knew I had tried to please the man for the entire duration of my life. When I was young, I had thought I could satisfy him in the sports arena. After all, I was reasonably athletic. Hell, I was a damned good athlete! But no feat had ever made me worthy. No awesome play had ever been enough to make him smile at me. No win had been sufficient to induce him to brag about me. Never had I heard a shouted "Good job, Robby!" or a "Thattaway, son!" as I'd raced up and down the courts and fields of my youth.

Dad had pretty much chosen my college for me, and I went where he told me to go without a single question, assuming my obedience would make him proud. It hadn't. And I didn't think I could have selected a career that would have met the rigorous criteria for what it took for my father to call me a success, as I was now fairly certain a career such as that didn't even exist. Because if I was going to call it as I saw it, our entire relationship was formed on the notion that I could never be good enough. No matter how much I tried.

Whatever I did, it had always been wrong. At the very least, it had never been enough. And it never would be. I had sacrificed my heart, Tristan's heart, and most probably Savannah's, in a futile effort to please a man who could not be satisfied.

But that wasn't even the worst of it. I was ashamed to admit it, but I had never even questioned whether or not my father possessed the right to mold my life in his own image, to judge my every move. Until Tristan and Savannah came along, I had lived my entire existence on a sort of autopilot, thoughtlessly doing what was expected of me. Never questioning anything. Playing by someone else's rules.

Those days were gone.

I rubbed my bristly chin with a dirt-caked, scabbed-up palm, tucked in my now-filthy yellow Ralph Lauren button-down shirt, and got to my feet. With an upward tug to the beltless waist of my pants, I headed for the exit, winking a thank you at the waitress who had helped me out in my desperate pursuit of coffee. I made a mental note to return to this very restaurant one day soon and thank her (and tip her generously.) I knew what I had to do now—no, no, that wasn't it at all. I knew, probably for the first time in my life, what I *wanted* to do.

And I headed off to do it.

CHAPTER 38

Tristan

IT HAD been quite a while since Savannah and I had sat alone together at the kitchen table for dinner. And trying to avoid the topic of Robby Dalton was like trying to ignore the elephant in the room.

"So, tell me about the group home, Savi. What are the kids like? What kinds of backgrounds do they have?"

Unfortunately, Savannah was distracted and, therefore, not feeling particularly chatty. "Like us, Tristan. They are kids *like us*. Kids with everything set against them and nobody in their corner."

I recognized her life-isn't-fair attitude; I'd seen it on her many times before. "Well, do you feel like you're making a difference by staying with them?"

"Maybe a little bit. But most of them have been through so much. Too much." I hadn't seen Savannah so visibly hopeless in a long time.

"Hey, honey, hey…." I placed my hand on the side of her face, and in a heartbeat she was crying. "What's the matter? It can't be all that bad, hmm?"

"What's the *matter*? *You* are asking *me* what's the matter?" She shook her head as if it would help her to make sense of me. "Tristan, Robby left you—*he left us!*"

I had already suspected that concern over me was at the root of her distress. That's pretty much the way Savannah operated. But it sounded to me like Robby's hasty exit had hurt her as well. "It's okay. We'll be okay." I had already questioned myself, my value as a person, my worth as a man; I had already cried. I'd even gotten a little bit angry.

But I knew it was now time for me to start living as my own man, and that meant I had to accept what was left of my life since Robby's retreat. And I had to help Savannah through her own feelings of abandonment and rejection. "You don't have to come home from the group home. Nothing has changed. You and me, we're big kids; we'll get through this."

She stared at me in disbelief but didn't offer me her thoughts.

"Robby did what he had to do, Savannah. And that is what each of us is going to do as well." I pulled her off of her chair, dragging her right onto my lap. "You are going to keep on helping those kids and I am going to continue to serve the finest food in Boston." I smiled at her sunnily, although inside I was still fighting back my tears. "And no matter where we go, Savi, we are each other's family."

"You are so good, Tristan. Such a good man. Robby's lost so much." I noticed that her tears hadn't slowed. "He'll never know how much."

"The man's a fool to let you go as well, honey." I wiped my palms across her cheeks to brush those tears away. "Now, this most certainly is not the reaction that I was hoping to elicit with my gourmet banana and Nutella crêpes, Savi." Picking up my fork, I fed her a small bite. "If you don't smile, I'll have no choice but to assume that my crêpes suck."

She finally gifted me with a reluctant smile. "I love you, Tristan. You deserve better than this."

I nodded. "You're right, I do." I'd never admitted anything like that before, but the time had come when I needed to start looking out for myself. For both of our sakes. "*We* deserve better."

What it boiled down to was one simple fact. All I really knew for certain about what went wrong in my relationship with Robby was that he and I had each been running from our own personal demons. And we'd been running for so long we'd stopped recognizing the fact that we were actually even in motion. I'd been running from my fear of closeness to a man, so I'd never given Robby what he'd needed from me: my complete trust. Robby had been running from any urge to please himself that ran contrary to what his father wanted, so he'd denied his sexuality. And he'd denied me.

Both of us deserved a partner who was able to stop running.

There was a soft knock on the front door. Just one single knock. And I'm pretty sure we both knew in an instant that it was Robby.

Without a moment's hesitation, Savannah was off my lap and out of the kitchen. And she didn't look back at me once as she made her way to the front door. I couldn't have stopped her if I'd wanted to; anything could happen now.

But no matter how this meeting went, my running days were over.

CHAPTER 39

Robby

SAVANNAH opened the door and the look she gave me…. Christ, all I can say is I felt *one* of my extremities, in particular, wither measurably beneath that glare.

"So here you are, huh?"

"Better late than never." I shrugged.

"Not funny." She grabbed the doorknob. "And speaking of being late, I think you may be too late. He's over you, Robby. He deserves better."

I reached out my hand and stopped her from achieving the satisfying door slam she so desired. "You're right. He *does* deserve better than me. And so do you, but please let me in, Savannah. Just let me explain."

I seriously thought she was going to try to force the door shut despite the fact that my hand was in the way, but after apparent reconsideration, she just spun around and started down the hall, mumbling something to the effect of "By the way, you look like crap." I could always count on Savannah for an honest opinion.

I stepped into the hallway, knowing beyond a doubt that I'd lost my right to be there. By running for the hills like a coward, I'd thrown away my right to be their family, to share their lives. And I wanted to kick myself hard in the ass for what I'd done, for what I'd *thought* I could do, but nonetheless, here I was, peering nervously into the kitchen. Tristan sat alone at the table, eating slowly, almost delicately, his eyes fixed on his plate.

I stepped through the doorway. "I'm sorry."

He looked up at me, his dark eyes huge and wary. "Don't be. You're just doing what's right for you. And that's what I want." His eyes moved back to the plate. "Savannah, uh, she... I made Savannah crêpes."

Beside his chair, I dropped to the floor on my dirty, scraped-up knees. "No. *No, Tristan*. What's right for me is *you*—I know that now—I love you."

He refused to look at me again, but spoke of what he'd seen just moments before. "Robby, you look, well, you look kinda terrible. Maybe you should take a shower and I'll fix you a crêpe. And, Robby, I know it's probably better for both of us if we're not *together*, like as in being a couple, but I'd really like to stay friends, as long as you... if you think it'd be okay."

At his words, the blood froze in my veins. Tristan was not one to casually throw away a friendship, but he was ready to move on romantically without me. I'd fucked things up with the only person with whom I'd ever felt complete. "No! No, Tristan, I'm trying to tell you—I want to be with you—I made a fucking major mistake when I didn't come home last night!"

"And then after you eat, you can take a nap if you want. I won't even go near the bedroom when you're in there, but you look so tir—"

"Tristan, listen to me. *Just listen*. I met with my father yesterday. Mikey told him about me living here and, and I freaked out that he knew. I denied that I felt anything for you. I insisted Savannah was my girlfriend and that you...." The confession rolled off my tongue with surprising ease. I guess it felt good to unburden myself. "That you—I told him you were nothing to me—*nothing*."

Tristan stood and almost robotically picked up his and Savannah's plates. Then he brought them to the sink where he turned and presented me with his back. "You don't need to explain any of this to me." He busied himself with the dishes for a minute or two and then he just stopped, his shoulders slumped down and his hands fell to his sides. Very quietly, he spoke. "And it hurts to hear you say those things."

Still on my knees by the table, I cringed at the subtle sound of pain in his voice. But I pressed on with my explanation. "He told me to dump you and I thought that I could, but, Tris, I just can't. *I can't!*"

His body seemed to have frozen in that slumped over, defeated position, and I knew my words weren't working; my confession was getting me nowhere. Before I knew it he was dragging his hands through his hair the way he did when he was really emotional. "Stop it, Robby! Don't you get it? I'm letting you go. It's okay, Robby. I'll be... we'll all be okay."

I got up and moved directly behind him, standing close so my dirty shirt brushed the back of his pristine white button-down. I leaned in so close I could smell his clean scent, and said softly into his ear, "I won't be okay without you."

Turning abruptly, Tristan pushed on my chest until I took a small step backward. With injured eyes, he studied my expression, almost as if he was trying to judge the truth of my words. And then a darker look passed over his face; Tristan was clearly angry. Finally, he replied, "I'm not gonna run any more, not from my own demons, and not from how I feel about you." His words seemed crisp and calculated, in the manner of a warning.

"You don't have to run! I don't want you to run." God, I loved him so much. He was the most beautiful person, inside and out, I ever hoped to know. I just needed one more chance to prove that I was worthy of him. "And last night I figured it out. *I don't have to run either!* You're all that matters to me, baby—you and Savannah are all I need."

Tristan was literally shaking now, from head to toe. I couldn't tell if it was out of anger specifically, or anguish in general. "B-but what about your family? And y-your father? And Mikey? I can't live with you just dropping off the face of the earth whenever you feel like you can't cope with—"

I placed my fingertips over his lips to still his rambling, but then remembering their filth from collecting change off the city streets, I jerked them away. "Shhhh, baby, none of them matter. *You* matter. And *Savannah* matters. I promise, Tris, I'm here to stay, and I'll tell my family about us today. Right now, if you want. But please, just say you still love me."

Now it was Tristan's turn to stumble. He seemed to trip over absolutely nothing, then collapse to his knees, and from there he slid onto his ass. Once seated, he stuck his head in his hands, as if it was too heavy to hold up any longer. Without a moment's hesitation, I joined him on the cool kitchen tile, and I pulled both of his hands off of his head and held them tightly in mine.

When he eventually looked up, I could see in his eyes how much the world, and more specifically, how much I had hurt him. "If we…. Robby, if we stay together, I'm, uh, I'm gonna need to trust you."

"Do you think you can? Trust me, I mean?" I squeezed his hands once and said a quick prayer. "I haven't exactly been model boyfriend material for the past few days."

Tristan withdrew one of his hands from mine and raised it to the side of my face. He looked quite pensive; I thought maybe he was buying time, so he could think it all over and answer my question honestly. "Somebody punched you." He traced the bruises on my jaw. "And you're, nothing personal, Robby, but you're filthy."

I wasn't about to let him change the subject. "Tell me—tell me you'll try to trust me—and say that you still love me, then I'll make all of this dirt go away."

"Robby, I love you even with the dirt." When he kissed the swollen place beneath my eye, I thought my heart would explode with relief. "And we are going to talk more about trusting each other and how much I hate disappearing acts later. But right now, I'm going to clean you up"—he touched a finger to my soiled shirt—"and feed you"—he touched my lips—"and hold you while you sleep."

"So you forgive me for skipping out on you last night? For hurting you, for thinking I could live without you?"

Tristan nodded. When he caught my eye, his gaze was clear and untroubled. And it was honestly the most gratifying moment I could remember.

"But do you think you're gonna be able to *trust* me?" Sitting in the middle of the kitchen floor, nose-to-nose with my lover, filthy as a kid fresh out of a mud puddle, hungry and exhausted and slightly beaten up, I had to admit I was about as happy as I could ever remember being. Only the right answer to this question could make me any happier.

"I already do." He said it so simply that I believed it was a fact. "Now, Robby, let's hit the shower."

For a second my head spun, as I marveled at how easy our problem had been to fix; Tristan's love for me was that strong. "Both of us? Uh, both of us in the shower *together*?"

Now Tristan nodded ever so slightly. He had never allowed me to see him fully naked before. His strong sense of modesty always had him hiding his body away from my view, in the dark, or deep within the sheets. One more time Tristan dropped his head shyly and his hands ruffled up his hair. Even with his head at that angle, though, I could still see his cheeks had blushed to a bright cherry red. "You bet your cute little buns we're hitting shower together, Robby!"

I smiled because I knew that this was our first step.

Tristan

ON OUR way to the bathroom, we had to pass by Savannah, who was sitting on the living room couch watching TV. I was worried she'd be angry with me for letting Robby off the hook so easily, but she offered us a rather sarcastic salute and then waved us away, so I guess I had no serious worries in that department.

As we stepped into the bathroom, Robby said, "I owe her an explanation too. I should really go talk—"

"Let's deal with Savannah after we... well, you know." I felt my face heat. "I want to show you something."

Robby looked at me curiously, as if he couldn't imagine what I could possibly come up with to show him in the bathroom. But when I moved to stand right in front of him and began unbuttoning my shirt, I think he got the picture. His eyes widened.

I was a little bit tense because I'd never intentionally displayed my body to another person, but since I'd made a promise to myself and to Robby that I wasn't going to run any more, I was going to do this. Letting Robby see me, all of me, was an important first step in letting him know I'd meant business when I'd said I was going to trust him. So once my shirt was unbuttoned all the way, I shrugged it off my shoulders and let it fall to the floor. Robby pretty much drank in the sight of my bare chest with very round blue eyes. But he didn't reach out to touch my skin. He just watched me, his hands clasped tightly in front of him.

Then I moved my trembling hands to the waist of my jeans. I wore no belt, so I didn't have that to struggle with, and my fingers went right to the buttons of my fly. I undid them one by one, probably a little bit too quickly to be considered particularly provocative, but I figured that if I didn't do this thing fast, I might just chicken out. When my jeans were unbuttoned, I pushed them down and stepped out of each leg.

I stood there in only my underwear, looking at Robby and shivering, partly from anxiety and partly from the cool air. And though I was close to being naked for the very first time in front of him, Robby now seemed interested in studying only my eyes.

"I'll turn on the water; you need to get in and warm up, baby." With a small smile, Robby turned away from me and bent down to the faucet to turn the shower on. As soon as I saw his back, I took a moment to slide my briefs down and kick them aside.

"Your body's perfect, Tris." He'd already spun back around, and despite the compliment to my physique, his eyes never seemed to leave my face. And since he didn't reach for me, I reached for him. But as soon as my fingertips made the slightest contact with his sides, Robby's arms came right up, pulled me against his broad chest, and held me there. "Now get in the shower, Tristan, and get warm. I'll join you. I mean, as long as you still want me to."

Once he released me, I nodded and stepped into the warm spray of water.

Exposing my body hadn't been as hard as I'd imagined. And since I'd bared my body, I was pretty sure that I'd be able to bare the rest of me when the time came.

Robby stepped into the shower behind me and I quickly turned to face him. Glancing up and down at his full length, I asked, "What happened to you?" He had several dark-red bruises low on one side of his chest, along with very nasty-looking skinned knees. "Where were you last night?" Again I was pulled against his strong frame. The light fuzz on his chest brushed against my hairless one, our groins were pressed together, and I realized that it felt good not to hide.

"I was trying to find my way back to you, and I did. That's all that matters, Tris."

I lowered myself to my knees, and taking a washcloth and the fragrant shower gel into my hand, I carefully cleaned the open sores on his knees, licking at the water droplets rolling down his thighs as I did so. When he moaned softly and placed his hands against my cheeks, I felt the scraping of new scabs on his palms, so, still on my knees before him, I cleaned those cuts as well. And then I lathered up my hands with soap and turned my attention to his privates, which excited us both so much that all

I could think of doing was bringing us relief. So I very enthusiastically tasted and touched and loved Robby's privates with my lips and tongue, and when he was close to the end of his endurance, he less than gracefully grasped me by my shoulders, pulled me up to my feet, and pushed me against the shower's back wall.

"My heart, Tris, my heart is yours." As he searched my eyes, he looked a little bit scared, and a lot like a little boy. "Forgive me, please. I'm so sorry."

The rims of his eyes had reddened quite a bit, and I knew I truly didn't want to see this man cry right now. "All I need is for you to love me. I need you to show me that you love me." And I turned around to face the wall. Pressing my palms to the dripping surface and pushing out my backside just enough, I uttered what I wanted him to do. "Make love to me, Robby."

"Like this? You want me to make love to you like this?" He pushed his privates gently against my backside. "'Cause, you know, I want you to take me too—it doesn't always have to be *this* way."

Robby sounded so unsure of himself, and insecurity seemed wrong on a man like him. A man who was handsome, successful, strong, and smart. And I was sure enough for both of us right now. "I want you inside me now, it'll be good for both of us because I'm already used to it. And I promise, I'll have my turn with you later in bed, where I can make your first time more comfortable. But now, please love me. *Please*." I nodded toward the shelf on the wall beside the shower. "There are condoms in the little drawer, and hurry, Robby, I really need you."

I didn't have to ask him twice.

Robby

STRETCHED out on the bedspread, both of us were naked, aside from the towels we'd wrapped loosely around our waists.

"Last night felt like a whole month without you." Tristan was as honest as Savannah but in a less brutal way.

I leaned over onto my side and allowed my eyes to feed on my lover's long, lean muscles and smooth tan skin. And better than that, I absorbed the trust that reflected out of his dark eyes. "I haven't kissed you since, Christ, Tris, since yesterday morning."

"Well, you haven't kissed my *mouth*. The back of my neck got quite a bit of attention from your lips when we were in the shower." Tristan shrugged a bit and I guess you might say he giggled. "But I think I can help you remedy that situation." He raised his arms, pulled me down on top of him, and our grinning mouths collided, causing our teeth to clash. I heard another giggle. "I thought you said that you wanted to kiss me, not *bite* me!"

After kissing rather seriously, though, for more than a few minutes, I raised my face from Tristan's. "I need to get things straight with Savannah. I don't feel right about hiding away in here with you, when she's out there all alone and probably still pissed off as hell at me."

Tristan sat up. "Yeah, you're right. We need to look out for her; Savannah's family, but she's the only person you are setting straight tonight. Everybody else can wait until I release you from our love nest, and I haven't decided exactly how long I'm going to keep you locked up in here."

"That's a deal, baby. And after I beg for Savannah's forgiveness, assuming she gives it to me, then how about we spend the rest of the night playing cards?"

"Kid's games?"

"What other kind of games *are* there?"

Without another word, we popped up and threw on our sweats. It was damned good to be home.

CHAPTER 40

Robby

I'D EXPECTED that she'd be pissed, but I hadn't expected the hurt. More than even Tristan, yes, Savannah appeared more wounded by my brief betrayal than my actual lover had been.

"So, you think that my heart is not involved, just because I'm not having sex with you?"

That was a very blunt accusation. It was also a fairly accurate estimation of what I'd assumed.

"I thought you said that we were all partners—the three of us, remember?" She was somehow able to spit out these statements without losing her train of thought, despite the fact that she was staring at some bloody crime show on television. "God, Robby, you told us you loved us—both of us! We even started our own Christmas tradition!"

Don't I just feel like a piece of royal crap?

And Tristan, who was sitting in his usual chair, flipping through one of his cherished cooking magazines, hadn't stepped forward to come to my rescue. But then again, why should he? If I was truly a partner of Savannah's heart, as I'd claimed, then I needed to own it; I'd made this mess with her and I needed to clean it up. "Savannah, you're right. I was most concerned with how Tristan would react to what I did. And that was wrong, because I love you too."

Still seemingly preoccupied by the TV screen, she asked, "Then my next question is for both of you: do you guys really want me to be part of this family? Because I know that having *some girl* hanging around might cramp your style—I might get in the way, or something."

All it took was for me to hear Tristan's panicked gasp of "*some girl?*" to set me into action. Before another split second passed, I had the remote in my hand and the television was snapped off. Tristan had already very predictably dropped his magazine, and was perched on the couch on Savannah's other side.

"It's good that we're talking about this. Obviously, it's very necessary." I spoke firmly, as Tristan and Savannah were staring at each other in an apparent state of speechless shock. I reached past Savannah to touch Tristan's knee because he looked like he might lose it. "I'll speak for just myself, and Tris, you can do your own talking after, okay?"

He didn't nod in acceptance, but then he didn't argue with me either, so I continued.

"This is a different kind of relationship than I'm used to seeing, or trying to be in. It's *unconventional*, know what I mean?" After a full twenty seconds of my partners' continued silence at that major understatement, I pressed on. "But being different doesn't mean that it's bad or wrong. In fact, I think it could be very good."

Finally, they snapped out of their trances and looked at me.

"I've always been kind of a loner, and I think you guys are sort of the same way. Other than each other, you keep mostly to yourselves, right?"

They nodded in unison.

"I don't think it would be a negative thing, for me, personally, at least, to have *two* people who I can trust and confide in and love." Surprisingly, what I just said actually made a hell of a lot of sense, proving that every once in a while, I got things right. "What about you guys? What do you think?"

Tristan spoke right up. "Well, I wouldn't want it any other way than what you just said. Savannah is already a definite family member to me, no questions asked, and now I love you, too, Robby, and it will only work if we all love each other and…." As he'd spoken, he'd unconsciously grasped Savannah's hand. I could see from the desperation in his eyes that he needed to be intimately connected to both of us.

It was clearly Savannah's turn to speak. She looked extremely uncomfortable, which hit me as very strange, since she'd always appeared so unaffected when it came to her own needs. I'd always thought of her as a person who existed simply to meet others' needs.

So I just came right out and said it. "Tell us exactly what you need from a relationship with us, Savannah."

She shifted her feet out from underneath her, stuck them on the coffee table, and leaned her head back. "I thought I already told you."

"Tell us again, Savi. So we can get it right."

Both of us now had a hand on Savannah, mine on her thigh and Tristan's over her hand. I urged her as well, "Go ahead. Tell us."

Taking care of her own needs was clearly as difficult for Savannah as it was for Tristan and me. "I just want... all I want is to *belong* with you guys."

We both held back our words, hoping she'd continue.

"See, I feel like I need to help people, or kids, really. Not just like I *want* to, but that I *need* to." She dragged her blue-green eyes from my face to Tristan's and then back to mine again. "I guess I hope that helping *them* will heal me from the pain of what my mother did, or more so, what she *didn't* do, when I was growing up."

I had to ask the question that was burning in my mind. "What about romance? Don't you want a *romantic* relationship?"

Savannah looked at me strangely, almost as if that thought had never crossed her mind. "No, no, not right now, at least. I mean, I'm not saying it'll never happen, but there are other things that I need to do and I can't give only part of myself to a man in that way. But I still need to have a family to stand behind me in the meantime. Someone I could bring a man home to someday, if I wanted."

Now we were getting somewhere. "How can we show you that we are your family? That we support you?"

Her eyes filled and I saw in her expression the very same vulnerability that I'd seen so often in Tristan's. "Just, when you guys think about me, no matter where I am, I want you to think of me as yours, like I matter to you. And if one of you has a problem, talk to me about it. Uh, and listen to me, like if I need to share." She blew out a long, slow breath through her lips, almost as if she was a little kid trying to whistle for the first time. "I want to know that I'm really home when I'm with you guys."

These partners of mine had been so very damaged by the twists and turns that their lives had taken. And so far, my track record with them hadn't been exactly stellar. But I knew now with an inexplicable certainty that I had been placed in their path to help right the wrongs they'd suffered. Beyond that, I was convinced that in devoting my life to these two broken people, I would find what my own life had been lacking for so long.

"I want to be in your life that way, Savannah. You'll be kind of like another sister." I had to smile at that thought. "And the only woman I've ever had a successful long-term relationship with is my sister, so I think that's a good sign."

As I spoke, a tear of simple emotion—whether it was from relief, joy, or gratitude, I couldn't say—trickled down one of her delicate cheeks. "Okay, Robby."

And Tristan, as I could have expected, didn't need to say a thing to show his accord. The pleased expression he wore spoke louder than words. (Plus the fact that he dove into the tiny spot between Savannah and me, landing pretty much in both of our laps.)

"So, it looks like now you have *two* brothers, maybe not by blood, but of your heart, Savannah Meyers. Do you think you can handle us?" I hugged them both at once and then bent to pull a deck of cards from off the table. "Go Fish, anyone?"

WE TUCKED Savannah in between us that night; somehow, Tristan and I had managed to agree without saying even a single word aloud, that she needed to be there. At the moment she was flat on her back, deep in a peaceful sleep.

I'd gained an incredible amount of appreciation for her over the past several hours. Out of all the men in the world, Savannah had selected me to complete their family circle. She had brought the three of us together with an open and generous heart, and without even a hint of jealousy. She'd been the bonding agent that had held our unconventional relationship together through all of its challenges, and we needed her to remain with us because she was an integral part of our small family's spirit. But despite her compulsion to give, I now knew Savannah's dreams and goals and needs were every bit as important as Tristan's and mine. Her need for love was equally compelling.

My hand brushed against Tristan's as we both smoothed her long curls back from her face. "We'll take care of her together, Tris." I felt energized and strong as I spoke those words. It was as if all of the fear and conflict in my heart had simply dissipated the moment I'd set my priorities in order and accepted my choices.

"Yeah, we will. Our little sister." Tristan took my hand and pulled it behind Savannah's head, to her pillow, interlacing his fingers with mine. "I like the sound of that."

"You know I'm sorry about yesterday, right?" I needed him to be sure of me and of my love.

"Yes, of course."

"And you may not believe this, but I'm actually looking forward to telling my family how I feel about you guys. Whoever cares about me will see how happy I am, and will be happy for me."

"And what about the people who aren't so happy for you?"

"Whoever can't love you and Savannah, can't love me either." I said it and I meant it. If someone wanted to be part of my future, he had to love and respect the two people I was planning to spend my future with.

I heard what I thought was Tristan yawning. "Neither of us got too much sleep last night, Robby. We should probably crash now." The blankets rustled a bit as Tristan turned onto his side to face us. "I love you; everything is gonna be fine."

"Nope, you're wrong there, buddy." Succumbing to a rather large yawn myself, I said, "Everything's gonna be great." I rolled onto my side and dropped one arm around Savannah, my fingertips landing on Tristan's chest. "Everything already is."

CHAPTER 41

Robby

I'D BE lying if I said I wasn't as nervous as an elderly horse at a glue factory as I sat in my family's formal dining room, waiting for my father to make his appearance. Trying to get my ass comfortable on those stiff overstuffed chairs, my elbows resting on the super-glossy mahogany table, in a room which had previously only been used for momentous family occasions—holiday meals, report card criticism, high school athletics performance evaluations—only added to my apprehension. Let's face it, a person doesn't morph from a compulsive people pleaser into a devil-may-care free spirit overnight. But I had set my priorities in order and had promised Tristan and Savannah that I was finished running.

I intended to follow through with my promises.

"More coffee, dear?" My mother appeared as anxious as I was. I wasn't sure if Dad had filled her in on the details of our last conversation, but she wasn't stupid, nor was she clueless, and she could sense that something was up. "It's decaf."

I supposed another cup of decaf wouldn't affect my nerves, so I said, "Sure, Mom. Thanks." She poured the coffee, and I have to admit I almost choked when she placed a tray of colorful Italian cookies on the table in front of me, because I knew who had brought them over to our house.

Earlier this morning, my roommates had surprised me with mimosas to go with the delicious mushroom and cheese omelets Tristan had made. After we'd enjoyed our little breakfast celebration, neither of them had risen from the kitchen table.

"It's time to talk," Savannah had said in her straightforward manner and had glanced expectantly at Tristan.

Blushing lightly, Tristan had added, "Robby, I want to tell you some things... about me. I want to tell you my story."

And he had proceeded to share with me the story of a boy who grew up in a truly dysfunctional family, where his greatest wish was that he would just be forgotten. Yes, he had suffered many years of his mother's neglect, which had certainly been bad, but when his youthful beauty had caught the eye of his reclusive uncle, things had gone from bad to worse, pretty much overnight. Several years of incestuous abuse had been followed by the better part of a decade barely surviving on the street; a lack of food, shelter, education, health care, physical and emotional security, and self-esteem. In fact, everything that made a person whole had been missing from his life.

Coupled with my newfound knowledge of Tristan's formative years was my one night of experiencing life on the street. In one measly night I had undergone a barrage of what had essentially been Tristan's way of life for so long—fear of the elements, fear for my safety, hunger, feelings of worthlessness and shame, and the list goes on. None of these sentiments was in any way positive. I had gained a new respect for Tristan that night—an admiration, really—and nobody would drive me from him.

My love for Savannah burned just as bright and intense, but in a brotherly way. But it went further than that, though. She was also the model on whom I would base some major "social changes" I wanted to make in my life. I was planning to adopt a kinder, gentler way of interacting with the world, I guess you could say.

"Martha, is that *decaf*?" After a single sip, my father slammed down his mug onto the dining room table, apparently repulsed. He hadn't even taken a seat yet and he was already criticizing. "For Christ's sake, make some *real* coffee."

"Oh, yes, of course, dear." She scurried from the room.

"Dad, I *asked* Mom to make decaf." That actually was a bold-faced lie, but it was for a good cause.

"She knows I detest that stuff." He pulled out a chair and sat down across from me. I fought off the "I'm so small" feeling and straightened my back against the taut cushion. "So, you look like you've been out all night." He smiled broadly. "Did you take me up on my suggestion to hook up with that nice fellow, Michael, and paint the town red last night?"

"No, Dad. That's not what happened."

His expression twisted in the same way as when he'd tasted the decaffeinated coffee, but he held his neck up high and stiff. "I hope you aren't here to further disappoint me, son."

Swallowing hard, I spoke. "I have a feeling that you may interpret what I'm going to tell you that way, but it is not my intention, not at all." I battled with my urge to close my eyes so I didn't have to see his fiery expression.

Just then, my mother returned with a fresh cup of coffee in her hand. Dad waved her away, mumbling, "Get the hell out of here, Martha. We are trying to talk man to…." He sniffed. "Man to *man*." She placed the mug in front of him and headed toward the doorway.

"No, Mom. Stay, please. I want you to stay."

The woman appeared as if she was ready to have a panic attack. She looked from Dad to me, and back again, not knowing which of us to please. I guess in our case, *my* apple didn't fall too far from *her* tree.

"Please, Mom. I want you to hear what I have to say."

My father shrugged and rolled his eyes, and then he nodded toward her curtly with what amounted to his permission to sit down beside him. "So what is this *big news* that you are here to announce, Rob? I can *hardly wait* to hear it." Yes, very sarcastic.

The moment of truth, well, it had surely arrived.

"Mom, Dad, I realize that it may be difficult for you to hear this, and I understand that you may need some time to absorb what I'm going to tell you." I couldn't say for certain, but I suspected that my father already knew what was coming. He pushed his chair back from the table a bit, as if to create some distance from me. "I've become, um, *involved* with Tristan Chartrand. You remember, Savannah's roommate. I feel very strongly for him and, uh and…."

My mom stared at my father and my father stared at me.

"And I am… Mom, Dad, I'm trying to tell you that I'm gay and I'm in love with Tristan."

The room was pin-drop silent. In fact the whole house, no, the entire *universe* seemed completely devoid of all sound, like we were all in one big noise vacuum. Mom continued to gawk at Dad, but now she clung on to the edge of the table as if she feared he'd overturn it. My father tried to stare me down, his eyes bulging, then squinting, and then bulging again.

I refused to look away. I had set my priorities; I had told the truth. The ball was no longer in my court. What happened now was my parents' decision.

Dad stood up. "Then I guess we have nothing further to discuss." My mother gasped. And he pulled himself up to his full height, towering over the table, and then he hesitated, as if he was waiting for something. As if he was waiting for *me* to do or say something.

But I just looked up at him, not allowing my expression to betray my disappointment in the man I'd spent my life trying to please.

"John, please, and Robby, you need to tell your father that... oh, dear." My mother was clearly uncertain just exactly whom to beg for what.

"Be quiet, Martha." My father dismissed her as if she was less than zero in his book. (If I ever treated my partners in that manner, I hoped they'd have the good grace to drown me in the bathtub.) "Robert, as I said, we have nothing further to talk about until you leave those two perverted gold diggers and move back in here. You know where we keep the key. I'll expect your things to be back in your old room by dinnertime."

It was my turn to stand. "Dad, and Mom." I resolved to treat my mother with complete respect from this moment on, and in doing so, I would address them both. "I know you'll need some time to come to terms with what I've told you, but please understand, I'm not moving out. My home is with Tristan and Savannah. He's my boyfriend and she's like a sister to me. I won't be coming back here to live."

"Then you won't be seeing any more of this family!" my father bellowed.

"John, please!"

"I understand, Dad, that you feel angry and disappointed right now, but I'm still the same person I was five minutes ago. I haven't changed. And you guys can call on me at any time; know that my door will always be open to you." I took one of my business cards out of my wallet and then found a pen on the sidebar. "Here, I'm writing down the address of our apartment. You are both welcome to come by at any time."

My father just stood there, utterly dumbfounded. I had never stood up to him before and I was fairly certain he was waiting for little Robby to crumble. And though I was perspiring, and panting, and a little bit nauseated, I had said my piece and I was glad.

My mother came to my side and grabbed my arm. "Are you sure, Robby? You never mentioned anything like this before about your being a *homosexual*."

"Mom, I'm almost twenty-seven and I've never brought home a woman for you to meet other than Savannah, who was actually my boyfriend's roommate. Hadn't you begun to wonder about me?" I looked her squarely in her eyes and she recognized my words with a small nod.

"And Lindsey, well, she's not gonna let you near Madison and the new baby when he comes! She won't let a bunch of perverts hang around her house!" His face was bright red. Hopefully not a heart attack waiting to happen, because that would just suck. But even a heart attack wouldn't change anything I'd said.

I turned to face him directly. "As a matter of fact, Dad, Lindsey has invited all three of us over to dinner tonight. I don't think our sexuality fazes her even slightly."

At that, my father stormed past me and continued up the stairs. A moment later I heard a door slam.

"I think you might need some new door hinges, Mom." It was an effort to lighten the mood, but she didn't bite. She was looking at me in this strange way, almost like she'd never seen me before.

"Mom? Are you okay?" I reached out and placed my hand on her arm. She covered it with her own.

"W-well, yes, dear.... I'm just surprised, I suppose." Her eyes had glassed over but she continued to study me. "And Robby, I-I think I'm proud of you. You certainly have grown into quite a man."

Suddenly I saw my mother in a way I'd never before seen her as well: as a woman with her own thoughts and opinions, rather than just as an extension of my father's will. "Thanks, Mom."

The woman hugged me briefly. "Now, I need to see to your father. And try not to worry about things with him too much." My mother wore a smug expression I'd never seen on her face before. "He'll come around when he realizes that you meant what you said." She smiled at me, evidently well satisfied. "It looks like our Robby is his own man now."

MY NEXT stop was the office. When I'd driven by on the way to my parents' house I'd noticed that Mikey's car was parked outside, and it was still there on the return trip, so I knew he was upstairs. Opening the door, I braced myself for the inevitable fireworks. Fireworks that should have happened a long time ago, if I'd been any kind of a man.

"Just got off the phone wit' yer old man, Dalton." As usual, Mikey did not remove his eyes from the numbers in front of him. "You sure shocked the shit outta him today."

I took a deep breath, and then said a quick prayer for patience. "Yes, I guess I did." And for some reason, I didn't feel as pissed off at Mikey and his bad attitude as I normally did. In fact, in some ways I actually pitied the man, as he had no idea of what love and friendship really meant.

"So now you're a fag, huh?"

He was trying to provoke me. I recalled what Savannah had told me about Mikey just this morning before I'd left. She'd said, "Mikey provokes you to get your attention. He's like lots of the kids I work with; he'd rather have negative attention from you than no attention at all." And she'd been right on the money. I took off my coat, hung it over my chair, and opened my briefcase on my desk in order to buy myself enough time to stifle a prematurely nasty retort, being extra careful not to play into his hands. I, however, did not take a seat.

"Not even gonna deny it?" He shook his head. "Well, ya better not make no sexual moves on my ass, ya hear? I'll sue yer skanky butt for sexual harassment at the workplace."

Sitting down on the edge of my desk, I said with a smile, "Don't worry about it. You are completely safe from my advances."

My comment seemed to rile him even further. "Why? Huh? Ain't my ass good enough for the likes of ya?" And when he said that, I knew that what Tristan had suggested this morning was true; Mikey was jealous of my feelings for my partners.

"Sit down, DeSalvo. We need to talk."

The look he sent me could've frozen hell over. "Ain't gonna have no chick-flick girly-chat wit' no queer boy." Nonetheless he placed his hand beneath his chin and looked up at me. Expectantly.

At long last, and for the very first time with my friend of so many years, in a situation where it really counted, I did the right thing. "I'm letting you go."

He didn't appear particularly surprised. "That pussy put you up to this?"

I swallowed back an angry retort, reminding myself that Mikey was pretty much an asshole, had always been an asshole, and would always be an asshole. Which was an insult to assholes everywhere. "If it is Tristan you are referring to, the answer is no. He doesn't even know I'm here. This involves us, DeSalvo, me and you." Truthfully, what Mikey had done to Tristan had been the motivation that inspired me to act on something that was long overdue. "But since you brought him up, my personal opinion is that you should find a way to apologize to Tristan for what you did to him. That was fucking wrong, man, not to mention that it was criminal."

"As if I'd go begging that pansy for anything." Until this moment, Mikey's eyes had remained for the most part stuck to the ledger in front of him. When he looked up at me now, I saw hurt in his eyes, but it was barely distinguishable beneath his sarcastic smirk. "Ain't gonna happen, man."

"I'm willing to admit that I played a part in our problems. Because I confess, when I finally met some people *of quality*, I couldn't dump your ass fast enough." I looked directly into his fathomless eyes, wondering if my inability to fully comprehend his nature was evident in my own expression. "I should have told you all of the things about you that pissed me off as they happened, but for more than a fucking decade, I kept my mouth shut. *My bad.*"

The man was plainly incoherent. His amenable pal, Robby, had never spoken to him in quite this manner, and he was quickly realizing what I'd already figured out: we barely knew one another at all.

"And I guess I used you, not really too different from the way you used me, huh? Just for different reasons. I suppose you were just an easy guy for me to hang with until I started to grow a backbone, you know?" It felt good to vent, but I reminded myself that venting wasn't the reason I was here. "In any case, I want you out of my office."

"Just like that? Yer firing my ass like I ain't nothing to ya?" He managed to stand up, but satisfyingly, he appeared a bit wobbly on his feet.

I took a step toward him. "Unfortunately, since we haven't been able to work together effectively enough to pick up any additional jobs, I no longer need an assistant. I can handle what limited work Dalton Builders has right now on my own."

Finally the meaning of this conversation registered in Mikey's brain. The stern lines on his face momentarily softened, and his cheeks turned pink, but it only took an instant for him to regroup and return to his caustic self. "You are one top-of-the-line, sorry ass-wipe, Dalton. I'm gonna have to make sure that ya, nah, that y'all pay for…. Shit, man, ya know, maybe it *is* time I made me a return visit to yer pretty boy-toy, Tristan Char— whatever-the-fuck his last name is."

This was crunch time. And I refused to let this man see me sweat. "The fact is, DeSalvo, you could've fucking killed him with that bat."

"*Wah! Wah! Wah!* Yer poor little fuck buddy!" Mikey pretended to wipe his eyes for effect. "I wasn't trying to kill him, Dalton," he sniffed, "'cause if I was, that faggot would surely be dead. I just wanted to teach you guys a lesson."

The man was fucking unbelievable.

How had I been his friend for so many years?

"And one more thing, before I forget to mention it. I want you to know that I've encouraged Tristan to press charges against you for assault and battery with a deadly weapon. After all, to this day he wears the proof of your attack on his chest and back, and even if he didn't, I made sure to take quite a few photographs when the marks were fresh. We have the bat sealed up in a big plastic bag too, with your prints all over it. So, at a minimum, I'm going to insist that he take out a restraining order on you."

Mikey looked at me blankly, and then his stubbly chin dropped.

"So if you're considering a return visit to *apologize* for what you did to my boyfriend, I'm going to have to insist that you reconsider. Just send him a nice little note. You can address it to him care of me, right here at *my* office. I'll see that he gets it." I wasn't sure why this apology meant so much to me. Maybe it was because I was fairly certain that Tristan wouldn't press charges and I needed him to know that his pain hadn't been overlooked. I needed Tristan to know that what he'd suffered had *cost* Mikey something, even if it was the voicing of a mere apology. And the loss of our friendship. Oh, yes, and his job.

For a moment, Mikey just stood there, apparently piecing together in his head the significance of what had just gone down between us. When it had all sunk in, he grabbed the laptop off his desk, stuffed some crap into a briefcase, and snatched up his coat. "Fuck you, Dalton! I fucking quit!"

Nodding amenably, I replied, "That's fine, but the laptop belongs to Dalton Builders, Mikey. You can put it back down on the desk before you leave." As predicted, it was slammed down with significantly more force than necessary.

Looking back…. Savannah

TRISTAN *hadn't ever looked as happy as he had when I'd left him last night. After we'd eaten dinner with Robby's sister's family, where the discussion had centered on outlining for them the dynamics of our unconventional little family of three, or, in other words, explaining how we fit together, we'd gone back home. While I'd packed my bag, Robby had recited one silly knock-knock joke after another, in an attempt to distract Tristan from the fact that I'd soon be leaving. Cheesy, yes, but also true. And Tristan had allowed himself to be distracted, which I'd considered a huge step in the right direction.*

Driving me back to the group home, my partners had sat together in the front seat of the Jeep, holding hands, and gazing at each other at every opportunity, trust and promises in their eyes. Each and every one of these sweet exchanges of their love had warmed my heart. For me, to have seen one decent man, a man whose life had been torn apart by unfair circumstances that had been totally beyond his control—smiling and laughing and loving—had satisfied me in a way I'd never imagined possible. To have seen a second good man who had never before known, let alone recognized himself for who he really was, accepting of and fulfilled in his relationship, had taken my satisfaction to a whole new level.

And as I'd watched them drive away, back to the place that was truly my home simply because they lived there, I had to smile because I'd been completely certain that my happiness would be looked after as well. The two men who'd turned practically all the way around in the front seat of the Jeep in order to wave like children and flash me four enthusiastic thumbs-up before I'd headed back into the dormitory, were my brothers with whom I'd share my life.

MIA KERICK is the mother of four exceptional children—all named after saints—and five nonpedigreed cats—all named after the next best thing to saints, Boston Red Sox players. Her husband of twenty years has been told by many that he has the patience of Job, but don't ask Mia about that, as it is a sensitive subject.

Mia focuses her stories on the emotional growth of troubled men and their relationships, and she believes that sex has a place in a love story, but not until it is firmly established as a love story. As a teen, Mia filled spiral-bound notebooks with romantic tales of tortured heroes (most of whom happened to strongly resemble lead vocalists of 1980s big-hair bands) and stuffed them under her mattress for safekeeping. She is thankful to Dreamspinner Press for providing her with an alternate place to stash her stories.

Mia is proud of her involvement with the Human Rights Campaign and cheers for each and every victory made in the name of marital equality. Her only major regret: never having taken typing or computer class in school, destining her to a life consumed with two-fingered pecking and constant prayer to the Gods of Technology.

Contact Mia at miakerick@gmail.com.

Also from MIA KERICK

http://www.dreamspinnerpress.com

Also from MIA KERICK

Unfinished Business

Mia Kerick

http://www.dreamspinnerpress.com

For more of the
best M/M romance,
visit

Dreamspinner Press

www.dreamspinnerpress.com

www.ingramcontent.com/pod-product-compliance
Lightning Source LLC
Chambersburg PA
CBHW051631260626
47170CB00004B/1129